TITAN
OF THE
STARS

ALSO BY E.K. JOHNSTON

The Story of Owen

Prairie Fire

A Thousand Nights

Spindle

Exit, Pursued By a Bear

That Inevitable Victorian Thing

The Afterward

Aetherbound

Pretty Furious

Star Wars: Ahsoka

Star Wars: Queen's Shadow

Star Wars: Queen's Peril

Star Wars: Queen's Hope

Star Wars: Crimson Climb

Dungeons and Dragons: Honor Among Thieves:
The Druid's Call

TITAN
OF THE
STARS

E.K. JOHNSTON

tundra

Tundra Books, an imprint of Tundra Book Group,
a division of Penguin Random House of Canada Limited
320 Front Street West, Suite 1400 Toronto, Ontario, M5V 3B6, Canada
penguinrandomhouse.ca

Published simultaneously in the United States of America by
Tundra Books of Northern New York, an imprint of Tundra Book Group,
a division of Penguin Random House of Canada Limited

*Publisher's note: This book is a work of fiction. Names, characters, places and incidents
either are the product of the author's imagination or are used fictitiously, and any
resemblance to actual persons living or dead, events, or locales is entirely coincidental.*

The authorized representative in the EU for product safety and compliance is
Penguin Random House Ireland, Morrison Chambers, 32 Nassau Street, Dublin
D02 YH68, Ireland, https://eu-contact.penguin.ie

Library and Archives Canada Cataloguing in Publication

Title: Titan of the stars / E.K. Johnston.
Names: Johnston, E.K., author
Identifiers: Canadiana (print) 20240433807 | Canadiana (ebook) 20240433815 |
ISBN 9781774884089 (hardcover) | ISBN 9781774884096 (EPUB)
Subjects: LCGFT: Science fiction. | LCGFT: Horror fiction. | LCGFT: Novels.
Classification: LCC PS8619.O48495 T58 2025 | DDC jC813/.6—dc23

Edited by Peter Phillips
Designed by Sophie Paas-Lang
Typeset by Terra Page
The text was set in Adobe Caslon.

Printed in Canada

1 2 3 4 5   29 28 27 26 25

Penguin
Random House
tundra | TUNDRA BOOKS

inked entertainment

*To Gordon Korman, who also stole a fault line.
There were more available than I was expecting!
We might be in trouble.*

The girl is tired. She lies on her bed and stares at the wall, trying to ignore the quiet movements from behind her. She doesn't want to be alone. Being alone would be worse. She is afraid, fear like creeping fingers on the back of her neck, but there's nothing she can do. They have run as far as they can. They have closed the doors that will close. There's nothing outside the hull but the blackness of the void. There's nothing inside but death and faint, faint hope.

She has taken stock of their supplies too many times. She knows exactly when they will run out of food. She knows how to be hungry, but she hasn't been hungry in a long time. She can already feel the burn of it, starting below her stomach. They will have water and they will have air, and if anything happens that they don't, it will be beyond her control anyway. She is on board to take care of the engines, not the plumbing or the air circulation. The engines cannot save her now. Can't save any of them, even if they regain control.

Control. She had it so recently. Control of her life and her future for the first time since the world shook apart under her baby feet. She had plans and the plans had been good, but now there's something creeping through the hallways and maintenance shafts that doesn't care. She imagines that she can feel it getting closer, and she tries to focus on more immediate fears.

She doesn't know where anyone is. She doesn't know how many corpses she'll find when she opens her door. She doesn't know if the ship will hold together long enough for anything else to matter. She can't relax, however much sleep beckons. There are too many thoughts in her head and there's no place left for her to hide. She is stuck in her room, and there will be no respite for her here.

The boy is tired. His body, his mind, his soul. This was supposed to have been a vacation, and even though he never expected to enjoy it, he didn't, in his wildest imaginings, consider the number of things that could go wrong. He had thought about normal problems: avoiding his parents, trying to make art in spite of their disapproval, perhaps a small malfunction in one of the ship's less important systems that resulted in cold breakfast. This is more than anyone could be expected to handle.

And he's not. As he has been for so much of his life, he's along for the ride. Useless dead weight while those around him do the real work. No matter how much he wants or how hard he tries, he simply doesn't have the skills to help. He's not even strong, raised in comfort as he was. He hasn't earned this exhaustion the way the others have, yet still all he wants is sleep.

It's a dangerous temptation, sleep. Like freezing to death in the snow, and all your body wants is to curl up or dig. He can't bring himself to do either. He doesn't deserve them. So, he'll sit here, horribly lost and uncomfortably found, in a small room that probably won't be safe for that much longer. Maybe, if he's very quiet, he'll escape.

The doctor is tired. There's blood everywhere, and other bodily remnants she doesn't care to name. She's alone, the only thing living on this deck of the ship. If she's lucky. If she's unlucky, then, well, at least it will probably be over quickly. Space is a system of hard lines that, once crossed, can't be walked back. She will last until her resources run out, or she too will end up with her viscera smeared all over the deck plating.

Her triumph has turned to ash, and worse. Her name might go down in history, but not the way she'd thought. Only a few hours ago, she had been at the top of the mountain. She'd been secure in the knowledge that her hard work would sustain her for the rest of her life. She'd just thought that life would be longer. And have better food.

She waits, the countdown clicking away on her wrist. She tries not to look at it. Looking at the door is no better. Neither is looking at the bodies around her. There isn't even a window for her to look out at the stars. She's not sure that would make her feel better anyway.

The sister is tired. There are thoughts she meant to have, advice she meant to give. Run. Hide. Resupply. Course correct. Instead, something is broken, and the pain makes her drift, dead in space, like every engineer's worst nightmare, no options for repair.

She holds her bag in her hands, even though it's on a strap around her body. Straps can break, and to be unmoored in space is to be lost. She cannot lose what she carries, even if right now she can't remember why. She had been running. She'd closed a door. She lost track after that. She's alone now, and everything aches.

She can hear the engines humming beneath her. They, at least, can still do their jobs. Engines mean air, light, gravity. Hope. She gave up on hope long ago, even after she'd been pulled from the shaking dark and given a safe place. Safety is what you make it, and she has been taught to make do.

Another sound, in addition to the engine. Steps. Feet. Not the boots worn by crew members or the soft shoes worn by the passengers. Something else. She can't run. She can't hide. She can't resupply. Her course is set, locked in by the blinding pain, and all she can do is wait for whatever is coming down the hall.

At least, she thinks before she drifts away into darkness, they have feet.

The queen is not tired. She has slept long enough.

ONE

CELESTE

The most ridiculous part about this last-minute panic is that synthetic brass polishes itself. It's cheaper. It's easier to install. And maintenance is a breeze. But this is *Titan*, not some regular transport vessel or, God forbid, a cargo hauler. The passengers on board don't care about how easy it is for the crew. They care about comfort and decadence. The authentic experience as inauthentically overblown as possible, but all the responsibility offloaded to someone they don't have to think about. And so here I am, polishing the fucking brass while passenger boarding is in progress, even though I'm supposed to be invisible.

Beside me, Ren Bailey sneezes as the smell of polish overwhelms her again. My eyes are watering, but I don't have time to stop. Ren spits on the rag she's holding, attacking the fitting with more violence than is really necessary. I understand the frustration, if not the action.

"That's disgusting," I say. "What if someone touches it?"

"It's going to dry," Ren protests. "And anyway, they'd deserve it if they get fingerprints all over my hard work, turning a knob that's entirely decorative."

I shrug, unable to deny that Ren is right. That's the other annoying part of our current job. The brass knobs don't *do* anything. They're just decorative, to add ambiance to an already over-decorated room. Because that is *Titan*: overdone in every way, and very, very proud of it. At the same time, I'm not about to give entitled rich people access to my DNA if I can help it. You hear stories, growing up in the Rupt—kids whose genes get scraped and suddenly they're found guilty of crimes they couldn't possibly have committed. That sort of thing. The poor and downtrodden are always easy targets, and most of us can't fight back. It's one of my least favourite things about the planet I was born on, right after the part where said planet had done its best to kill me.

I wipe my eyes on the sleeve of my jumpsuit, carefully avoiding any of the polish I might have brushed against, and go back to work. I'm so close to my dreams now. I'm not about to let a few random scuff marks stand in my way if I can help it. I won't let them stand in Ren's way, either. We've both come through too much together for that.

A chime sounds on the comm secured around my wrist. It's echoed in stereo by a chime from Ren's. We both look down, even though we know what the notice is going to say. Sure enough, the passengers are almost fully boarded and will soon be given free access to the whole first-class section, including the room we're cleaning. We don't have much time to finish up.

"Celeste, we have to go," Ren says. She throws her polishing gear into the tote without sorting it, but she does take time to make sure it's all organized.

"I'm almost done," I say.

I rush through the last four knobs, skipping the undersides, which no one is going to see anyway. It goes against protocol—even the unseen parts of *Titan* are meant to be perfect—but there's no way I'm going to risk encountering a paying customer if I can possibly avoid it. Besides, the voyage is going to last for a week. Surely no one will expect a performance from the crew for the *entire* time. I grind my teeth. They definitely will.

Ren stops, waiting for me in the middle of the room and standing near the four display cases that are the main feature of this particular salon. They are covered with large pieces of fabric—the colours coordinate with the brass, of course. No one knows what's inside. Ren is obsessed with it because she doesn't like surprises, and I'm happy to leave it alone because I don't like confrontation. I'm going to keep my head down as much as possible, get paid, and find a new job the minute we land on Mars.

"Come on," Ren says, peering out the door. "We can make it to the hatch if we go right now."

I throw the rag and the bottle of polish into my tote and hurry to catch up. Ren deliberately leaves one large fingerprint on the inside doorknob as we duck out of the salon and into the hallway. It's first class, so the hallway is wide and well-lit. The floor is panelled dark-stained wood from actual trees, because everything has to be real, and the walls are painted light-yellow gold, with large mirrors placed every few metres to give the illusion of more space and the benefit of reflected light. We walk as lightly as we can in our workboots so as not to scuff the floor and dive into a crew hatch without being seen by the family that's loudly opening the door to their suite down the hall.

In the privacy of the service corridors I pause to catch my breath. These hidden tunnels are my favourite part of *Titan's* design. There's no artifice, no unnecessary baubles. Everything is functional and small, and I feel utterly at home here. They're intended, of course, to make it possible for the crew and hospitality staff to move about the ship without being seen by our betters. I dislike that part, but I love the maze of secret entries and exits, how I can go anywhere and see anything, all without being detected. As long as I'm careful, at least.

Several members of the crew are in the corridor already, some with trays of refreshments and some with luggage carts. A few are in the same state as Ren and me, on their way belowdecks after finishing up on final tasks. We all look tired—it's a nerve-wracking job, getting ready for a maiden voyage of this magnitude—but excited. *Titan* is an adventure, after all, even if you only scrub her decks.

Ren winces and I follow her gaze to see our superior officer glowering at us.

"You're late," says Anthony Davis, a senior engineer who acts like he hates all apprentices on principle. He isn't a terrible boss. He just isn't very patient.

"No one saw us," I say. "And we got it done."

"Probably did a piss-poor job," Anthony grumbles. "If there's a complaint, you're getting all the blame."

"No one's going to notice the damn knobs, Senior Engineer Davis," Ren says. She leans against the wall of the service corridor in an exaggerated pose. We aren't supposed to sit down during our shifts, but Ren grew up in the Rupt too, and she knows how to bend the rules. "They'll be too busy looking at all the other expensive, pointless things."

"Get to the engines." Anthony dismisses us. "And don't forget, you'll need your dress uniforms tonight for the inspection."

Titan is a new model of spaceship, the first to be built entirely in orbit. Before, only parts of ships were built in space. It's dangerous work, welding together pieces of metal while wearing a spacesuit and floating in the void with a limited supply of oxygen. The engines of those ships had to be assembled on the ground. They were flown into orbit as the shuttle that brought the passengers up, a small craft that would slot into the space-built habitat areas and then propel the ship forwards. Only after the interlock would the ship have oxygen and gravity throughout. *Titan* is a new thing, a ship built all at once, with atmosphere and gravity the whole time, which means a lot of attention can be given to small details like brass knobs. The passengers have arrived more leisurely on light craft, which will return to Earth once everyone is aboard.

The newness of *Titan*'s construction principles also means that even the most experienced engineers are a little thrown off balance by the design. *Titan* is a true spaceship, built without ever having to account for planetary gravity beyond that which maintains its orbit. This makes parts of the design extremely counterintuitive, even though they make nominally logical sense. Passengers will never have to think about it, but the engineers do all the time, and it takes some getting used to. That's probably why Anthony is in such a bad mood. I don't think he's just a dick.

Ren takes our totes and heads off to the janitorial storage area while I go straight to the engine room. The engines are the heart of *Titan*, both literally and metaphorically. They control the ship's speed and generate the power that keeps the lights on, and they're located in the very centre of the ship. A chute straight through to the stern vents the exhaust, but even that is limited because other systems siphon off the waste gas to use. *Titan* isn't entirely self-contained, but she's close. An intricate arrangement of interwoven systems allows the ship to function with incredible efficiency, despite its size and the wastefulness of its passengers.

I pause for a moment at the door of the engine room to reorient myself. Since it never had to endure planetary forces, *Titan* is more or less a perfect sphere. This means that no matter where you are on the ship, and no matter how much your brain relies on earthly directional concepts like behind and starboard and bow, the engine room is always down. The centre point is weightless, which is what allows the engines to work so cleanly, but it always takes me a moment to get used to it when I cross the boundary.

The belt of my jumpsuit has a carabiner on each hip. I take one in each hand, pulling out the beginning of the retractable cable built into my uniform. When the engine room's trapdoor-style hatch opens, I clip one carabiner to the hook beside the bulkhead and climb down the ladder into the room, the cable unspooling as I go. I have to keep moving my lines as I descend—the clips detach either manually or at the press of a button on my toolbelt—until I reach the first platform. Other engineers are milling around, waiting for any orders about last-minute pre-launch tasks. Some of them are prepping their own safety lines for a jump to another platform. Weightlessness makes the actual jump pretty easy, but the timing and direction are still important. A lot of things in the engine room would be damaged if a human crashed into them.

Below me, in the centre of the room, the massive engines hum like they're excited to be underway. I completely agree with them. As much as I try to be jaded about this whole experience—which is definitely easier when I'm looking at pointless opulence than it is when I'm looking at revolutionary tech—the truth is that I'm very excited to be in space, very excited to be leaving orbit, and also *very* excited about the excellent job qualifications I'll have when we finally make port on Mars.

After years of scrambling and scrounging on Earth, finding decent work when I could and trying to study late at night when I would have rather been sleeping, I'm finally in line to get a job I actually want. I have a real shot at a good future, far away from everything that haunts me. No more Earth. No more Rupt. No more paltry government living allowance. No more being at the mercy of people who pretend they want what's best for me when what they really have is employment quotas to fill and they don't want to use their own kids to fill them. I'll be free. I just have to make a good impression on literally everyone I meet. I want to learn from the senior engineers. There's enough time on this voyage for me to be promoted, if I play my cards right. As for the passengers, well, I won't meet very many of them if I'm lucky, but if I have "Engineer on *Titan*" on my resumé and they have fond memories of the journey, maybe they'll be inclined to hire me.

I look down past the engines just in time to see Ren arrive through another hatch. My comm chimes with new orders before I can plot the trajectory that will take me to Ren's side. I don't get vertigo from the weightlessness, and I don't fear it, but I have to plan my movements pretty carefully. I always make sure to enter the engine room through the hatch that's closest to where I'm going, even if it means walking around the deck above. Ren, on the other hand, is a natural, and always takes the shortest route, flinging herself wherever she needs to be with absolute confidence.

"Dress Presentation," the comm reads. Because *Titan* is too civilized for the comms to be vocal. I'm not going to be near the passengers very often, but God forbid they hear anything besides a discreet chime if I am. "Main Salon."

I groan. That's even worse than Inspection. At least then the passengers would be on our turf, trailing along behind whatever officer is giving them the belowdecks tour. I'd pretend to be working, in a uniform that's far too clean, and they'd all marvel at how advanced the ship is and wonder if it even *needs* a crew, because they don't know how anything actually works. Dress Presentation means stepping into that polished-brass world and being paraded around like a mascot.

I can tell by the expression on Ren's face that she's received the same set of orders, even though she's too far away for me to hear. She waves at me and I nod. The engine room is so noisy that the engineers use a lot of hand signals across any distances. Our wrist comms only work one way—honestly, I don't know why they bothered calling them comms—and we don't always have time to log in to the nearest console. It's like when I was in the dorms—our guardian could yell for anyone and we'd have to come running, but if we needed *her*, we'd have to go and find her and use our "inside voices." I understand Ren's signals: she's going to come to me.

It's beautiful to watch Ren navigate the engine room. She careens around the other workers, passing effortlessly through that weird space where down becomes up, until she lands with complete assurance next to me. She's grinning, as always when she's weightless, and I can't help but grin back. We're finally leaving. Yes, it'll be a week of travel, and yes, we're going to be working the whole time, but what waits for us at the end will be worth it. Even if it kicks off with Dress Presentation.

"I wonder if they picked us because we're pretty?" Ren yells into my ear.

I laugh. We're both underfed and undergrown, and we've been in orbit long enough, working on *Titan*'s construction, that our skin has taken on what lifelong engineers refer to as "stellar pallor." Ren wears it better than me, with her rosy cheeks and vibrant hair. I just look like I've been wrung out.

"They picked us because we're charity cases," I tell her. My voice has a stronger pitch so I don't have to yell as loudly as she does for my words to carry. "A nice reminder of how they've invested in a future for everyone, not just their own bank accounts."

"You're no fun," Ren says. "I want French braids, though."

I cut my hair short when I was hired on, but Ren has kept her long chestnut brown hair as is. This means it's usually wrapped up in a messy knot on the back of her head, but sometimes I braid it for her. It's nice to do something just for comfort, to help someone else. A pretty thing that I can offer, and that Ren loves, in a world where we don't usually have access to pretty things.

"You'd better move, then," I say.

We ascend to the hatch that leads to deck one and the crew quarters, and haul ourselves out on to the deck, feet back firmly on the ground now that we're out of the engine room. As some of the lowest-ranking people on board, our shared room is on this deck, right above the engine and close to all of the noise. Even the most senior officers only rate quarters on deck three, two above us. With time ticking down, we head out to change into our dress uniforms. Duty calls, even if it's tedious. It doesn't really matter at this point: we get paid all the same.

two

DOMINIC

I stand helplessly in the middle of the room, watching my valet hang three suit jackets I don't remember packing in the carved wooden wardrobe that dominates the wall of my dressing area. This is the smallest room in my suite, but the wardrobe, a dressing table, an overstuffed sofa, three giant suitcases, and two people fit quite comfortably in it. Comfortable is what *Titan* promises, and comfort is what it delivers.

Physically, at least. Emotionally, I'm so on edge that I might just claw out of my skin. No amount of warm wood panelling is going to make that go away.

"Dom, are you in there?" Adam Jeffers, rumoured heartbreaker and current inexplicable boyfriend, never asks questions he doesn't already know the answer to. He also doesn't bother knocking. Where the hell else would I be?

"I'm coming," I say, well aware of the face my valet is pulling at hearing Adam's voice. I don't blame him. I started to feel the same way a while ago, and sometimes I have a hard time remembering what attracted me to Adam in the first place.

"Don't threaten me with a good time," Adam says, salaciously. I don't have to see his face to guess his expression. "Ugh, the colours in your rooms are so much nicer than mine."

I arrive in my sitting room just in time to see Adam flop sideways into a chair and throw his feet carelessly over the arm of it. As soon as I'm in range, he reaches out and hooks his hand around my waist, pulling me close. I would have gone all the way into Adam's lap except I resisted at the last moment, so instead I'm just standing awkwardly next to the chair.

"Not even a kiss?" Adam grouses. He's like a cat with its belly exposed, claws at the ready. "Why do I bother with you, anyway?"

He's clearly expecting a funny answer, but I don't have one to give him this time. I would have, once, content to play yet another part in someone else's idea of life, even though I chafe at the role. I pull away and sit down in a chair by myself instead.

"Whatever," Adam says, clearly annoyed. His face turns suddenly pious and I brace myself. Adam only behaves himself when there are witnesses, and even *that* is up in the air most of the time lately. It's on the list I'm not keeping about why I'm starting to hate him. "Do you like the colours in here? I feel like they coordinate so much better than the maroon and turquoise in my suite."

The doors on *Titan* are ornamental, made to look like they're heavier than they actually are. Accordingly, they are beautiful and quiet. Yet I don't have to turn around to know that my father has come into the room, no more inclined to knock than Adam had been.

"The colours are fine," I say shortly. I know I'm being set up. Adam's smirk is a dead giveaway, but it is far, far too late to avoid the situation. We're in orbit, after all. All of our baggage is on board. "I'm sure yours will be fine too—you just you have to get used to them."

"I hope so," Adam says. "It's so nice to talk about it with an expert, though, don't you think, Mr. Reubens? Mother had to consult with *so many* experts while she was creating the blueprints for this ship that I lost track of them all. When it got to the decorating, maybe she needed someone with more of an artist's eye."

No one else can get away with baiting Benedict Reubens like that. He's rich and important, but he only designed part of *Titan*, and not a particularly functional part, from what I've been able to determine. A systems engineer, my father's work is always shrouded in confidentiality agreements, but this time was even more opaque than usual. Adam's mother had designed the entire thing, revolutionizing engines and space travel in the process. There is no doubt who *Titan*'s owners prioritized when it came to public accolades, and I know it grates at my father's soul.

"Dominic has better things to think about than colour matching," my father says coolly. A seething anger still rolls off of him.

"Then why did he bring so many of his drawings?" Adam asks, all innocence, even as his eyes slide sideways to make sure the hit has landed.

I curse at myself for not helping Peters unpack and getting all of my things squared away before my space was invaded. I hadn't been able to leave my entire portfolio behind, despite the promises my father had extracted from me before we left our house the final time, so I had selected a few of my favourite pieces to bring. I'd meant to put them away before my father saw them, but I left them on the table outside the door to my bedroom when I got distracted by the dressing room. I'm too mad at myself for the mistake to be mad at Adam for calling them "drawings."

"Dominic, we talked about this," my father says. He stalks over to the table and sweeps up the offending papers. "It was a nice hobby, but we agreed you would focus on your real future now. Especially given your lack of talents in your mother's arena."

It hadn't exactly been a conversation. My father only knows one way to talk. I hadn't said anything during his tirade. It was easier to let him complain about my many failures in the Youth Parliamentary Program and fuss that I would be just as embarrassing when I followed his path instead. I certainly didn't agree with his declarations . . . I just know better than to fight when he's on a rampage.

"I wanted to be able to decorate my room," I lie. Not my best work, but it might be enough for now. "I know we're starting fresh, but you brought some sentimental things with you, and I know Mother did as well. I didn't think I was excluded."

My father makes a face like my art personally offends him, but he lets the folder slide back onto the table. I'm going to pay for this later, but at least I've saved the last of my work from one of *Titan*'s incinerators.

"You are a part of this family," my father says. "We gave you that respectability, along with your education and everything else. We allowed you to have some fun when you were immature, but I expect you to start acting like you actually belong, beginning with the launch ceremony. You haven't even started getting dressed yet."

"That's my fault, Mr. Reubens," Adam says. It isn't a save, just a way to extract a debt later on. "I distracted him."

"I'm sure your mother expects you to be turned out too," my father says. It isn't quite an order to leave, but it's as close as he can get.

"Of course," Adam says. "I was just about to be on my way. I'll see you later, Dom."

My father and I both stand by and watch him leave.

"I wish he wouldn't call you that ridiculous nickname. We gave you a three-syllable name for a reason," my father says.

It is one of the only things I agree with him about, though I don't actually mind the name, just that it comes from Adam. I imagine my father is projecting. There's limited dignity in shortening Benedict.

"Get dressed. We'll have to have yet another talk about your wasteful hobby, I suppose, but it'll have to wait."

My father marches out of the room, leaving me to my preparations. My valet coughs politely, letting me know that everything in the dressing room is ready for me and that he's heard the entire conversation.

"Thank you, Peters," I say. "I'll come get you for the cravat. I can do the rest of it myself."

"Of course, sir," Peters says. I hate that. It used to be just my name, but my father had overheard and forbidden such familiarity. Peters has to follow the rules to keep his job. "I'll find a place for your artwork."

At least someone appreciates my talents instead of constantly berating me. I sigh and go to pick a suit.

The launch party is in full swing by the time I make it to the salon. All five hundred passengers—plus the crew and staff who are required for the launch—fitting comfortably in the lavish space. Adam is waiting for me near the door, sharp pleats and sharp smile with a tie as narrow as his conscience. I let him link arms with me because I hope he'll pull me away from my parents, but then Adam's mother sees us and that's the end of that. Sylvie Jeffers is elegant, brilliant, powerful, and entirely new money, which means my parents can barely tolerate her. They couldn't forbid me from dating Adam because they're ambitious enough to encourage dynastic moves, but I don't think for a moment that they like him.

And that's it, of course, no matter how much I try to ignore it: why I started dating Adam in the first place. He'd been a reckless rebellion with a pretty tongue, someone who annoys my parents but is too important for them to push away. I thought I was gaining an advantage, but I've never been very good at playing my parents' games. Now the veneer is fading and I'm casting about for escape routes that seem to be rapidly disappearing. There's no way off *Titan*, after all, and we're going to be breathing and re-breathing the same air as each other for a week.

Our two families parade through the party in a group, Sylvie and my mother, Alodia, pretending to compliment each other's dresses while my father puffs out his chest so far that the starch in his shirt is stretched as far as it can go. Everything about *Titan* is modern at the core and gilded with early-twentieth-century affectations. The passengers have been encouraged to follow the trend for the duration of our cruise, and most of them have clearly gone all out for the launch. At least I can entertain myself by internally criticizing everyone's attempts at period dress.

"Dominic?" says my father, imperiously waving me closer. I have to push Adam to get him to change direction, which earns me glares from both of the people I'm currently disappointing.

"Yes, Father?" I say, dutifully giving my attention.

"This is the programmer I was telling you about, remember? The junior systems engineer who designed our environmental code." The prompting is clear: I am to ask a clever question to make my father look good.

"I do remember," I say, shaking the young woman's hand. She's only a few years older than I am, and clearly this is her first fancy party. I don't mind playing along with this part of my father's act. He does employ genuine geniuses, and talking to them is always fascinating, even if I don't share their interests. "You said it was especially smart because she figured out a way to get the fog to be clear, which meant the display was visible while preserving the humidity."

My father had an NDA, and despite what I'd told Adam to get him to leave me alone, he had let a few things slip. Nothing that gave any detail about the *contents* of the display cases he and his team designed, but enough for me to know that the atmosphere behind the glass had been delicately built to preserve both the mystery and the objects inside.

"Thank you." The programmer blushes, though that might have been due to the champagne flute clutched in her hand. "I must say, though, your father has the ideas. It was an honour to code them into reality. And we always had enough money to work with too, which is an important part of any equation."

My father and the programmer exchange facile compliments for a few more moments and then he makes our excuses to her and directs us farther into the crowd. He hadn't even bothered to introduce the programmer by name. He only wants to be seen as a good superior in front of Sylvie, who is trailing along behind us with my mother.

"The real trick was stitching everything your father imagined into the *Titan*'s main system," Sylvie says. She leans into me like she's telling me a great secret. "I don't deny that your father created a perfect display for our little surprise, but it's a big draw on the ship's power, and it was my engineers who made it possible for the containment system to work on board."

"Do we get to meet any of your people?" I ask, even though I know my father will be furious at the idea of being outshone.

"The crew, yes," Sylvie says. "I believe the captain has arranged for a few of them to come up for a bit. Not to the whole party, of course, but for the speeches."

My father's chest reinflates. His engineers are invited passengers—a reward for their work on the project—and are attending the actual party, not hovering around below-decks, waiting to be summoned. Sylvie's engineers—the ones who are actually making the voyage with us—aren't really engineers, in his view. Sylvie is an aerospace engineer herself, and there were others who worked with her, but most of them have already moved on to other contracts and aren't making the trip. The engineers who are on board are the kind of engineers who have their name because they work with the engines. Having the same word for both jobs lets my father exercise quite a bit of pettiness, but I don't think Sylvie cares that much right now.

There is a buzz at the front of the salon and a man in a naval-style uniform steps up to a raised podium. *Titan* is a civilian vessel, so the captain's uniform isn't quite military, but it definitely gives the impression of authority. On any ship, the captain's rule is absolute. Even Sylvie will have to defer, and she's the reason *Titan* exists.

"Fellow travellers, welcome," the captain begins, voice ringing out around the room through the sound system. "Welcome aboard *Titan*, a new way of travel with all the familiar comforts of home. I am Captain Bernard, and we're pleased to get this maiden voyage underway. But before we do, there are two people I would like to thank."

An expectant sort of hush ripples through the room, even though everyone knows exactly who is about to be mentioned.

"First, Dr. Sylvie Jeffers, our engineer, designer, and dreamer," Captain Bernard says. "Without her, *Titan* would be just another ship of the line. Instead, she has built the future of travel. Dr. Jeffers took on the laws of physics and won, my friends, and now we all get to enjoy her dream made reality."

There is polite applause. Sylvie smiles what she clearly thinks is a modest acceptance of the praise.

"Second, I would like to thank Mr. Benedict Reubens," Captain Bernard continues. "We're not going to tell you exactly what he has designed just yet, but let me assure you, he has worked very hard to make this voyage to Mars like no other before it, and probably no other again."

This round of applause is slightly confused, but still enthusiastic enough that my father doesn't grumble at being less effusively acknowledged. I know that he loves the mystery, and that makes up the rest of the applause in his head.

"I would ask both of you to come forwards to help me launch *Titan* for all of us." Captain Bernard gestures to the small console beside the podium. It isn't the real launch mechanism, of course, but it will signal the bridge that we're ready to go.

I watch as my father and Sylvie stand shoulder to shoulder and place their hands on the button. You'd never guess that they hate each other with the kind of burning fury that powers stars. Adam squeezes my hand too tightly. We need to break up as soon as possible. I should have done it before Adam decided to come on the voyage, but there's nothing I can do about that now. I won't be able to avoid him all the way to Mars, but I don't want to be automatically associated with him anymore.

"To Mars!" says the captain, and the button is pushed.

There's a slight jerk as the ship slides forwards, and then a projection screen rolls down so that we can watch the external cameras. Adam told me that rumble plates were built into the floor of this salon for this exact moment. *Titan* moves so smoothly that no one would notice the launch otherwise, and Sylvie wants to make sure that everyone has an experience.

Cheers echo through the salon. Adam leads my mother and me over to meet the captain while Sylvie steps away for a moment. She returns with five crew members, all dressed in immaculate uniforms. They all look a little uncomfortable and stand stiffly in a row. No one has offered them drinks or hors d'oeuvres. I smile, hoping that will help set them at ease, but they all ignore me, except for the short-haired girl at the end of the line who rolls her eyes.

"These are just a few of our engineers," Sylvie says, waving carelessly at them. They may as well have been props in her ongoing battle with my father. She's daring him to scoff at their job titles to their faces, but he doesn't take the bait. Now she turns her attention to me. "Most of the senior engineers are busy with the launch, of course, but these five are part of a special recruitment program, so I thought you would like to meet them especially."

In a flash, I see the rest of the evening play out in perfect detail in my mind. It can't be stopped or slowed or turned: Newtonian inevitability at its finest. There is no mistaking the age of the engineers or the victorious edge to Sylvie's smile. She means to poke at my father again, and I am going to be her collateral damage.

"You know we wanted *Titan* to be a humanitarian ship as much as it's a passenger vessel. Our apprenticeship programs are the best on Earth or Mars. For this voyage, we specifically sponsored engineering hopefuls who were survivors of the St. Lawrence Rupture." The smile she turns on me is more artificial than the gravity. My father freezes and my mother turns red. The engineer girl looks at me, her eyes fierce.

"Just like you," Sylvie says.

quiet, quiet, quiet

just a little longer

just a little warmer

just a little closer

we are almost ready

we are almost hungry

she is almost hatched

three

CELESTE

I don't remember the St. Lawrence Rupture. I was only two years old when the Ottawa Valley rift system finally collapsed, taking almost everything from Montreal to Sudbury with it in the sort of disaster San Andreas could only dream of. While Ren and some of the other kids we grew up with claim to remember the horrible shaking and terrifying sounds of that day, I have nothing. I'm almost grateful for it. Some of the girls in my dormitory screamed themselves awake in their beds if there was a thunderstorm, and most of the older kids didn't like to sleep inside for years after the quake.

For something I don't remember, the Rupt has shaped my entire life. Fifty-five kilometres wide and seven hundred kilometres long, the only thing that prevented the Rupt from being a globally memorable disaster was the relatively low population of the area. Yes, Montreal and Ottawa were tragedies, but west of that, there were simply fewer people to crush. Whatever the world thought or remembered or didn't, the town of Renfrew had been where I lived, and when it was almost completely destroyed, it affected me very deeply, even if I was too young to remember it happening.

I had been one of a few hundred kids pulled from the wreckage. The youngest babies were found under family members or pushed into small, stable niches by dying hands. Some of the rescued were old enough to know their names and who their families had been, but I didn't have that either. I'd been renamed by the orderly at the hospital in Brockville who was assigned a whole group of survivors and told to label them for record-keeping purposes. Everyone in my group had a bird last name and a first name that could be easily pronounced by anyone in either Ontario or Quebec, just in case.

They'd still been optimistic in the first few months after the quake, sure that extended family members would come forwards to claim the kids. They could have done DNA testing as they did the few times an adult came forwards to claim a child as theirs, but there were simply too many dead bodies to bury and living mouths to feed to spend time on identification that wasn't absolutely necessary.

Ren had been able to say her name, or at the very least she'd screamed "Ren!" long enough that they had written it on her ident card, along with "Wren," because sometimes gallows humour is all you have. Ren Wren became Ren Bailey when she and I were five and Ren was adopted out of the dorms, but the Baileys lived in the Rupt resettlement, so we weren't separated.

At the end of the day, only two kinds of people survived the St. Lawrence Rupture: those like the Baileys, who would stay to help rebuild, and those who somehow managed to escape. As another one of the former, I spent my whole life trying to scratch my way out, and most of my friends and not-exactly-official family had done the same. I spent years focused on the goal, working as hard as I could and trying to avoid the pitfalls that surround a life of poverty. And I had finally made it, not just into a job, but onto a ship bound for Mars. I hadn't done it entirely without help and handouts, but I *had* done it in such a way that I could wear my uniform proudly in a room full of people who didn't care about me in the slightest.

And Sylvie Jeffers *still* made me feel like a charity case. It's one thing when Ren or I say it. We're joking. We know what our lives have been. But hearing this rich woman admit that the only reason we had been brought up to the party is because of where we were born is infuriating. Especially because, as soon as Sylvie finishes talking, every eye in the group turns to one of the well-dressed boys, ignoring us altogether.

He's moderately tall, with ruddy skin and a shock of blond hair that probably came out of a bottle. He certainly doesn't look like he's ever been hungry. Before Sylvie spoke, he'd looked bored, like there were a hundred places he'd rather be, even though he had tried to be polite when we were introduced. Now that Sylvie's done, though, his eyes take on a strained look.

The boy next to him has a mean smile that only turns sharper. "That's right, Dom!" He says it like he's suddenly remembered something, but it's clear he's simply playing a part. "*You* survived that horrible earthquake too."

I feel like a bowl of acid has been overturned in my stomach. I don't look at any of the other engineers in line with me but I can imagine their responses well enough. David Hawk—who'd been with Ren and me in the bird orderly's ward—and Wendy Jackson are twins who only found each other two years ago when David needed a kidney transplant and kids from all across the Rupt had tested in hopes of finding him a match. Jackson wasn't their original name, so changing their official identities had been ruled too troublesome. Michael Jenkins grew up with both parents— an oddity in the Rupt—but he still has nightmares of watching all three of his siblings get crushed under a steel girder his father hadn't been able to lift. Ren probably had the most stable childhood of any of us, but she's still the oldest of a pack of foundlings, and her dads lean on her for help without meaning to. All of us had struggled and grown up in spite of our surroundings, making the most of what little we had. None of us are particularly patient with outsiders.

I know exactly who the boy is now, and who his parents are. Everyone knows him, even if they don't recognize him anymore because he's grown up from the adorable, fat-cheeked toddler he used to be. After the quake, there had been a lot of really fast adoptions. It was considered humanitarian. Ren's case was different—she was adopted a few years later and only taken three houses down the block from the orphanage. Most of the adopted kids had just disappeared, "rescued" from the horrible mess left behind, with no thought as to where they might end up. A few of them were taken in by public figures and paraded around by politicians as good-will success stories. One of those politicians had built her entire career on the image of having taken care of some poor, unfortunate survivor.

Dominic Reubens's parents could have built a dozen schools and still had money left over to repair half the sewers and roads in Montreal. Instead, they adopted one child and the whole country hailed them as heroes. Alodia had risen to power in the government, and later in the private sector, on the coattails of the son she'd "saved," and Benedict always managed to mention his son when he talked about his work in interviews and lectures. And now I'm stuck on a spaceship for a week with *all of them*.

"How wonderful to meet you," Benedict Reubens says. He speaks too clearly, as though he isn't sure we understand English, even though his wife co-sponsored the bill that encourages all the kids in the Rupt to be bilingual. And then sold all the educational packets that made it possible. "It is always good to see young people make the best of bad situations. We are very proud to have you on board."

I get the distinct impression he will actively ensure he never sees any of us again.

"Hello," Dominic says quietly. There is nothing cruel about him, like there is with the other boy, and nothing forced, like the adults. "I hope you have smooth sailing. Or whatever it's called in space."

"Sailing works just fine," says Ren, who never worries about things like talking out of turn because her wide brown eyes get her out of almost every problem she ever encounters. "But I'm not going topside."

"They'll manage," Sylvie says. "My engineers are highly trained and supremely competent. They're not just here because of who their parents are."

I almost flinch at the rapid turnaround of Sylvie's treatment, and then again from the spitefulness of the barb about parents. Before I'm fully at attention again, I realize that neither I nor anyone in the lineup had been the target of the insult. It's directed at Dominic, or maybe his parents. The air between all the adults crackles, like there's too much oxygen in the mix and someone is holding a match ready to strike. This sort of petty squabble is far, far above my pay grade, and I'm pissed off that I'm being used in the fight.

"Will you be leading the tour tomorrow?" Dominic asks, apparently desperate to change the subject. He looks straight at me when he speaks, but I just blink instead of answering him.

"No," Ren supplies, when it becomes obvious that I'm not going to say anything. "That will be one of the senior engineers."

"Ugh, that just means it'll be boring," the cruel boy says. "Mum, can't we have a tour with kids our own age? The perspective would be so much more interesting."

I wrack my brains, trying to remember the name of Sylvie Jeffers's brat and coming up completely empty. Then I remember reading a gossip magazine in the weeks of shuttling back and forth between Earth and *Titan* before we could live on board, something about the dynastic matchup of Dominic Reubens and . . .

"Adam, they have to work," Dominic says. "They can't waste their time keeping you busy."

"No," Sylvie says, looking directly at the five of us and clearly expecting at least one of us to agree with her. "I think it's a good idea. Maybe the two of you will learn something about personal responsibility."

"We'd be happy to have you belowdecks," David says, a touch over-formally. I'm impressed he's spoken at all. Usually Wendy does all the talking—before Wendy, David just hadn't said much of anything at all. "We'll just have to sort out the schedule."

"I'll set it up with the captain," Sylvie says. "Now, why don't you five mingle a little bit. Answer questions. Try the canapés. You can go below at the next bell."

That's three quarters of an hour away. Wendy pulls David off to look at the fancy navigational charts that are set up for any passenger who might care about our actual route. Ren goes straight for the food, which is so predictable that Michael follows her without asking where she's going. I'm blocked in by Dominic, who realizes about three seconds too late what he has done. Now I'm alone facing down people I already know I don't like. At least he looks apologetic.

Sylvie excuses herself to talk to the captain, and someone calls out to Benedict, who leaves with his wife on his arm and without bothering to say goodbye. Adam looks at me expectantly, like I'm about to give a performance.

"Do you have any questions?" I ask, hoping the answer is no.

"Of course not," Adam says. "I just wanted to get rid of our supervisors. We're going to be on this ship for a week. I don't want my mother hovering over my shoulder the whole time. You can just show us a place to hide and we'll be set for the whole cruise." He waggles his eyebrows, letting me know exactly what he plans to do with his hiding place.

I look at Dominic, who winces. Clearly one of them has a surprise for the other, but I'm not about to get involved in that mess.

"I actually do have questions," Dominic says. "But they can all wait until tomorrow. I don't imagine you thought you'd be working up here tonight. You should enjoy the party."

"Thank you," I say, barely managing to not make it a question. Then something occurs to me. "Wait, I have a question for you."

"Oh?" Dominic visibly steels himself, and I realize he probably thinks that I'm about to ask him about how he grew up. I do want to know what it was like and how his parents justified their decisions, but my immediate concerns are more pressing.

"What did your father build?" I ask.

"I would really like to tell you," Dominic says. "It seems like you know how to keep secrets. But Adam doesn't, and my father would kill me if I was the one who let his big surprise out. Also, he didn't tell me either."

"Wait, your mother didn't tell you?" I turn to Adam, who's starting to look annoyed about being left out of the conversation. He grins at me. It isn't very nice.

"She thinks I'm unreliable," Adam says. "Besides, she got to do her whole reveal with the ship. Benedict should have his fun too."

Ren catches my eye, waving at me to come over and try the hors d'oeuvres. I make my escape without any further conversation, but I don't fully relax until I've made it across the room to where Ren and Michael are waiting for me.

"I can't believe we're going to have to spend time with those brats," Michael says, handing me a glass of something fizzy and a serviette.

"Watch your tongue," Ren says. "Their parents can buy you without ever missing the money."

"It just makes me mad," Michael says. "They get to act like children, spoiled and petty. We have fucking jobs."

"It's not their fault we didn't get to be kids," Ren says philosophically. "And even if they are dickbags, they still have money, and that means we can take it from them."

"How?" Michael asks. "Pickpocketing?"

"Don't be stupid, no one carries cash," Ren says. "I mean by getting them to hire us. Or recommending us to someone else. Or, I don't know, maybe one of them would marry you."

Michael rolls his eyes, but he does blush a little bit.

I listen to them banter. It's comfortable, a welcome opposite to the loaded conversation that Sylvie and the Reubenses had exchanged. Now that we're away from that particular group, the party isn't actually all that bad. Yes, my uniform is too tight, but no one is looking at us like we don't belong. As we mingle, several people actually ask me very smart questions about ship operations, and no fewer than three children inquire as to where their poop is going to go when they flush. Their parents always look shocked, but I'm happy to not only answer the question but commend them for asking it.

"There are almost two thousand souls on *Titan*, including the crew, the passengers, and all of the scientists that are here with Benedict Reubens," I say, smiling at the third child as he nods attentively at me and his father stops turning pink. I decide at the last minute not to point out that about half of those two thousand people are neither passengers, scientists, nor crew. No one likes to be reminded about those particular people. "It was important to think about how that stuff works. We actually have it a little bit easier than old-fashioned cruise ships. They used to have to carry it around with them in tanks until they got to port. *Titan* has special waste containers that are fired right into the sun!"

I leave out the part where a substantial portion of all waste products are recycled. That always upsets people, but the flowers and trees in the arboretum and the vegetable garden in hydroponics have to get fertilizer from somewhere.

As the family walks away—the kid still chattering happily about spaceship design—I find my gaze wandering back to Dominic Reubens. Adam hangs off his arm, and his parents are right there with him, but he looks very alone. No one speaks to him directly, and even Adam only seems to use him as a prop. It's not in my nature to feel sorry for rich people. Anyone who says you can't buy happiness is lying. Money buys a *lot* of things that can make you very happy. But Dominic is clearly miserable. Sure, he'd been saved from the Rupt, but the rescue clearly hasn't been for free.

My parents died when I was two. I have no memory of them at all, not even the vague and dreamy kind of memories some people have of their younger years. I can't even pretend to remember them, because I have no idea what having parents feels like. Usually, I wish for something, even though I don't know what that is. Something like what Ren has with the Baileys. But watching Dominic is an example of a whole opposite direction. For the first time in my life, I'm not only grateful that I'm going, I'm also glad that I have no one to leave behind.

four

DOMINIC

I'm used to adults looking at me speculatively. Strangers always look back and forth between me and my parents, their gazes flickering as they come up with the polite way to ask the obvious question. People who know my parents look at me with judgement, constantly. My own parents have stopped looking at me lately, which is almost worse, because their judgement of me is never going to change. For a while, I'd liked the way Adam measured me up, but now it just feels weird and overly possessive.

The girl from engineering is different. Most of her compatriots barely paid me any attention. The girl, on the other hand, had run through the full gamut of emotions during Sylvie's little display. At first, she'd tried to ignore me out of spite, then she'd been annoyed with me, and finally she looked at me like I was a mystery. That one is my favourite, if I had to choose. It's definitely better than how she's currently studying me from across the room: like I'm an object of pity.

If anything, our positions should be reversed. I should pity her, and we both know it. She'd had to grow up in the squalor I had escaped, and she's probably had to work herself to the bone to get out. And yet here we are, and she's still looking at me. It makes me nervous that I don't even know her name. There probably isn't a way to talk to her again without causing a scene. Adam will definitely protest if I go over there, as if hard work is contagious, and my parents will not understand why I would talk to the grunts while my father's "legitimate" engineers and programmers are sipping champagne with the wealthy elite of Earth all around me.

"And what are your plans when you arrive?" A question from the woman talking to my parents pulls my attention back to my immediate surroundings.

"Oh, I don't get to stay," Adam says breezily. "I mean, I want to, obviously, so I'll have to spend the whole trip trying to convince my mother. She wants me to go back to Earth and start an aerospace degree."

"There are always arguments to be made for staying on the frontier," the woman says. I finally remember who she is: Adelaide Connor, one of *Titan*'s financiers. Her father had died shortly before we left, and she'd inherited everything the Connor Mining Corporation had had on two planets—much to the rumoured dismay of his executive board. She'll be staying on Mars because she owns a mine there now. "You can take school online. There's no reason to be there in person all the time. And the opportunities on Mars will be so much more interesting."

"I'll tell her you said so," Adam says. He's the absolute picture of politeness now, since he's tracking down something that he wants: to get away from his mother. And it's not like Adelaide gets nothing, with someone as promising as him owing her a favour.

"And what about you, Dominic?" Adelaide turns towards me.

For a second, words fail me, even though I've had all of Adam's time answering to prepare. Then I see my father take a breath to answer for me and I say the first thing that jumps into my mind.

"I'll be shadowing my father, of course, at least to start with," I tell her. My father doesn't smile approvingly, but he does look vaguely mollified. "There are so many integrated systems on Mars. I think it's best to familiarize myself with them before I choose a particular direction. Some of the things we need on Earth are irrelevant on Mars, and vice versa. By observing my father integrate and redesign the environmental systems in the habitation domes, I'll learn a lot."

"That is definitely clever of you," Adelaide says. She takes my answer at face value as though I haven't scrambled to give it. "Mars is wonderful and vicious in turns, and the domes are quite elegant in the way they house and protect us."

I do my best not to look too outwardly relieved. There's no way my father will accept a generalist, but with the weight of the opinions of someone like Adelaide supporting me I can put off getting tied into some boring environmental engineering program as soon as I get off the ship. It's not art, but the longer I can keep my options open, the better I'll feel. I don't even mind owing Adelaide a favour. I think. Business people can be wonderful until they're vicious.

Adelaide goes back to talking to my parents, something about mining and labour relations and her father. My attention drifts off again, watching the room instead of listening to the adults. The girl from engineering has moved on from staring at me. Now she's over by the display my father designed, standing too far away to touch it but obviously interested in whatever lies beneath the fabric that's draped over it. It kills me to admit it, but I find I'm pretty curious too, now. An NDA has to be *incredibly* tight to keep my father from bragging or dropping hints at the dinner table, and aside from knowing that whatever is inside must be sensitive to temperature change, I don't know anything. One of the other girls, the one with the long braid, goes over to her.

"I'm hungry," Adam says, right in my ear. I nearly jump with surprise but manage to stay still. "Let's go back to the buffet table before all the real food is gone."

There's absolutely no way that anyone on the upper decks of *Titan* will be eating anything but the best food available for the entire trip to Mars, but I'm perfectly fine to have a good excuse to split off from my parents. I let Adam pull me towards the table. It's set up in a style meant to be reminiscent of the early twentieth century American east coast, which I find uncomfortable. Those cities had been the first to sink when the sea level started rising in the mid 2000s, and no amount of nostalgic glamour can make those memories appetizing for me. It doesn't even make Adam pause, and I watch my boyfriend load up his plate while I debate when the best time to break up would be. Not here, obviously. I like Captain Bernard, and he deserves to have a smooth launch. But soon.

I look around for the least busy part of the room to stand in while Adam eats and am pleased to see that it's near my father's display, where the girls are still hanging out. Adam follows me without protest—possibly because his mouth is full. The case is roughly two metres wide and about four and a half metres long. The top of it is just over my head, which gives us a false sense of privacy. The girls look up when we arrive.

"Still won't tell me?" the one with the braid asks. "I can't believe you don't even have a guess."

"Sorry," I say. It never occurred to me to find out. I'd been shadowing my mother while my father was working on this project, and I didn't want him to think I was interested in case he made me take part. I don't like politics, but I like it more than systems engineering. "My father would actually put me out an airlock."

She laughs, but the other girl doesn't react at all. She only goes back to staring at the case, fascinated.

"What are your names?" I blurt. "Sorry, it's weird when people know who I am and I don't know what to call them. You don't actually have to answer me."

I can feel Adam roll his eyes. He won't talk with his mouth full at a fancy party, but apparently he's decided that his manners are wasted on the crew.

"I'm Ren Bailey," braid identifies herself. "That's Celeste Sparrow."

Celeste nods at me absently without looking up. It's starting to get a bit awkward, if I'm being totally honest, but it still beats standing near my parents and enduring their polite conversation.

"It's nice to meet you," I say, because I *do* feel like the crew deserves good manners. "I hope the tour tomorrow doesn't inconvenience you too much. I know you have schedules to keep."

"It's fine," Ren says. "We're only junior engineers, and the senior ones can call us if they need us. Now that we've launched, it's mostly maintenance anyway."

Titan is designed in such a way that her engines run constantly. Unlike an old-style solid fuel rocket, which fires a massive burn and then maintains speed with inertia, *Titan*'s engines are calibrated to push the ship gradually faster. At a carefully calculated midpoint, the engines will reverse, slowing the ship down so that we arrive in orbit around Mars without needing extreme measures to stop. It's not wasteful, because the engines also power all the other ship systems. Even though they require constant supervision from the onboard crew engineers, the cost of paying them is worth the benefit of getting to Mars in a week instead of in seven months. Still, the part of the voyage between launch and landing is the least exciting, even with all the onboard entertainment, and it's going to last for a while.

"That's good to know," I say. I hate to sound like I am patronizing them, but I can't help what comes out next. "I know this voyage is important for all of you."

Celeste is better at rolling her eyes discreetly than Adam is.

"What about you?" Ren asks, deciding that turnabout is fair play. "Are you just out here for a tour?"

"No, we're moving," I admit. "My father has been hired to oversee the life-support systems in the domes, since they're expanding and getting more complicated than the original design called for. My mother resigned her seat in parliament last year, so it made sense to take the opportunity."

"Mars doesn't have an official government," Celeste says, speaking for the first time. There is no hint of French in her accent, so I surmise she grew up on the English side of the Rupt. "Right now, it's all corporations. Your mother might have more to do than she expects. I don't think the unions are comfortable. Company towns have a bad reputation."

I blink. Thinking about Mars as a company town seems ludicrous. It's a technological marvel, a triumph, even. Almost a million people live in the domes, and more are expected as soon as space allows. It's why my father was offered a job. And here's this girl, compressing all of that achievement into something as antiquated as the design aesthetic of the ship. Yet something about how she says it strikes a chord in me: there's no way my mother will be on the unions' side if it comes to that. She can make more money from the corporations.

Adam gives up the conversation as boring and wanders off to look at the art on one of the wall panels. Ren doesn't say anything, but it's clear she's surprised. Not by what Celeste is saying, but by the fact that she's saying it out loud.

"You really think it's not going to be a problem?" Celeste presses. I must look confused, but the truth is that I'm already well into *resigned*. "*Titan* isn't a cargo hauler, but do you know what half the ship is given over to carrying?"

"No," I say. I've seen the specs, obviously, but not every section of the ship is labelled on them. Officially, *Titan* is registered as a cruise ship.

"Let's just say that of all the people who plan to use this trip as a way to get to Mars for work, Ren and I are in the lucky group." Celeste bites off the words with a strange sort of resentment. "We're getting paid and we're getting experience. We won't have anything to work off when we get there."

I wince, wishing I'd paid more attention to what Adelaide had been saying about labour issues. No one likes to talk about the indenture program that brings the bulk of the workers to Mars. It's highly regulated and supervised, of course, but it's highly regulated and supervised by people like my mother. There are always cracks, even in the best-designed systems, and the same old stories about human greed are already circulating.

"I don't think my mother is the sort of person to set up a government," I say. It isn't quite a subject change. "But she might be okay with consulting. Do you think the unions will work with her?"

Ren looks at me like I've said the most ridiculous thing imaginable.

"No, I don't," Celeste says. She sounds cold. "I don't think for one moment that your mother will be on our side."

I open my mouth and then close it again. I had already reached the same conclusion, and I know that Celeste is right. Alodia Reubens would charge a steep fee if she were a consultant, and she wouldn't be interested in helping workers get *out* of the control of their corporations. She always follows the money.

"We're going to Mars for a lot of reasons," Ren says. "Money is a big one, obviously. But there are a lot of dangers there, especially for people with no connections or job security like us, and not just because there's no breathable atmosphere outside the domes."

"Are you scared?" I ask. I'm definitely being forced to do something I don't want to do, but there is no denying that mine is the most gilded of cages.

"We've spent our whole lives dodging the kind of work programs that end in indenture," Celeste says. "That's how most kids get out of the Rupt, but you never hear good things about what happens to them later. Thankfully, we weren't that desperate, and we can take care of ourselves."

As a rule, my parents only ever talk about the Rupt in a roundabout way, usually to guilt me into doing something. Like giving up art and going to Mars. Hearing about it from people who grew up there, people I might have grown up with if things had gone differently, is another matter.

"Do you mind talking about it?" I ask quietly. "I know you have no reason to explain yourselves to me, but I—"

"You want to know how the rest of us lived?" Celeste asks. Her tone is dark and I know I'm on dangerous ground.

"He might still have family, Cel," Ren says softly. "Even if he got out, we can still tell him what it was like."

"Ren's story is better than mine," Celeste says after a moment. "The Baileys adopted her when she was five, and so she grew up with two parents and a whole pack of siblings. Her dads got a government stipend for each kid, but they're a real family. Ren's aged out of the government money, so now she's making her own."

"That's commendable," I say. The word is wrong, but I can't think of any other way to phrase it. My parents don't need my help—they need my compliance. I don't want to sound patronizing when I genuinely think Ren is doing a good thing. "I mean, that's what should have happened after the earthquake. That sort of co-operation and coming together."

Celeste snorts.

"Celeste wasn't adopted." Ren takes over the story. "She grew up in the dorms just south of Ottawa. When she still got her government stipend, she had no control over it at all. If she wanted to withdraw money, there was this whole lengthy process. And then the payments stopped. She managed to get work that paid well and didn't trap her in a contract of any kind."

"What happened when you aged out?" I ask. The stipends only last until Rupt kids turn sixteen. That must have been at least a year ago for both of them, if my guess of their ages is correct. Ren's siblings must be close to her in age, even if she's the eldest. That means her parents will lose a bunch of stipends all at the same time, which won't be easy. I can't even imagine the pressure she's under, even though it sounds like her dads aren't exerting any of it. Everyone likes to pretend that no one adopts for the money, but the economics of disaster get bleak very quickly.

"We were finally allowed to transfer whatever was left to a real bank," Celeste says. "It wasn't much."

There are so many things that I grew up with that I treated casually. I got to be careless and reckless as a kid. These two were required to be on their toes at all times to ensure they didn't get snapped up by some "well-meaning" dead-ended government work contract.

"Thank you," I say.

"You want to know what you missed out on?" Celeste asks, still testing me. "A quick glance down the road not taken?"

"No," I say. "I'm not sure what I want. It's hard to explain. But thank you anyway."

"Are you still here?" Adam swings back into the conversation. He's carrying another full plate. This time when my stomach turns it has nothing to do with the design aesthetic.

"We were just talking," I say.

"With your people?" Adam sneers.

"With our tour guides," I say through my teeth. I turn back to apologize to the girls, but they're already gone. "You didn't have to be so rude to them."

"Oh, who cares," Adam says. "They're part of the crew."

"Did you know that there are indentured miners on *Titan*?" I ask.

"I hadn't really thought about it," Adam says. "But it makes sense. Even with all the people who bought tickets, a trip to Mars is still expensive. They have to make it worthwhile somehow, and there aren't enough engineers like your friends to do that. They'd never let *Titan* haul cargo. It would go against their marketing plan. People is the only other option."

The calculated way Adam draws his conclusions makes me feel tired. I'm useless. I can't change any of the things that I think are wrong. All I know how to do is what's expected of me, and that just means reinforcing a system that splits people into groups so that some of those groups can be swept out of sight . . . and I'm not even good at that. I can't fix anything, and my inability to help just makes me feel worse. On Earth it had been bad enough, but on *Titan* there's no escape. There are literally people beneath my feet and I can't do anything to make the system treat them better.

"Dominic, there you are!" My mother appears from nowhere, wrapping her arm around my neck and kissing my cheek. She has definitely been enjoying the champagne, which is unlike her. She's probably annoyed that, after years of being the public face of the family, my father is about to overshadow her. Her withdrawal from parliament hadn't been entirely voluntary, after all—merely a way to avoid a mounting number of unpleasant questions about the connections between her bank account and the government committees she oversaw. She still wants to be at the centre of things. "How clever of you to save a good spot for your father's reveal. We're right up front!"

I had meant to disappear for this part, to leave my father to stand alone in his spotlight. The project hadn't interested me while he was working on it in secret, and something about the case makes me uncomfortable now that I can see it. But now it's too late, and I can't avoid my father's big moment.

As he steps up to the microphone, I look into the crowd for the crew engineers. Celeste and Ren had been standing right beside me a few moments ago, but by the time I find them in the crowd, they're already pushed all the way to the back.

we were cold

we were still

we were alone

we are moving

we are hunting

we are so, so close to finding
what she has sought

five

CELESTE

"**I can't believe** you spoke to him like that!" Ren buzzes in my ear, a little too loudly but not enough that I pull away from her. "What happened to keeping your head down and not offending any of the rich people?"

My face flushes and I resist the urge to look down at my shoes. I'll keep my head held high. It's very unlike me to confront anyone, let alone a stranger, but something about Dominic Reubens makes me want to punch him in the face. Or maybe something else. I don't know, and I don't like it. Against my will, my gaze is drawn back to him, even now that he's off hobnobbing with the other guests and has probably already forgotten I exist. He looks sad. He has no right to look sad.

"I don't know," I whisper back to Ren. I'm more considerate of her eardrums than she is of mine. "He just got under my skin for some reason."

"It would have made more sense if you'd gone off on Adam," Ren says thoughtfully. "That boy is a grade-A asshole. But he'd probably retaliate. Dominic seems almost..."

She trails off, and I know that Ren is feeling sorry for him, same as I am, and is just as annoyed about it. The boy is infuriating. He probably doesn't have calluses on his palms or unexplained bruises from hard work. It's maddening that either of us feel sorry for him. But we always have each other. Dominic only has, well, all of *that*.

"I don't like it," I say shortly. I stop looking at him and return my gaze to the covered display in front of us. I can tell Ren is itching to find out what's inside. I can't help looking at the brass knobs we had polished mere hours ago, and am then immediately annoyed because no one is paying them any attention. They're barely even looking at the delicate food while they eat it.

"The good news is that you don't have to," Ren says.

David and Wendy cut through the crowd towards us. I'm torn between hoping we'll be dismissed soon and wanting to stay. The guests are frustrating, but this is undeniably more entertaining than another round of cards in the mess. And the food is undeniably better.

"We should move to the back of the room," Wendy says once she and her brother are close enough to be heard over the ambient hum. "The science-types are going to announce what's under the damn sheet, and if we're at the front, they'll send us away. If we have to put up with this party, I'm seeing the grand reveal live."

Ren almost bolts to the back of the room. I twist my hand

in the fabric of her jacket to keep her from taking off and she drags me forwards a few steps. There's no way Ren is going to miss this, even if she has to be farther away. Wendy and David follow us more sedately, and Michael joins us as we lean against the wall.

"What wonderfully clean knobs," Michael says, almost keeping a straight face. "I can almost see my reflection in them."

"Shut up, we cleaned the other gallery," says Ren, but I appreciate the acknowledgement, even if it is a bit of a joke.

Any smart remark Michael might have replied with is cut off by a sudden hush in the room. People shift as the covered display case finally becomes the focus of attention instead of the thing everyone in the room is trying to politely ignore. Benedict Reubens is standing proudly next to the captain, along with Dr. Jeffers and several others who aren't dressed quite fancily enough to be guests.

"Travellers, if I could have your attention, please," the captain says. All talk ceases immediately when he speaks. "I am pleased to reintroduce Benedict Reubens, who will be announcing the crown jewel in *Titan*'s design."

Benedict steps up to the mic, a wide smile on his face. He looks genuinely pleased and excited, a far cry from how bored and almost petulant he had been earlier when he'd mingled with his family in tow. Dominic and his mother, along with Adam, are in the crowd. I find it easier to look at the back of Dominic's head. Ren strains to see, stretching up on her toes until David finally helps her step up onto one of the chairs that have been placed around the room. No one's using them, not even children who might want to sit for a bit of a rest.

"My friends," Benedict says. "I am truly honoured to tell you our secret. Much like *Titan* herself, it is the culmination of several years of hard work by all kinds of scientists, engineers, and programmers."

He's a charismatic speaker. In spite of myself, I'm hanging on his every word. He had been rude to all of us literally half an hour ago, but here I am, wanting to know what he says next. I look at Ren and her eyes are shining.

"Ten years ago, federal geologists working in the Canadian Arctic uncovered a section of newly thawed permafrost," Benedict continues. "They were looking for aquifers and sites for new mines, so when they found an impact crater, they were very excited."

Trust the government to find the bright side of melting permafrost.

"But it wasn't just an impact crater, my friends." Benedict is clearly enjoying himself, winding up the crowd. I can't even be mad that it's working on me too, because I really want to know what he's leading up to. The enthusiasm is catching.

"Here to tell you about the incredible scientific discovery is pre-eminent ethnobiologist Dr. Alexandra Ripley, from the New College at the University of McGill." Benedict gestures to one of the people standing next to him, and a woman in a crisp maroon business suit with a pinched, pale face and straight black hair steps up to take the mic.

"Thank you, Mr. Reubens," she says. She surveys the room and takes a deep breath. "I'll be honest with you, travellers, I never expected to make this sort of announcement. Ethnobiology is the study of the intersection of culture and living things. In humans, this can be as simple as the average height of a population compared to its geographic location. We don't do a lot of ethnobiology outside of the study of humans, though sometimes we apply its principles to animals like orangutans and dolphins. When I was called to the Arctic, I was expecting perhaps an unusual whale or a hunting technique that hadn't been observed before."

Alexandra Ripley is clearly very, very excited. Even though her delivery is calm and collected—as if this is just any other public lecture—she's flexing her fingers and transferring her weight too frequently. It's like she can't keep still. Her behaviour doesn't match her appearance at all. No one this enthusiastic about anything should wear maroon.

"Travellers, officers, crew members," she continues. "Usually, this sort of announcement would be made in the halls of academia, but when I was asked to wait and make the announcement here on *Titan*, I immediately agreed that it was a better location. As humans reach for the stars in new and innovative ways, what better time could there be to discover that there are beings out there reaching back?"

There's a moment of confused silence as the audience processes her words. Surely it can't be, I think. There's no way—

Benedict Reubens steps up to the display and reaches for the heavy fabric that lies overtop of it. I'm not entirely sure what the expected response is, and apparently no one else in the gallery is either, though the confused silence shifts to include confused murmuring. With a dramatic flourish, like he's baiting a bull to charge him, Benedict sweeps the cloth aside. It rises up into the air and then settles behind him, leaving the interior of the glass case visible for the first time.

The case itself is beautiful. It's made of polished brass right up to waist height, where the glass takes over. The craftsmanship is exquisite. Exactly zero people are paying attention to the case. Every one of us—passengers, crew members, even the other scientists who already know—is looking *inside*.

Those closest react first. At least one person shrieks, and a man next to Dr. Ripley laughs shrilly like he can't believe what he's seeing. They press forwards, curious for a closer look, but the scientists have moved in front of the case and hold them back. By then, the people in the middle of the crowd are able to see. This time there's a great deal more screaming, and instead of pressing forwards, most of them try to move away. They're blocked by those of us at the back of the room who still can't see what's going on.

"Travellers!" the captain calls out over the din. "Please remain calm. The case is completely sealed."

"What the hell is in that thing?" Ren asks, pushing on my shoulder to see if she can get a little bit higher.

But I'm no longer interested in what's in the case. There's genuine fear in the eyes of the passengers who are trying to get away from it. In the crush, I look around for an escape route and lock eyes with Dominic Reubens. He's totally calm, which makes me feel better for some inexplicable reason, even though Adam is gripping his arm tightly. I relax and he nods at me. Then he waves at me to come towards him and his relative safety along a gallery wall that's not in direct line of the crush. I grab Ren's hand, pulling her down from her perch, and we push through the crowd at an angle to meet him. We're shoved and cursed at more than once, but eventually we make it.

"Are you two okay?" Dominic asks. He's managed to shake off Adam's grip while we were moving towards him.

"Yeah," I tell him. We've been bounced around, but it's hardly worse than missing a jump in the zero-g engine room, and we've both done that more than once. "What's happening?"

"A failure of crowd control, mostly," Dominic says. "Come over here and you'll be able to see."

Ren steps into the place Dominic clears for us, dragging me behind her. Adam is pressed up against the side wall of the gallery room, his hands all over the brass as he uses it to stay on his feet. He doesn't look scared, necessarily. It's more like disbelief. His mother is totally ignoring him, standing near the case with Dominic's parents and the captain, trying to keep the crowd from rioting.

"Everyone calm down!" Dr. Jeffers manages to make the order sound soothing. "You have been chosen to view history in the making, and when you tell this story to your grandchildren, you won't want to tell them that you helped cause a stampede instead of observing decorously."

The crowd quiets some, shamed into silence if nothing else. Adam regains his composure and grabs on to Dominic's arm so tightly that I see him wince.

"Let's try this again, shall we?" Alodia Reubens has not lost her gift of speaking to a large crowd. "Thanks to my husband and his team, the co-operation of Dr. Jeffers, and the generosity of Captain Bernard, we are pleased to present the passengers of *Titan* with the scientific discovery of this age. Not just proof that we have neighbours in this galaxy, but actual specimens for you to look at."

This time, I have no idea how the audience reacts because I'm too busy reacting myself. It shouldn't be a surprise. They've told us what's in the case in extremely clear terms. But it's so hard to believe. Impossible, even. Until I can no longer deny it. I can see over Ren's head clearly enough, and the two of us stare in awe at the sight in front of us:

real

actual

extra-fucking-terrestrial

life.

I have exactly one moment to be furious that this has been revealed in a crowded room *on a spaceship*, but then I remember that we're nowhere near the hull or anything of mechanical significance, and I breathe a little easier as I take my second look.

The bottom section of the case is a raised platform to conceal the tech and so that viewers can see the contained items more clearly. Above that, the bulk of the display is clear glass. Even from the crowd, I can see the creature inside. It's big, nearly as long as the case, sinuous and spiky. Far from a little green man, it's more like a giant purple squid. It has multiple limbs—tentacles?—protruding from its thorax, and all of those have pincers at their terminus. The head seems to be almost entirely gaping maw, the lack of teeth somehow creepier than if it had been rows and rows of razor-sharp dentition. The third body segment is the smallest, like it was an afterthought in the creature's design. It has nothing sticking out of it.

Behind me, I hear Adam throw up. I try not to gloat.

"This is only one case," Ren hisses in my ear. "What the fuck is in the other gallery we cleaned this afternoon? It's in the room right next to this one."

As if in answer to her question, Dr. Ripley takes the mic again.

"I know it is alarming, my friends," she says. "I promise you, when my colleagues and I saw this beautiful creature for the first time, we all had similar reactions to yours. To know, all at once, that we are not alone in the universe is quite something, and it is not made any easier by the fact that our visitors are so alien."

"Is it alive?" someone shouts from the back of the room. I think it might be the man who laughed.

"Oh, no," Dr. Ripley says. "They have been dead for millennia. They were preserved so meticulously in the permafrost and we were able to save them before they deteriorated in the thaw."

They. This isn't the only creature. Ren is right. There are other cases on *Titan.* I'd stood right next to them. In the haste of getting ready for departure and then preparing for a Dress Presentation, I hadn't given much thought to where in *Titan*'s layout the launch ceremony was being held, but Ren remembered. This gallery is right next to the one with the other cases, and they are even bigger.

The passengers seem to be having similar thoughts because the murmuring rises up again.

"Travellers," Captain Bernard says. His voice is the most reassuring, possibly because he spends a lot of time in space. "Benedict Reubens and his team have designed a comprehensive display of these aliens. Each case maintains its specimen in perfect stasis and allows you to observe it. You, the first passengers on *Titan*, will be able to explore the exhibit at your leisure as we travel. Dr. Ripley and her team will be available to answer any questions you might have. The journalists on board will have the honour of breaking the news on Earth, even as they report on *Titan*'s premiere voyage."

"It's a fucking museum," Ren says. "They brought aliens on this trip to make it a giant flying museum."

As she speaks, the wall behind the case rolls up into the ceiling, revealing the second gallery behind it. The lights come on a moment later, and the other cases are illuminated. Dr. Ripley looks absolutely thrilled, and Benedict is smiling like all his best dreams are coming true. *Titan* might be groundbreaking, but now she'll be a footnote in the greatest discovery in the history of humankind.

Ren reaches out towards the case, her eyes wide but fearless. She looks like she had the day the Baileys had adopted her, like she knows everything is changing now and will never be the same again. I want to pull her back in, to throw the cover back up and bring the wall down. The crowd moves forwards and I'm swept towards the display cases with them.

For the first time, I wish I was back on Earth.

six

DOMINIC

The mood belowdecks is incredibly subdued, even for this time of the morning. We're about three hours into *Titan*'s day shift, which means up in the dining room passengers are starting to think in terms of brunch. I know better than to expect the sort of display of happy workers one might see in a commercial or used for propaganda, but the crew of *Titan* works quietly and does their best to stay out of the way of our scheduled tour. I wonder what it was like when the aliens were announced down here yesterday. The launch party had ended shortly after the reveal, and I'd escaped to my suite. Now that I think about it, breakfast conversation in the dining room had been a little strained too.

Sylvie Jeffers is nominally our guide, but she lets a senior engineer named Anthony do a lot of the talking. Anthony is gruff but informative, even if it's clear he'd rather be somewhere else. I do my best to listen astutely since the man has taken time out of his schedule, but Adam feels no such compunction and tries to chat up Celeste and Ren. To their credit, neither of the girls seems to be falling for Adam's particular brand of charm.

My father is right up front, supplementing Anthony's answers whenever he feels it's necessary. He's so loud that any interesting person we might talk to is scared off well before we make our way down the corridor. My parents don't care, and Adam is yawning openly, but I'm actually interested in the ship's design. Not enough that I'm going to throw myself into my father's plans for me. I still have no desire to go into the family business, despite what I said to Adelaide Connor at the party. But it's undeniably pretty cool . . . and it's beautiful.

"You'll remember that *Titan* is a sphere," says Anthony. "Because she was built in orbit and will never have to make planetfall, the normal constraints placed on ship design by gravity could be ignored. Her shape is actually irrelevant, but the sphere does have a few advantages."

"I find it all terribly confusing," my mother says. She's not reacting well to space travel and looks a little green around the gills. "How can every direction be down?"

"The same way it is on Earth, ma'am," Anthony explains. "Though, admittedly, it's not quite that simple. If the ship was rectangular, with a top and a bottom, you still wouldn't know how you were oriented in relation to Earth."

My mother blinks and her face pales a little bit more as she tries and fails to make her brain understand what her body is experiencing, and to identify a direction that makes sense.

"It does get a little easier, the longer you're on board," Anthony says, a little awkwardly, in an attempt to be kind. "Just remember that the engines are always below you, and they're taking you to Mars."

"Mother, do you want to go back to your room?" I ask. I don't want to leave, but I also don't want one of these people to have to clean up her vomit. "I have the ship's plans downloaded into my comm, so I can take us back if you like."

My wrist comm is basically only good for receiving alerts about what activities are underway, but there *is* a map to help me get to said activities. Which is good, since for some reason the comm doesn't allow me to talk to anyone and ask directions. The staff and crew are, we were informed, more than happy to help us if we need anything, and it's so much nicer to ask a person than your wrist.

"Oh, she'll be fine," my father says. "Go and talk to those young engineers. Maybe some of their work ethic will rub off on you."

My mother doesn't look like she wants to keep going, but she lets my father pull her back to the front of the group. Sylvie is smirking, as though my mother's space sickness is somehow *her* personal victory. Adam goes to walk beside her and I fall back a bit. Celeste and Ren are bringing up the rear, and soon I'm walking just ahead of them.

"Is it always this quiet?" I ask. I had been expecting the ship to make more noise when it wasn't being muffled for passenger sensibilities.

The girls look at each other. I hope they haven't been ordered not to answer questions or something. I don't want to get them in trouble. But then Ren shrugs.

"No," Celeste says. "You know how, in adventure stories, sailors are always really superstitious?"

"Yes?" I haven't been allowed to read much fiction since I was ten, which means I've taken every opportunity to do so on the sly.

"Well, we're not superstitious exactly," Ren says. "But last night we found out that there are aliens on board our ship, and it's not like any of us can leave."

"The passengers can't leave either," I point out. "But I think I see what you mean. You signed on for a job, and now the job is very different."

"Yeah," Celeste says. "Don't you think it's creepy? Not just the fact that aliens exist, but the fact that they told us while we're all isolated on a spaceship?"

"I think they wanted to get them off of Earth," Ren says, conspiratorially. "Can you imagine if this was in some big city down there? People would panic. Up here, there's nowhere to run, and if something goes wrong, there's only one target."

"What could possibly go wrong?" I ask. "The aliens are dead."

"Ignore her," Celeste says. "Her family is very nice, but they are kind of prone to conspiracy theories."

"It's called being prepared for all eventualities," Ren says.

I laugh. It is clearly a conversation they've had before, and it makes me feel welcome to see this iteration of it. Ren is pretending to be affronted, and Celeste's teasing is gentle.

I've wondered what it would be like to have a friend like that, who didn't want anything from me. Everyone I go— went, I guess—to school with is like Adam: competitive and ambitious. We'd all grown up comfortable on our parents' money, and we all intended to stay comfortable.

Up ahead, Anthony is explaining the hydroponics bay. *Titan*'s air is recycled through that section to pick up new oxygen from the plants, so it's connected to a lot of the ship's other systems, including the alien display. My father is asking a million questions—and answering half of them before Anthony has a chance to—so no one is paying attention to us.

"What was it like?" I blurt without thinking. "Growing up in the Rupt, I mean. I'm sorry, I know that's really personal. I don't even know what I don't know. I feel like I was cut off from something, that's all."

"It's not much of a thing to be cut off from," Ren says. "You're one of the lucky ones."

"Oh, my parents make sure I remember that," I assure her. "That's why I want to know what it was like. I don't want to be like them. Not if I can actually help, you know?"

Both of the girls look at me like I'm nuts, and I probably am. I'm an artist who's been forbidden from making art and I'm probably going to be disinherited the next time I step away from the family plan. But I still want to know.

"So, the actual earthquake was the Ottawa Valley expanding really fast," Ren says. "All that pressure stored up for*ever* and then torn apart quickly. A lot of the land just collapsed."

"Right," I say. "The epicentre was all mudslides and that sort of thing."

"Those people died immediately," Celeste says. "Or so we hope, in any case. Ren and I lived away from the epicentre, so our families were killed when the buildings all collapsed."

Ottawa had been as prepared is it could have been for an earthquake. The nature of the plate movement in the area remains a mystery, even years after the Rupt, so nothing can be predicted with any accuracy. It had been difficult to prepare people for a disaster no one could pin down. "The big one" had been a topic of discussion for decades before it finally hit. Buildings had been moderately reinforced for quakes, but the magnitude had flattened everything for kilometres. The Library of Parliament had fallen into the Ottawa River, and the rest of the Parliament Buildings had fared extremely poorly. The Peace Tower had collapsed straight down, which was a blessing since the bricks could have done a lot of damage if they'd been thrown. The American Embassy had exploded. The top two thirds of the Rideau Canal was unusable.

And that's just a small section of the downtown. The secondary wave of damage had been considerable as well. There had been fires and flash floods, but it had also been late January when the quake hit and temperatures were below -40 degrees Celsius at night.

"But you were rescued?" I ask.

"Eventually," Celeste says. "I don't remember it, so I can't tell you about that part."

"I don't really remember it either," Ren admits. "Just a noise that was so big I could feel it, and so much screaming."

It seems ridiculous to talk about Earth instead of the aliens or the ship, but I want a distraction. It feels like the aliens have been scratching away at my brain ever since I saw them, and *Titan* has been scratching at my spirit for even longer, though at least the ship is a tangible thing. Everything about the aliens, from their existence to their vibrant shade of purple to their presence on board, makes me uncomfortable. If the girls don't mind humouring me, I'm happy to talk about literally anything else.

"I don't remember it either," I tell them. "I was found in Orleans. My parents were at home in my mother's riding, in Alberta, so they arrived two weeks later, and that's when I was adopted."

"Dominic, what in the world are you bothering those girls about?" my father asks. He's still at the front of the group, so his voice is very loud and impossible to miss.

"I was just asking them some questions," I say.

"About the ship?" my father presses.

I don't answer because I'm terrible at lying. My mother rolls her eyes and turns back to Anthony, but my father makes his disappointment very clear.

"You could at least pretend to care about their jobs," my father says. "They had to work very hard to get them."

Both Celeste and Ren look like they wish they could disappear into the deck plating.

"This one, for example." My father gestures carelessly at Celeste. "She grew up in the dorms, from the time she was a baby. She had no one, but she applied for every scholarship and grant the government made available to her, and look at her now."

Celeste flinches as my father's full attention falls on her. He must have read her file, I realize, and I don't think that's very fair. My own private information is public thanks to my parents, but they have no right to pry into someone else's life.

"So many people in her situation would just take hand-outs and never strive to get out of the Rupt, but not her. She's got ambition. She's the kind of young person we want to see growing up and out of that disaster." My father's rant brings the whole tour to a halt. Everyone is staring at Celeste now, and she's starting to look as ill as my mother does.

"Engineer Sparrow is indeed one of our best apprentices," Anthony says stiffly. "Both she and Engineer Bailey are astute and thorough in their work."

He's trying to help, I know, but he's only making it worse. Once my father starts in on something—especially me—there's no making it better, and there's frequently collateral damage. Suddenly the aliens don't seem so bad. They don't question my worth. They just make my skin crawl.

"And you can't even manage to ask them pertinent questions," my father says, turning his attention to me fully. "It would be embarrassing if it weren't so predictable."

I make sure my face stays as neutral as possible in the face of my father's wrath, the girls' pity, and Adam's spite.

"You, Sparrow, was it?" my father says. "I read your file. Come up here and talk to me instead."

Celeste can't say no. She goes to the front and Anthony

starts the tour again. This time, my father makes sure to direct his questions to her, looking pointedly at me when her answers are given. She speaks robotically and is clearly uncomfortable, but I know my father doesn't care about that sort of thing.

"Yes, this is exactly what we want to see in Rupt kids. Don't you think, dear?" he says to my mother. "This is what so many of your bills were about—making sure everyone had the same opportunities we gave to our son."

I tune out my mother's answer. I fall into step beside Ren, who does me the mercy of not apologizing. I feel like the walls of the ship are closing in on me, the sphere constricting more and more until I'm about to be squeezed down to nothing. At least we're almost at the end of the tour.

We end up back in the main display gallery. The double room is now revealed in its full glory with bright lights and shining brass accents everywhere. There's no one at the cases at this time of day. Official admittance to the room won't begin until this afternoon, and from what Ren and Celeste have said, I imagine the crew will avoid the place as much as possible once they get their first view of the aliens.

Anthony steps up to the case with visible reluctance, keeping his gaze firmly away from it. My father drags Celeste forward.

"You know, when Dr. Ripley first contacted me, I thought she was off her rocker," he says.

"It's not hard to understand why," Dr. Jeffers says. She's standing close to the case, Adam beside her. "When they came to me, I thought it was a prank."

"Aliens on a spaceship does sound like something out of a story," my mother admits. Maybe it's just the lighting, but she looks healthier now that we've returned to the opulence of the passenger area. I can't imagine she's *more* comfortable close to the aliens, though. "But I'm glad you were able to set everything up. The reveal was strange, but I think it went well. What do you think, Sparrow?"

"Um," says Celeste, caught off guard. "I mean, I think everyone was very surprised, so the reaction might have been a little stranger than you expected?"

Her answer ends up coming out as a question, which I understand completely.

"The captain said afterwards that he thought for a moment there would be a riot," Dr. Jeffers says. She laughs, like a riot on a spaceship isn't incredibly dangerous to everyone on board. "But I think he was letting his imagination get away from him. The passengers on this cruise are some of the best and brightest minds on Earth. And we've learned that the crew is pretty incredible too." She smiles blindingly at Celeste.

"We try," Anthony says, when it becomes apparent that Celeste isn't going to answer the compliment.

"You can go, engineer," my father says. "Thank you, I am sure you have work to do."

"Yes, thank you, sir," Anthony says. He nods and then steps aside. He would have pulled Celeste with him, but my father intercedes again.

"Oh, she can stay," my father says. "I want to talk about the display case with her. Neither of the boys care about it, but I know *she'll* want to know more than was in the general briefing."

He has clearly forgotten Ren exists, and the other girl takes the opportunity to disappear with Anthony, shooting Celeste a sympathetic look as she goes. Sylvie Jeffers and my mother leave together, talking about ways to combat space sickness, with too much sweetness towards each other. Adam takes a seat, clearly prepared to listen to whatever my father is about to say, if only out of spite. There's no way I'm leaving Celeste alone with these two, and despite my father's scorn, I do care about the aliens. I'd just rather care about the aliens from a distance. Reluctantly, I take the seat next to Adam's. When Adam links fingers with me, I don't fight it, even though I want to.

"Well," my father says. "What do you think, Sparrow?"

"To be perfectly honest, sir, I don't know yet," Celeste says. Her tone is perfect. She clearly knows how to talk to men like my father. She's used to being on display because she's a subject of interest—a diamond plucked from so much muck, and all that. I don't know if I'm supposed to be furious on her behalf, but I can feel the anger building. No one should have to perform.

"No harm in admitting that," my father says. "As I said, it took me some time to get used to it as well."

"It's very impressive," Celeste says. "The aliens themselves, but also the habitat you've built for them."

My father preens. Fully revealed, there are five display cases arranged in a U-shape extending out from the first one we saw last night. The other four cases are longer, but contain smaller alien specimens, each arranged with samples of the permafrost they'd been found in. The smaller aliens don't have the big thorax segment the big one does. I'm trying not to jump too far ahead of the official information, but it's pretty straightforward to draw a hypothesis from that observation. There's no reason the aliens should follow Earth insect behaviour, but it's not an unreasonable guess and it's easier to think about them with some familiar context. Even though they're smaller, the other aliens are about a metre long and have the same maw and tentacles that the big one does. I shudder and look away.

Celeste reaches out a hand and hovers her fingers near the glass. The alien she's closest to has been posed so that it's rearing up like it's going to strike—the way a snake would, but with too many arms. Its maw is open as if it might be screaming in stasis. The expression on Celeste's face is inscrutable. A chime sounds on her wrist, pulling all of us out of the moment.

"I'm sorry, sir, I have to get below for my shift," Celeste says. This whole debacle of a tour is in *addition* to her workload.

"Of course, of course," my father says. "You have my permission to access this room whenever you like, even if there are passengers here. And if you want to see any of the plans, I'm happy to let you take a look."

"Thank you," Celeste says, in the tone of a person who doesn't want to accept a favour from a man like my father but will do so because she doesn't have another option.

If my father notices, he gives no indication. Celeste hasn't even fully exited the room when he turns back to Adam and me and begins lecturing us on how his brilliant preservation system works. I watch Celeste go. She has no reason to, but I hope she'll come back. It's nice to talk to someone who doesn't care about me at all.

some of them touch the stars

some of them burn them

all of them are delicious

one by one

we eat

she grows

seven

CELESTE

"**I need a shower,**" I say.

The tour ran past lunch so I had to eat quickly and go back to our quarters to get ready for our shift. We're on afternoons, which is the worst for routine. You're rushed at lunch, working over dinner, and tired at breakfast. The upside is that it's an eight-hour shift instead of a twelve-hour one, but we're at everyone's beck and call. Instead of working a station for the whole shift, we get sent wherever we're needed.

I pull on my work belt and do a quick safety check on my carabiners. My feet already hurt. At least I probably won't have to talk to anyone I don't like for the next few hours.

"We haven't even started yet," Ren says. "Or, wait, do you mean because Benedict Reubens touched you?"

"Why are rich people so gross?" I know I'm whining, but I can't help it. "Like, they are physically incapable of not being disgusting. I wasn't even a person to him—he just wanted to make Dominic feel bad."

"At least you got us a free pass into the display whenever you want," Ren says. "I mean, I am assuming I get to go with you and we'll just go in the middle of the night when there's no one to bother us, yeah?"

"Yeah," I say. "I still wish he'd remembered your name instead of mine, though."

"Please, my story is nowhere near as good as yours," Ren says. "I have two parents and a name that wasn't some guy's weird hyper-fixation."

"François is very nice and you know it. And birdwatching isn't that weird," I tell her. "I met him, like ten years later, and he recognized my name as one of his."

He'd been retired by then, only the money was too good for a health care worker to leave the job if they weren't burnt out. I was getting my annual checkup, mandated for Rupt survivors—and he was still at the hospital.

"Couldn't you have got something cool? Like Egret? Or Peregrine?" Ren checks her own carabiners and then turns around so I can do the double-check.

"I like Sparrow," I say. "It's interesting, but not too interesting."

"Yeah, and memorable, apparently," Ren says. "Come on, we'll be late."

The two of us head down to the engine room for our shift. Usually we'd be coming off of a rest period, but the tour request has thrown everything off. Anthony is probably going to be grumpy too, just to put icing on the cake. At least we'll only have to deal with him for a couple of hours before the day shift is over.

Life-altering revelations aside, the journey is going well thus far. It has been almost eighteen hours since *Titan* left Earth's orbit and everything is going exactly as it should. We're due to pass the moon in another few hours. It isn't exactly on the way, given relative orbital positions, but the cruise planners had felt that if they were going to be sort of close, they might as well let people see it. It's been endlessly complicated for the navigators and, by association, the engineers. We have to go slowly because the moon isn't in the direction we're actually heading, and we won't be able to pick up speed until after we swing around it. Then there will be a final course correction and then it's straight on till morning. The detour adds almost a million dollars to the overall cost of the fuel, and no one will see the moon through an actual window, but none of the passengers care about that part.

We pass under the locked section of the ship where the indentured workers are making the crossing. Already there are horrible rumours circulating about what's going on on those decks, how it's lawless, and since they have no way of keeping track of time they all went insane immediately.

"Can't you read the blueprints?" Ren had bellowed at one of the hydrobiologists in the mess at breakfast as he told some lurid tale. "They've got screens and access to the same tech we do. It might be a bit cramped and the food will probably get boring, but they'll be warm, and that's not nothing for some of them."

The hydrobiologist had spluttered at her and then immediately begun to tell the story again, only quieter this time.

"Fancy plumber, and he thinks he knows how people work," Ren had groused.

The threat of indenture always loomed on Earth. Scary stories about it were normal, to evoke pity for those who were desperate or foolish enough to sign their life over to some rich person who had very little reason to care about them. It's no different from the cautionary tales we'd whispered as children in the Rupt, but the locked doors on *Titan* just make everyone more paranoid about it. The simple fact is this: no one on those decks has started to work off the cost of their passage to Mars. Whoever owns their contracts needs them alive to recoup their investment. They won't be travelling in comfort, by any means, but they're safe enough.

"The dads actually had to lock Chels and Glory in the basement to keep them from taking the indenture tickets," Ren tells me. "I understand why they wanted to come, but I'm glad our parents didn't let them."

You only have to be sixteen to sign an indenture contract—to make it possible for people to get work and support their families, of course, not to exploit children who can't even vote yet—and two of Ren's younger siblings are old enough, with the rest coming on fast. I'm glad they have their dads to protect them.

We pass through another doorway and reach the mustering room, where each engineering crew meets before shift. It would have been faster to take the straight path through engineering proper, but now that we're underway, it's better to keep the engine room free of random traffic. An accident or collision in Earth's orbit is one thing, but we have a week in space ahead of us, and everyone knows exactly what resources are on board.

"There you are," Anthony says as we come in. "I knew you couldn't be lost, since you were giving a tour, but I was starting to wonder what was keeping you."

"Do you want me to spell his name?" Ren asks. "You were there, Senior Engineer Davis."

"I am aware," Anthony says dryly. "And you're not late yet anyway. You've got, like, three more minutes."

"Wait, did we pass a hazing ritual or something?" I ask. "Why are you being nice to us?"

As soon as I say it, I know why. Rumours spread like wildfire on *Titan*—even faster than the oxygen cyclers. Everyone will know that I have an all-access pass to the alien exhibit. I'm sure I'm about to make all kinds of new friends.

"Oh, we are definitely going to make money on this," Ren whispers to me. "Or at least get a lot of favours."

"We?" I ask.

"Yeah, because you're such a people person," Ren says.

It's true. I would probably just have taken people along to make them stop talking to me. Ren will make sure I get something for it.

"Hot showers," I say. "Definitely hot showers."

"If you two budding criminals are done planning your black market scam?" Anthony says. "I have some assignments to hand out."

If Anthony is looking to gain my favour, my task list certainly isn't his way in. On one hand, I'm relieved—I don't want my boss to suck up to me for something I don't even want anyway. On the other hand, now Ren and I have to run supplies up to the bridge for the next eight hours. At least the service passages run between engineering and the bridge, so I'm unlikely to encounter any more passengers.

The first delivery is fairly straightforwards. The requisition is from Captain Bernard, and it's for six boxes that the quartermaster wants taken far, far away from the galley.

"Fish food?" Ren says, heaving a box onto the trolley.

"And tank decorations, a few replacement bulbs for what I'm assuming is a heat lamp, and whatever it is you clean out fish tanks with," I add, skimming the manifest we were given. "I wonder if the captain likes fishing when he's on Earth or if he just likes having them as pets."

"You can ask him," Ren says. "Fish in space. It sounds like a terrible movie title. Why does he need fish?"

"I don't know," I say. "He's going to be making this run for years, probably. Maybe they stop him from getting homesick."

"How long do fish live?" Ren asks. She puts the last box on the trolley and catches the strap I throw her. In a moment, we have the load secured. It isn't a bumpy trip, but if we have to manoeuvre around people, we won't have to worry about stability.

"You can ask him," I suggest.

Ren doesn't dignify that with a response, and the two of us begin to push the trolley. All the other gear in this room just needs to be dropped into engineering when it's required for repair or something, and that can be done by opening a hatch in the floor. The storage room wasn't intended to hold bridge material, but with the now-revealed aliens being brought on board as a surprise, a few things have been stored in unusual places. Once the fish food has been removed, it'll be back to business as usual.

There's a freight elevator three sections over, and once we reach it, our job will be significantly easier. It would be nice if there were more elevators, but *Titan* is only nice for a limited crowd.

We make it through all three sections without meeting anyone other than a few of our shift members. Everyone is too busy to talk, even though they're all clearly dying to ask me questions about the aliens. I keep my eyes down, which is fairly necessary given that I'm steering the trolley, and avoid them. Ren opens the freight elevator and we push the trolley on board. It's only big enough for the cart, which means we now face a climb, but I don't mind.

With Ren leading the way, we tackle the first ladder. It's the shortest one, because the crew deck is only slightly taller than a normal person's height. The second ladder, which brings us through the deck where the hospitality staff are quartered, is almost nine feet of climbing, which we repeat for deck three, home of the mess and various galleys, along with cabins for officers and onboard science-types like our medical staff. After that comes two decks of storage for luggage, the ugly version of hydroponics, the waste recycling vats, and the water tanks. Then we're into the passenger levels.

These ladders are twelve feet high, and there are three of them. Twice, we have to wait while the hospitality crew uses the ladders to move between decks on passenger orders. Those always have precedence, unless there's an emergency, but it's still kind of annoying.

At last we reach deck nine, *Titan*'s outermost layer. It's still separated from space by several metres of metal and machinery, not to mention shielding against various forms of radiation, but it is as close to the "top" as *Titan* gets. Any time someone on board thinks they're looking out a window, they're actually looking at a very well-designed screen. It's how the passengers will view the moon later on, and also how they can stare into the vastness of space if they ever feel like doing that instead of watching a program or putting up a soothing painting to look at.

Our trolley has been pulled off the freight elevator by someone else who needs to use it, but that's to be expected on a ship that has prioritized passenger movement over the crew's ability to do their jobs. Everything is still packed in place, so we head toward the bulkhead that leads into the bridge. I scan my wrist comm, whose limited function does include opening locked doors if the wearer is allowed to. Usually I don't have bridge access, but Anthony has given us clearance for this delivery. The door slides open and we push the trolley the last little bit into the room.

I haven't seen the bridge since my orientation tour, and it had only been half finished at that time. Now it's full of people and flashing lights and bright panels. If engineering is *Titan*'s heart, this is her brain. It takes me a moment to get used to the buzz of activity in the room. In engineering, everything is muffled by the sound of the engines, but up here, the conversations layer on top of each other without interruption. It's actually quieter, in a way, but it's harder to listen to.

"Ah, there you are." Captain Bernard waves at us. "Right this way, if you please."

I blink. I didn't expect the captain to meet us personally. He must really like these fish. Beside me, Ren shrugs and the two of us push the trolley in the captain's wake. Everyone gets out of his way, of course, and then they have to take a few more steps to let us through with the trolley to follow him. It's kind of funny to watch.

"I know it's a bit of an extravagance," the captain says, ushering us into his ready room. "But my family have been captains of something for generations, and leaving the ocean behind entirely seemed like pushing my luck."

I put the safety lock on the trolley and look up. I had been expecting a fair-sized tank, but what I see takes up almost the entirety of one of the walls. There are flashes of all different colours as the fish mill around—blues and reds and silvers. Most of them are large. None of them look particularly tropical.

"Did Mr. Reubens design that too?" Ren asks, brazen as always. Then she adds, "Sir?"

"No, this was built into *Titan*'s original design," the captain says. "After I was assigned, they let me pick some features for my ready room. The other choice was a vertical greenhouse thing that made me want to sneeze just looking at it."

"It's very nice," Ren says politely. "Um, what kind of fish? I read about that breeding program for new fish stock for that reef that used to be near Australia that they're trying to rebuild, but those fish don't look like these ones."

"This is a cold-water tank," the captain says. He helps us unload the boxes, leaving them by his desk so he can sort everything later. "Mostly in the herring family. They've been bred not to eat each other, but if they were normal fish, they'd basically be the base of the whole North Atlantic food chain."

Captain Bernard smiles at us like his favourite thing in the whole universe is talking about fish with people, and for all I know, it probably is.

"So, do you go fishing when you're on Earth?" I ask.

"Yes," the captain says. "It's a strange hobby, but it's quiet and I find it relaxing."

"I can understand that, sir," I say. There's a beat of silence where I wonder if I should ask more fish questions or get back to work, but then my wrist comm chimes.

"I'm sorry, sir," says Ren, whose comm has also sent her a notification. "We've got to get going. There's a lot of traffic in the freight elevator while we reshuffle the lower storage areas, and we're on a tight schedule."

"Of course, don't let me keep you," the captain says. He helps us push the trolley back out into the main bridge before nodding in farewell and going over to one of his officers.

Ren and I move the trolley back to the elevator. Since it's empty, we can sit on it and ride down—it's much faster than climbing. It's still a tight fit, but both of us are on the small side. We settle in as the doors shut, and Ren turns on her wrist beacon to give us some light. I meet her eyes and see that they're glinting in the beam.

"Fish," Ren chokes out before dissolving into giggles.

"Mostly herring," I say sagely.

I don't usually laugh as much as Ren does, but in this case her amusement is contagious, and by the time the freight doors open to the lowest level we're both laughing.

eight

DOMINIC

Adam throws himself into one of the chairs in my sitting room with the sort of drama that's usually reserved for Shakespearean death scenes. I find it even more annoying than usual. Yes, my feelings are hurt by how my father acted during the tour, and presumably Adam is feeling slighted. Not because he actually *is* interested in following in his mother's footsteps, but because he's not a fan of being lectured by anyone. Still, there's no reason to take it out on the furniture. Instead, I hand my jacket to the waiting Peters and then tell him I'll be fine until dinner. There's no need for both of us to suffer.

Our tour had lasted from after breakfast until just before lunch. I had almost been able to enjoy it. Celeste and Ren are both fun to talk to, even if my questions had been a bit awkward. I hope I'll be able to speak with them again, and that they won't mind more talking about the Rupt. For the first time in my life, I'm close to people who know a lot about where I came from—the real stories, not the politics my mother peddles—and I want to take advantage of it. Politely.

"I can't believe how much your dad fawned all over that wretched girl," Adam says. "Why should she get special treatment? Anyone can grow up in the dirt."

"You know how much he likes to grandstand," I say. I don't know why I'm still trying to humour Adam. I'm about three seconds from breaking up with him, I just don't know how I'm going to do it.

"I like it better when I'm the good example," Adam says.

Adam expects a sly "Because you're *such* a good example," or some other smart comment, but instead it feels like I'm finally able to slam shut a door that's been letting in an annoying draft. I sit down in the chair opposite him, put my hands on the armrests, and summon every bit of cold dignity I can muster.

"I don't want to date you anymore," I say, and it's easy to say it. I feel flat and emotionless, but there's a sort of determination in me that I'm not used to.

"What the fuck are you talking about?" Adam asks. He sits up straight and puts his feet on the floor. Leaning forwards, his edges are back but he isn't smiling—so the threat of his sharpness is all too apparent.

"I don't want to date you anymore," I repeat. It's even easier the second time. "I understand that the nature of ship accommodations means we'll see each other every day, but that would have happened on Earth anyway. I don't want you in my room or touching me."

"Dom," Adam says, "come on, man, who else am I going to hang out with on this heap? We're expected to be together. Hell, even our parents are on side with it, and I know yours hate me as much as my mother thinks you're pathetic."

My parents might hate Sylvie Jeffers with the cold fury of the void, but they love their own power enough to like the idea of a dynastic arrangement between our two families. Sylvie and my father built *Titan* together, and they don't even like each other. If their sons work well with each other, each parent could imagine their own names shining with the fresh glory of their sons' accomplishments.

"Yes, and why would I want to get out of a relationship like that?" I ask dryly. "It's not like there's no one else our age on board."

"But you're such a good fuck, Dom. And who else have you got?" Adam leans back in the chair, crossing one foot over his knee.

I had suspected that his reasons for keeping me around were pretty base. And maybe sex and the power trip of dating someone he can usually control is enough for *him*, but it isn't something I'm going to put up with anymore.

Over his shoulder, I can see Peters hovering just outside the room, even though I had told him he could go. If things go bad, at least my valet will be here to help me.

"I don't care." And I *don't* care. My voice is stronger than ever. "I hate the way you treat other people, and I hate the way you treat me. It was fun for a bit, because it was something my parents couldn't stop, but it's not fun anymore. You're not fun, Adam, and I don't want you here."

It's so much more than that, but Adam will never understand. He's not built for empathy. I thought that would make me stronger, help me develop that skin of cynicism everyone else I know seems to have graduated high school with, but I was wrong. He's just a dick.

"You are unbelievable," Adam says. He gets to his feet and begins to pace back and forth, staying out of arm's reach. "You wait until we're on this godforsaken ship—which I only came on because you were here—and now you expect me to just leave?"

"I hoped we could make it work," I admit. He's still lying. He's only on *Titan* for thrills, and for the chance of maybe breaking from his mother when we get to Mars. "But *Titan* just brings out the worst in you. Do you even remember the names of the engineers who took us on that tour? You're about to head to a nice lunch buffet, but they have to go to work. You add to people's problems, and you make me a worse person, and I'm done."

I haven't even got out of my chair. For the first time in a while, I feel like I'm in control. Of the conversation, of the moment, even a little bit of my life. Adam's callousness towards other people won't be my problem anymore, and his crude remarks about sex won't be something I have to worry about. I still have to get him out of the room, but, so far, I feel like things are going pretty well.

"The only reason your father has tolerated your behaviour the last few months is because of me," Adam hisses. He stops pacing and rounds on me, all but splitting at the seams with rage. "If you stay with me, you might get to keep your stupid art as a hobby. Without me, your father is going to crack down, and you'll probably never see a bright colour again."

It's an extremely valid threat. But the offer Adam is making isn't good enough. I lean back in my chair and cross my arms in front of me.

"I'll take my chances, thank you," I say. I muster up every bit of snobbery and superior attitude I possess and look Adam in the face. "Do you need Peters to show you out, or can you find the way yourself?"

Adam looks like he has a hundred things to say, each more venomous than the last, but instead of lashing out, he goes cold.

"I can find the door, thank you," he says. "I can't wait to hear what your parents think. I'll see you at lunch, Dom."

He strides out of the room with his head held high, but I know I've stuck a thorn in his paw. Adam Jeffers does not get rejected. There will definitely be consequences, both from my father and from Adam himself, but I already feel lighter.

"Would you like me to have a lunch tray sent up?" Peters asks from the doorway. My valet looks oddly proud of me.

It's very tempting. But staying in my room for lunch will too easily lead to staying in for supper too, and then never leaving until my father breaks the door down. It will be better to face it head-on.

"No, thank you, Peters," I say. "I think I should just get it over with and move on as quickly as possible."

"Of course, Dominic," Peters says, laying extra stress on my name because there's no one here to care if my valet approves of my life choices. Or that I'm proud of myself because he does. "I've left one of your pullovers out for you. Lunch is supposed to be less formal."

"How formal can you make a buffet?" I ask.

Peters is far too professional to laugh, but I would have sworn I heard a soft cough.

I pull on my sweater and then look in the mirror to straighten my collar and hair. Some measure of rakishness is considered stylish these days, but I think that having my hair tousled just makes me look younger. Once I'm sure everything is in place, I pick up my room card and tuck it into a pocket. Then I take a deep breath, like I'm getting ready to dive into very cold water, and open the door.

The three passenger decks on *Titan* all use the same dining room and entertainment areas. The first-class galleries are grand, with high ceilings that encompass two levels of the ship. The outermost deck accesses the rooms by walking down grand staircases. The second deck is all in a straight line. The third deck has to do a little bit of climbing, so obviously their tickets are cheaper and their suites aren't quite as nice. My suite is on the second deck, deck seven, so if all I ever want is to eat in the dining room and entertain myself in the galleries, I can just stay on one level.

The dining room is a section over from my rooms. It's not labelled, but the actual seating area only takes up about half of the space. The other section is a concealed galley to prepare all the food. It's much easier than carrying everything up from a lower deck, but the real reason is less about making it simpler for the wait staff and more about ensuring the food is hot when it gets to the table. Dinner is a full-service production, but breakfast and lunch are self-serve. The buffet is gigantic for both meals, with almost anything you can imagine. *Titan* might be registered and built in Canada, but she's an international ship, so there's food for every culture. Towards the end of the journey the selection might dwindle, but right now there's plenty of everything.

I get a plate and fill it with sandwiches and fruit. There are a few appealing dishes in the non-Canadian parts of the buffet, but I know that this meal is going to be a challenge to get through, so I want to stick with comfort food. There's nothing like a good sandwich, and everything on *Titan* is the best.

There's only assigned seating at dinner—the better to ensure everyone's drink preferences are met—but I know my father already considers his table his own personal property. That is where he'll sit, and if another passenger gets there first, it will probably be very uncomfortable. When I sit down, I'm the only one there. Three bites into my first sandwich triangle, I see my parents come in. A server appears with a selection of pops, but I wave her away. The last thing I need in my stomach right now is more bubbles.

I'm finishing my second triangle when my parents take their seats. My mother has recovered enough to try a variety of sushi and my father has gone for salad and vegetable soup, with a plate of halved hard-boiled eggs.

The same server brings them their tea and I steel myself.

"Your father and I were disappointed with your behaviour on the tour this morning, Dominic," my mother begins. She struggles to get her sushi from the soy sauce dish to her mouth because she sits too primly in her chair and grips the chopsticks incorrectly.

"I'm sorry, Mother," I say. "I suppose I let the excitement of meeting others who grew up in the Rupt get to me. Don't worry, I'll make sure it doesn't happen again."

"I don't know why you bother so much about that wretched place," my mother says carelessly. "I had to because it was my job, but we freed you from it. Put it out of your mind, my love."

"I agree with your mother," my father says. "You don't need to worry about what goes on in that mess. We pulled you out of it, and you should act accordingly."

I nod as uncommittedly as I can. I fully intend to talk with Celeste again, but I'll be sure to do it when my parents aren't around.

Across the dining room, Adam comes in. He looks in our direction and then stalks to the buffet. He piles his lunch on a plate without much thought to the food itself and then goes and sits at a table on the far side.

"Are you and Adam having a fight?" my father asks, his concern almost sounding genuine. "I probably shouldn't have admonished him this morning. He'll grow out of his laziness someday, and his ambition is already there. I suppose you didn't attempt to mollify him and that's why his feathers are still ruffled?"

"We broke up," I say.

"I beg your pardon?" my mother asks. She sets down her chopsticks.

"I told him I didn't want to date anymore," I elaborate. "He's not thrilled, but he left my room. We're over."

"This is intolerable," my father says. "That boy is the only good thing about you lately. He pushes you. He makes you focus on the right things. I'll admit, I am not entirely fond of him, but I can't deny that you make a good pair."

"I agree with your father," my mother says. "You'll meet with him after lunch and say that you were over-emotional after the tour. He'll believe that. Then you can apologize and convince him you didn't really mean it when you broke up. You have to consider our future, dear. The two of you together is a powerful factor."

I am such an idiot. I knew that their ambition outweighed their dislike, and I still tried to annoy them by dating the son of Dad's rival. Of course they'd rather I was miserable if it means our family reputation stays elevated.

"I will not," I say. "He didn't make me a better person. He is mean and vindictive, and he hurts people on purpose."

"I don't care," my father says. "Your relationship with that boy is the only advantage I hold over Sylvie Jeffers, and I won't watch you squander it."

I take a bite of sandwich to avoid committing a murder, and my father takes it as acquiescence.

"Excellent," he says. "We were going to take you to the bridge with us after lunch, but instead you and Adam can go find a dark corner to kiss and make up."

"No," I say. It comes out much more clearly than any of us had been expecting.

"We have given you everything," my mother hisses. "And you refuse to co-operate with us when we consider your future."

"You just said it was *our* future," I remind her. "I don't want to be a game piece that you trade around when it's useful."

"Because God forbid you're actually useful," Father says. His voice is starting to rise, which is attracting attention. He gets himself under control with some effort.

Doing this in public had definitely been the right call. If I had skipped lunch and had this confrontation in my rooms, there would have been a lot of yelling. Since we're in full view of all the diners, my father has to restrain himself.

"This is not over," my mother says. She has her politician smile on, which is always bad news. "But in the meantime, you are certainly not joining us on the bridge. I expect you to go back to your quarters and think about how you want the rest of this voyage to go."

"I'll have my valet go through your room, as well," my father says. "Any contraband that you smuggled on board will be removed and destroyed. You will not spend one moment engaging in your childish hobby."

I hadn't forgotten his threat, but it still hurts. I wonder if Peters has hidden anything. It's possible. Peters has a fine line to walk, but he does what he can, and in return, I go out of my way to be as easy to work for as possible.

"I understand, Father," I say calmly in the face of their combined wrath. "I knew there would be consequences, and I accept them."

For the first time in years, or probably ever, if I am being honest, Benedict Reubens looks at me with some measure of respect. He had clearly been expecting more complaining or pleading. Receiving acceptance is not something he had been prepared for, and that's what I was banking on.

"Well," he says, "at least you're not a total pushover."

"Thank you, Father," I say. I pick up the final sandwich triangle and take a bite. It isn't a lot of leverage, but it's a place to start.

silver scales around us

silver scales inside us

silver scales will not sustain us

but the taste is enough

the feel is enough

the promise is enough

she'll begin

nine## nine

CELESTE

By the end of my shift, I'm even more exhausted than usual. I can't even blame the tour. Ren and I have been up and down ladders way more than usual, delivering equipment all over the ship. A run or two during a shift is not uncommon, but usually on-duty engineers spend most of our time in the engine room. I would have given anything for a regular assignment, but every time we came back, the senior engineer on duty sent us off again.

"Who decided this ship should have ladders?" Ren asks, bending over to massage her calves when we're finally dismissed from duty just after 9:00 p.m. ship's time.

"Someone who was never going to climb them, obviously," I tell her. It's hard to imagine Sylvie Jeffers spending eight hours the way we just had.

"I wish we could just go to bed," Ren says. "Well, after I eat something, of course."

"Why *can't* we just go to bed?" I ask. I'm not even sure I'm going to make it through the late dinner sitting in the mess hall, though not eating would be foolish.

"Because someone has a free pass to the alien room, and we should take advantage of it," Ren reminds me. "I didn't get a good look the other day, and I want one."

"Ugh, I don't," I say. "They look like giant squids, and it's creepy to have dead things just hanging around on board. Like those deer heads in the cabin your dads rented the summer we were twelve."

"Alphonse and Gertrude were great!" Ren says haughtily. "And they never complained about the mosquitoes."

"There were so many mosquitoes," I remind her, a phantom itch creeping up my arm at the memory.

The Baileys had always done what they could to give their kids holidays, and one year I had been able to come, because Ren and I were old enough to contain the younger ones if we worked together. The cabin was northeast of Ottawa, clear of the Rupt completely, on a little lake that reflected blue sky out of dark water. There were three rooms with nothing but bunk beds. I was comfortable enough, but the screens on the windows were in disrepair, and a lot of bugs came in before the dads could go into town and fetch mosquito netting. I had been too grateful to complain to the adults, but I was more than happy to complain to Ren. The taxidermied deer in the great room had scared the littlest kids, and the stories Ren made up about them didn't help.

"Please?" Ren says. "The passengers will be at their fancy dinner by now. I talked to some of the wait staff. They said dinner starts at eight and will be three hours by the time they do all the courses and the musical performance. We'll have the place to ourselves."

I roll my head around on my neck, feeling each of my cervical vertebrae press against the one below. There'll be no distracting Ren from this. I may as well do it now, because otherwise she'll never stop talking about it and I'll never get to sleep again.

"Fine," I say. "But we're eating and changing first."

Dinner in the crew mess is always a loud affair. All four of our daily meals are served buffet style, and there's a storage unit just outside the kitchen that keeps food hot for people who work non-shift hours like the medical staff, the catering and kitchen crew, and can't make it to regular meals or the late dinner. The food isn't as varied as the food the passengers get is, but there's still a selection. I had discovered curry on board *Titan*, and I'm slowly working my way through every variety the kitchen can serve.

Ren is more of a meat and potatoes type, though the ship-grown tubers leave a great deal to be desired, by her account. For the first time in both of our lives, we can eat without worrying where the next meal will come from, how much what we're currently eating costs, and how we'd make sure other people also get fed. It's incredibly relaxing. At first, we'd bolted down our dinners like we always had. The twins and Michael had been the same. But after a few weeks, it became easier to remember that we aren't on the clock when we're in the mess, and that we're allowed to have seconds if we want them.

Ren eats efficiently, having secured the promise of going to look at the aliens. I don't hurry, but I keep up. Wendy Jackson—who's on the day shift because she works in hydroponics but prefers to eat with her brother—tells us about her misadventures in the Medical wing. Since she gave David a kidney, they both have to be monitored for any strain or related issues. *Titan* only has one Medical bay, which means that passengers and crew alike are treated there, and, according to Wendy, the medics don't take class into account when doing their triage. She'd been seen ahead of at least four passengers with space sickness, and none of them had been happy about it.

"One of them might actually complain," Wendy says, gesticulating with a fork full of fish and chips. "I doubt the others will, though. They were kind of embarrassed when David started waxing on about how awesome I was for giving him an organ and how miraculous it was that we found each other after being separated."

"I'm going to milk that story for the rest of our lives," David says. He adds his carrots to his twin's plate and takes her zucchini in return.

"I didn't say not to," Wendy tells him. "I just thought it was funny."

"Do you think the complaint will go anywhere?" Michael asks. He's technically eating breakfast, since he and David are on the night shift, but that doesn't stop him from piling his plate with mashed sweet potato and baked chicken.

"No," Wendy says. "The head doctor looked ready to shut them all down. Even if it goes to the head steward or the captain or something, I wouldn't bet against the medical staff."

Ren finishes her last bite of dinner and looks meaningfully at the last few bits of rice on my plate. I try not to roll my eyes as I clean them up with my flatbread and wipe my hands on a serviette.

"Are you two going somewhere?" David asks.

"Of course they are," Wendy says, her eyes bright with excitement.

"Oh, right," David says. "Your 'special circumstances' pass."

None of them bother to hide their disgust at his remark. It's all too common when someone finds out where we're from. It's the reason no one is going to get away with complaining about Wendy being ahead of them in line in the infirmary, and it's the reason I can go see the aliens whenever I want to. People always seem to find it inspiring, our lives and accomplishments, never mind how many people had died to give us those circumstances to overcome.

"I'll take you all up eventually," I tell them. "I don't even want to go tonight, but Ren is pushy."

"It's all right," Michael says. "Some of us know how to be patient."

Ren and I take our plates to the return counter and make our way out of the mess hall. We are almost entirely on the opposite side of *Titan* from where the gallery is, so we walk around the service corridor to get to the hatch we need. With everyone either working or at dinner, the halls are as quiet as they ever get. I can hear the engines humming, a constant sign of life beneath our feet. It's a comfort and a reminder, of what we have achieved and what we still want.

The hatch is open when we arrive, which isn't unusual. Theoretically, we're supposed to close hatches for safety and containment, but no one wants to open the damn things every time they're on a ladder, so the senior officers let it slide. The scientists and special guests that Dr. Ripley brought with her have started eating with the crew already, even though they can eat with the passengers in the fancy dining room. I can't say that I blame them. I check to make sure no one else is on the ladder and then I start to climb. My shoulders ache every time I lift an arm, but I keep going.

"I might have a tiny regret," Ren says, panting for breath a few rungs below me. "Not enough to turn back, but if it makes you feel better to know that I'm in pain, I am."

"It does," I tell her. "And thank you."

At last, we reach the second passenger deck. We emerge from the same hatch we had fled into before the launch. It's extremely creepy to think about now, how close we'd been to the aliens without knowing that aliens even existed. My mind still shies away from the enormity of the idea of life on other planets, but it's hardly something I can deny. We haven't had time to check any of the newsfeeds from Earth, but I'm sure they're crawling with conspiracy theories and all sorts of nonsense. Maybe getting the aliens away from Earth for the reveal had been a clever idea in more ways than one.

I scan my wrist comm and the door opens to let us in. Until I hear the click, I was certain it wasn't going to work, that Benedict Reubens hadn't actually done what he'd said he would and given me access. It would have made far more sense if he'd forgotten me immediately once I was no longer in his line of sight. Yet my pass works, and we step into the gallery.

The lights are dim, since no guests are expected at this time and the official viewings haven't started yet. The room is still set up much the way it had been for the launch celebration, though the large table full of tiny snacks is gone.

We move closer to the display, Ren eagerly and me with considerable reluctance, though I couldn't have explained why if someone asked. The case really is an engineering marvel. The systems are totally self-contained, preserving the specimens within as perfectly as they had been when they were frozen on Earth. There are spotlights on certain parts of the cases to draw the eye. Little placards have been added so that viewers can read information about what they're looking at, although the introductory placard is quick to inform us that much is still unknown.

And then, of course, there are the actual aliens.

From across the room, it had been possible to dismiss them as a novelty—something else for the wealthy passengers on *Titan* to enjoy. Up close, it's impossible to deny that these creatures are real, had been alive, and had probably eaten things that are about the size of a human, if the mouthparts are being displayed correctly.

"I thought it was going to be like looking at dinosaurs," Ren admits, her voice quiet and a little overawed. "You know, like the natural history museum."

"Those are fossils," I point out. "Petrified organic matter. These were frozen, so there's still tissue. And they weren't found in pieces, so there's not a lot of guesswork when it comes to putting them together."

Ren looks at the thing's giant mouth.

"You think it really looked like that?" she asks.

"I don't imagine it walked around with its mouth open all the time, if that's what you mean," I tell her. "But it's probably close."

Ren shudders but presses on towards the other cases. I follow her, trailing one hand against the glass casing just to prove I can. The containment field tingles; it's definitely not something we're supposed to touch. The passengers probably consider themselves too fancy for a warning sign. It doesn't make me feel any better.

"I think it's because they're purple," Ren says out of nowhere. I jump. It's easy to be startled in this room. "Purple's supposed to be a friendly colour, but these things look absolutely terrifying."

I can't disagree with her. The display lighting is museum-soft, but the aliens are almost phosphorescent. Neon purple shouldn't exist this . . . much.

"Ew, are those eggs?" Ren points to the corner of the display case farthest from the big alien.

Sure enough, nestled in the corner of the case in a reconstructed nest is a clutch of eggs. They look intact. They're beige with purple veining, one much more veined than the others. The truly distressing thing is how much they look like normal eggs. The colours are all wrong, of course, but they're familiar in size and shape, even though they are utterly off-putting.

"Yeah, that's too much," I say. "I don't want to think about baby aliens and what they eat and how they grow."

"The placard says that they were found in a nest like this, but that the scientists had to build their own version of the nest for the display," Ren says, her eyes trailing over the information as she reads it quickly. "Yuck, I hope they wore gloves when they picked them up."

"We wore hazmat suits," says a voice from behind us. This time we both jump. "Don't worry, I don't mind it when tourists come by. That's the whole point."

Dr. Ripley steps into the light, a kind smile on her face.

"We have permission," Ren says, automatically defensive. Our uniforms give us away instantly.

"Everyone should have permission," Dr. Ripley says. "I agreed to this venture because the funding they offered me was astronomical—pun absolutely intended—but I have no intention of hiding these creatures away so that only the rich and privileged get to see them."

"Thank you," I say, even though I would have been quite happy to never know these things existed. Beside me, I feel Ren relax.

"I'll tell you that there is going to be a lecture tonight, though," Dr. Ripley continues. "They're cutting the music short in the dining gallery and everyone will move down here. You're welcome to stay, of course, but I can't promise you'll have as good a view as you do now."

"We won't stay," Ren says. "We're just off shift, and we should turn in. But I do want to come back!"

"Any time," Dr. Ripley says. She looks at me. "You're the girl Benedict Reubens gave a pass to, correct?"

I nod.

"Excellent," she says. "He's an asshole, but at least he accidentally stumbled into charity and landed on decent people."

She glances down at her watch.

"You have about fifteen minutes, girls," she says. "I'm going to lead the horde in from the dining room, so you'll have to show yourselves out."

We nod and watch as the elegant scientist sweeps out of the room. She's playing a part on *Titan* as much as we are, and somehow knowing that she has managed to secure academic funding in return for all of this pageantry makes me feel better.

"Ten minutes," I say. "And then we have to go."

Ren goes back to reading the display cards, but I can't take my eyes away from the aliens themselves. They're upsetting—too many arms and too much mouth, frozen in the cases but active in my imagination—but also compelling. I want to run screaming and move closer at the same time, and the longer I look at them, the stronger all of my feelings become.

Behind me, the door opens, and I turn quickly to face the latest intruder. There shouldn't be any passengers for a few more minutes.

"It's only me," says a familiar voice, and sure enough, when I turn around, there is Dominic Reubens.

ten

DOMINIC

"Sorry if I startled you," I say. I fight off the urge to hold my hands up like the girls are scared birds and I have to prove I'm harmless before they'll let me close. "I thought I would get here early and find a seat in a corner somewhere."

"We'll get out of your way," Celeste says deferentially. She takes a step towards Ren and the other door.

"No, you don't have to do that," I say. "I mean, if you want to stay for the lecture, don't let me stop you."

"We didn't even know there was a lecture," Ren says. "Dr. Ripley told us about it a few minutes ago."

"We were about to head back down," Celeste tells him. "It's been a long day."

"Yeah," I sigh. "No thanks to me."

"You're not that bad," Celeste says. I can't help brightening a little at her extremely meagre praise.

"Definitely not the worst person in that tour group," Ren adds, her voice carrying from the back of the room. Her voice is good-humoured, and I'm glad to know I haven't *completely* alienated the two people on *Titan* that I actually want to talk to. "Celeste, are we staying or going?"

"We're going," Celeste says firmly.

I want to argue, to convince her to stay, but I know better. She needs her rest, and after today's extracurriculars, I'm not about to get in her way.

"Maybe you could meet me back here tomorrow?" I hear myself ask. "I could tell you what the lecture was about, and you could have more time in here. It'll be easy to duck out of dinner again."

"Won't your parents miss you at the dinner table?" Ren asks.

"I'm a bit more of an embarrassment than usual right now," I admit. "I broke up with Adam."

"Good," Ren says shortly. "Because he *was* the worst person in that tour group."

I laugh. It feels good to loosen my chest. For most of the day, it had felt like something was sitting on me, pressing me down. I'd thought maybe I was having trouble adjusting to the artificial gravity or something, but when the feeling had started to lift after the final argument with Adam, I realized it was all in my head. And now it is out of my head. A little bit, at least.

"My parents do not agree with you," I say. "But it does mean I can make a getaway. What do you say?"

The two girls exchange a look. Ren shrugs.

"There isn't usually much to do after eight if you avoid senior officers," Ren points out. "And Dominic can order us up here, if we need to smooth anything over."

"But you're engineers," I say. "Why can I give you . . ." I trail off as both of them look at me. Of course. A passenger can order them around, even if they're supposed to be doing something else. That's how we'd ended up getting our belowdecks tour. I do my best not to wince.

"All right," says Celeste. "We'll meet at eight tomorrow, and Dominic will cover for us if we need him to."

We all hear a murmur of voices growing steadily louder. The passengers are almost here for their lecture.

"Good night!" Celeste says, and then they're gone.

I'm so distracted by having spoken with them that I almost forget why I'd come early. I remember my goal only a few seconds before the door opens, and am safely hidden in the back of the far gallery by the time my parents come through and take their seats in the front row. They don't even make it look like they're thinking about saving a chair for me. Sylvie Jeffers is also alone. Adam is probably sulking somewhere. Or already making out with someone he deems expendable.

I slump down in my chair and prepare to give my full attention to the lecture. Seated out of the way, I can see a part of the case I haven't noticed before. There's a little nest with a bunch of egg-looking things in it. I guess alien babies have to come from somewhere, and eggs are a less disgusting option than several movies I've seen, but I wondered why they'd been shoved in the back. I'd have thought people would want to see them. Maybe it has to do with preservation and my father's containment systems. I'm not going to ask him about it.

After a few more minutes of milling around and general conversation, Adelaide Connor steps up to the lectern—old-fashioned, like everything else in the gallery that isn't from another planet—and taps the mic a couple of times to get everyone's attention. Silence falls, and Adelaide smiles.

"Good evening, fellow travellers," she says. "I am once again pleased to see you all back in this gallery, and happy to welcome you to the first in our planned lecture series. They won't all be about the aliens—we have to let Dr. Ripley save some surprises for her journal articles—but tonight's talk is about those very creatures. The Connor Mining Corporation is proud to sponsor these lectures, and we hope that you enjoy them and find them informative."

She pauses for a moment while the Connor Mining logo appears on a screen behind her.

"Without further ado," she continues, "please welcome famed ethnobiologist and alien expert Dr. Alexandra Ripley."

There's polite applause as Dr. Ripley steps up to the lectern. She's a tall woman with short hair and tonight she's wearing a modest suit that makes her look authoritative and well put together. It's probably labelled in some academic handbook as a style that says "trust me and give me adequate funding."

"Hello, everyone," she begins. "I am absolutely thrilled to be speaking to you tonight, not just because I am on a spaceship that is headed to Mars, but because I stand in front of one of the greatest scientific discoveries of our era. Like most discoveries of this magnitude, it isn't just about the science. There's a reason they brought along someone with 'ethno' in their title. I told you yesterday that I examine cultures as well as biology, and that doesn't just mean the creatures in the case behind me. That means how you, the audience, interact with them. I know you didn't sign up to be part of an experiment, but I trust you'll find it very low-impact, and the perks are much better than whatever you got for that undergraduate psych lab you signed up for once upon a time."

The atmosphere in the room had been tense as people thought about the aliens, but as Dr. Ripley speaks, everyone calms down a bit. They even laugh at her joke. From my place behind the cases I can see faces in the crowd. It's fascinating to watch them relax as the doctor continues to speak.

"Yesterday I told you a little bit about how we found the aliens," Dr. Ripley says. "Tonight, I am going to give you more details, and then my colleagues and I will tell you some of our initial findings."

Behind her, the Connor Mining logo changes to a map of the Arctic with a red dot on it. It's zoomed out so that the audience can clearly see reference points they'll recognize, like Baffin Island. And then the map focuses in on the dot. The view gets closer until an island just north of Baffin is highlighted, Bylot Island, and on it Sirmilik National Park.

"The original team from our friends at Connor Mining went to Bylot Island to investigate melting permafrost," Dr. Ripley says. "Since the island is a national park they knew they weren't going to be able to mine it, but they were hoping to learn what they could from the permafrost."

Adelaide preens in her seat. I think it's very unlikely that a corporation would conduct scientific research on a protected island out of the goodness of its heart, but I can't think of another immediate motive. Maybe those rumours about her being different from her father are true.

"Three days after they began their investigations, I got a personal message," Dr. Ripley says. "No one is ever fully prepared for a helicopter to land in the middle of a university campus, so I knew that whatever they needed me for, it was very important."

The slide changes again. This time, it's a picture of the work site. At first glance I would have thought it was just regular tundra, but there are surveyor's stakes in the ground and a plastic sheet over part of the exposed terrain.

"Now, the Canadian government hasn't had the best track record of finding things in the Arctic," Dr. Ripley says. "This is because they never asked for directions."

A few people in the room laugh. The Canadians in the room shift uncomfortably, though we definitely deserve that particular jibe at our expense.

"There was a famous shipwreck that was lost once upon a time, for example," Ripley says, "and the government spent thousands of dollars finding it. The local Inuit community had known where it was the whole time. To avoid similar embarrassment, I decided to bring in local experts as soon as possible."

Two of the other scientists stand and join Dr. Ripley at the front of the room.

"My fellow travellers, allow me to introduce Dr. Gilly, geologist, and Dr. Booth, ethnohistorian." Dr. Ripley's colleagues step forwards to be acknowledged by the crowd. "Each of them will be lecturing about their specialities at a later date, both in relation to the aliens and more generally."

The two scientists take their seats again after briefly mentioning that they are happy to answer questions during the day, should anyone wish to approach them.

"Working with the Connor geologists, the local scientists, and my team of archaeologists, we soon fully uncovered the first alien." The screen behind Dr. Ripley changes again. This alien is one of the smaller ones. Even on the ground, surrounded by shovels and scientific equipment, it manages to look dangerous. "We had to be careful extracting the creatures, since they had been at a constant temperature for millions of years. Conservation was our highest priority, and, thanks to Connor Mining, we were able to recover everything you see before you."

The lecture continues for almost an hour after that, with Dr. Ripley showing pictures of various stages of the excavation and providing small details about each individual creature. She saves the big one for last, and doesn't mention the eggs at all. Maybe they're going to be part of a different lecture. I can't imagine that no one has taken any pictures of them.

"We can't really assign gender to these creatures," Dr. Ripley says. "At least not in the traditional sense. However, when we found this individual, all of us immediately had the same feeling. This is the queen. It's not scientific, and I certainly couldn't defend the designation academically, but I think you'll agree with me: she's infinitely impressive."

There are murmurings of general agreement throughout the room. I find myself inching away from the display case, even though I'm rapidly running out of room on my chair. The faces I can see in the crowd all look uncomfortable or awed or some combination of the two. It's a strange feeling. I know it's completely illogical, but I can't deny that Dr. Ripley has a point. The big one is definitely the queen. Even as I move away, I can't take my eyes off of her.

"There is so much we have yet to learn about these aliens," Dr. Ripley concludes. "As scary as they look, and as grateful as I am to have them behind glass, part of me does wish that we had living samples to examine. I have plenty of unanswered questions, but looking at these creatures makes me want to ask even more. I hope you will join me and my colleagues here as the lecture series continues. We look forward to sharing what we've learned with you, and maybe even learning something from you in return, if you have questions, comments, or new ideas."

There is more polite applause as Dr. Ripley concludes her speech, and then the screen shows the Connor Mining logo again. It's almost a relief not to see giant pictures of the aliens anymore, even though they are literally right in front of where I'm sitting. Everything about them is confusing, from their existence to the way they make me feel too many feelings. I wonder if everyone feels the same way or if I'm the only one who's a mess. It will be absolutely typical if I'm unique in my reaction. If there's a way to do something backwards, I'm pretty good at finding it.

It's very crowded by the lectern as passengers come forwards to ask questions of the scientists or get a closer look at the aliens. I decide it's time to leave before too many people make it into my little sanctuary at the back of the gallery. It's simple to get into the corridor, and then the map on my wrist takes me back to my suite. I know that by the time we arrive at Mars I'll have *Titan*'s layout memorized, but I don't mind relying on my comm in the meantime.

I make it back to my room without encountering anyone. As soon as I'm inside, I turn around and lock the door. My father can probably override it, but at least this way I can pretend I have some privacy. Peters has left my pyjamas on my bed, along with a tray of snacks on my bedside table and a bag that I don't recognize. I peek inside the bag and smile, but I make myself take a shower and get ready for bed before I indulge myself.

Inside the bag is a pad of paper—clearly taken from a drafting supply box at Connor Mining—and several charcoal pencils. I have no idea how Peters got them, though I suppose Adelaide did seem to like me for some reason, and right now I don't really care. I usually work with colour—I like making things bright and beautiful—but I am extremely grateful for what Peters has been able to find. I'm going to make sure my valet gets whatever job he wants once we get to Mars. I will give the best reference in the history of giving references.

I put a piece of paper on the table in my sitting room and prep one of the pencils. I take a deep breath, forgetting my anger and frustration with my parents and Adam, and begin to draw. It takes me a moment to get into it. It always does. That horrifying feeling of beginning and wondering if everything that I've ever done before has been a fluke, lightning I had failed to bottle and would be stuck chasing forever. But then the scratch of the pencil beats against my heart and the shapes begin to come out of my fingers.

I draw the gallery, of course. It's the subject at the top of my mind. I draw the cases and the shadowy forms within them. It's almost more than I can bear to make their horrible shapes, like drawing the lines means I can no longer deny their existence. I have to accept them. Aliens exist, and they have been on Earth with us for a long, long time. With each stroke, the truth is carved into my soul.

And because I don't want it to be all serious and world-altering, I draw two human figures looking at the display cases. They lean forwards curiously, one of them even reaching out a hand like she has nothing to fear at all. I don't draw their faces, but I do draw the engineering uniforms. One girl has a long braid, and the girl reaching out has hair that's cut short.

I set the pencil down and stare at the drawing I have made. It isn't my best work. I am out of practice at sketching. But the intent is unmistakable. My life has changed dramatically since I boarded *Titan* two days ago, and the reasons are in charcoal grey under my fingers. I gently touch the figure of Celeste and wonder if there are any non-governmental pictures of her in existence. I can draw her one, if she wants. There isn't a lot that I'm able to offer, but I know what it feels like to not be seen, and if she wants people to notice her, even if it's just as a potential employee so that she'll have financial freedom, I am more than happy to help.

the lights are cold, but the air hums

the ground is hard, but the metal hums

the beings are strange, but their voices hum

with their hands, touch

with their mouths, speak

with their eyes, see

with their brains, grow

grow to what we need to be

eleven

CELESTE

I give serious thought to never going back to the gallery. I certainly have enough work to do. Suddenly being friends with everyone who serves belowdecks on *Titan* doesn't get me out of shift work, though I do notice that several senior engineers give me the right of way when it comes to crossing paths in the engine room. And neither Ren nor I is assigned to run errands between decks again.

"I could get used to this," Ren says, happily running maintenance checks on the exhaust manifolds to make sure they're looping back into the main recycling system at peak efficiency. It's a much more sedentary job than we're usually assigned.

"You are welcome to it," I tell her. I don't like being given favours, and I really don't like the thought of owing people something, even if it's something as simple as a trip up to the gallery.

"You can't blame them," Ren says. "It's fucking *aliens*. People want to see that sort of thing."

Everyone on board is scheduled to have a viewing time, though crew time is limited, and the people travelling on the indenture decks will only view the aliens remotely. The times are slotted around the crew's work shifts and spaced out because the paying passengers have precedence. Anthony isn't scheduled for several days, which I know because he had sighed loudly about it at breakfast.

"They might change their minds when they actually get to see them," I say. I can't quite supress a shudder.

I've never been the type to dream about life on other planets. I think about space travel a lot, obviously. Everyone in the Rupt does, hoping for a place in the Connor mines, however much it costs us to get there. I planned my path to *Titan* with precision, outlining each goal and not letting up until I had either met it or exhausted all of my possibilities and begun the search for a contingency plan. But all of my variables had been *human*. I never imagined that there might be other forms of life in the universe. It's simply too frivolous and outlandish for me.

I don't have to see the news from Earth to guess how the response is going, though. There will be plenty of people who don't believe the discovery is true. Denial will take many forms, from religious fervour to convoluted conspiracy theories, and the fact that the aliens are on *Titan*, heading for Mars, instead of being available on Earth, probably exacerbates the situation. I also know plenty of people who simply won't care. There's life on Earth that needs taking care of.

Some freeze-dried alien specimens on a departing spaceship aren't really very important to people who are concerned with feeding their kids.

"I think they're fascinating," Ren says. "Like, they don't look anything like aliens do in movies. And I was not prepared for that colour of purple."

"They don't creep you out?" I ask. "It doesn't bother you that the secret was kept so tightly that people like Benedict Reubens were able to install them on a spaceship without the general public finding out?"

Ren pauses, her console beeping at her softly as it waits for input.

"Well, when you put it like that," Ren says. She grins. "Maybe they're on the spaceship because no one wanted them to stay on Earth, and we're a closed-lab experiment on how different social classes will react."

"Now you sound like you should run an anti-government website," I say. I fight off another shudder. Ren's suggestion rings uncomfortably true. "They just make me very unsettled. And now I have a free pass to see them whenever I want, and a whole crew of people clamouring to come with me."

"You haven't made any promises yet," Ren says. "And as much as I'd like to barter this for social capital, I don't want you to be uncomfortable. We're going to be on this ship for a week. You don't have do everything immediately. In fact, go up by yourself tonight and just see how you feel. If you want to bail, you can. I'll stay below so you won't feel like you have to stick around for my benefit."

Since Ren genuinely wants to see the aliens and benefit from my special treatment, this is a generous offer from her. I mull it over for a couple of hours before concluding that she's got a point. Despite my revulsion, I *am* interested in knowing the full story. And, to be perfectly honest, I want to see Dominic again. I just find so many things about the circumstances off-putting. So, even with Ren's encouragement, it's with some reluctance that I climb up to the gallery at the appointed time. I'm not going to be entirely alone, after all. Assuming Dominic can escape his parents again, he's going to tell me about what he learned at the lecture. Or something. He probably just wants to talk about the Rupt again because he feels like he's missing something important from his childhood.

When I open the service hatch that leads into the gallery, the lights are still low. The display glows. As I step into the room, the lights turn up, only to be quickly dimmed again by something I can't see.

"Hello?" I call out.

"Oh, I'm sorry," Dominic replies. He must be sitting on the other side of the case. "I was used to the lower light and I just fixed it with my tablet. I lost track of time."

He sounds focused on something, which makes his voice different . . . more compelling. I can't tell what he's doing from where I'm standing.

"It's fine," I reply, closing the hatch behind me. "I can see well enough."

I cross the floor and step around to his side of the display cases. He isn't sitting in a chair looking at the aliens, as I'm expecting. Instead, he's crouched on the floor with a portable desk in his lap, surrounded by sheets of paper. I look down at the one closest to my feet.

The drawing is stark, done in heavy lines with no hesitancy. The shape of the alien is unmistakable, its form curled in on itself but its maw gaping, like the one in the case. It's black and white, the colour of the aliens' skin left to memory, and the stark contrast of graphite and paper, but there's no question as to the talent with which the drawing was made.

"Wow," I say. I haven't met many artists at all, and none who are as good as Dominic is. "How long have you been here?"

Dominic looks up, blinking owlishly. Even though we've spoken since I came into the room, it's like he's really seeing me for the first time. I've pulled him out of some kind of creative fugue, and I immediately feel bad about it.

"Um," he says. "Well, if you're here and that means it's dinner time, then since breakfast."

"I'd say I think you need a hobby, but is *this* your hobby?" I ask. "You're very good."

His fingers are smudged from the graphite and there are a few marks on his face from where he must have brushed his hair out of his eyes. It's not the same as engine carbon, though it speaks to his willingness to work at something. It might be a talent that only someone with money can spare time for, but he's clearly put in the work.

"Thank you," Dominic says. "And it's only kind of a hobby. I wanted it to be my job, somehow, but my father has other plans."

"Is this why he's so cruel to you?" I ask. He makes a face. Clearly, he's not as invested in his dad's plans as his dad is. "It was pretty obvious on the tour."

"You think?" Dominic says. He laughs painfully. "And yes. One of the many misunderstandings between my parents and me is how I could throw away everything they've done for me on such a useless fancy."

He pulls a fresh sheet of paper onto the desk and keeps sketching. It's mesmerizing to watch the aliens appear.

"You could argue that the only reason you *can* do this sort of thing is because of what they did for you," I say, without really thinking about it. "I mean, no one has time for this sort of thing in the Rupt. You do a bit of art or music in school, but once you hit grade ten, it's all trades unless you've been pulled for a gifted program."

Dominic looks up at me again, and for the first time since we started speaking, his focus is fully on me. I can tell he has a million questions.

"I don't think my parents would go for that argument," he says, finally. He sounds wistful, like he'd given himself a moment to hope and then was crushed. "Even if it is true."

Silence hangs between us for a moment and I make a decision. This boy hasn't suffered like I have, but he's suffering now. If I can make him feel better, I will. I don't believe in much, but I do believe in making the world brighter for another person if I can.

"You can ask, if you want," I say. I carefully shift some papers and sit down on the floor beside him and cross my legs like we're little kids at a campfire. "I don't always want to talk about home, but tonight, you can have a free pass."

"I don't even know where to start," Dominic says. He leans back against the legs of the chair behind him, resting his head on the seat. He closes his eyes for a moment, and it's quiet in the gallery except for the hum of the display cases.

"Do you know exactly where you're from?" I ask. Almost no one does, but it seems like a good place to start.

"Orleans, but nothing more specific," he says. "I was adopted out of one of the emergency hospitals, but they were taking cases from all over the place by that point. I had a name, but my parents changed it when they adopted me."

Of course they did. They don't strike me as the types who would tell him, either. A name meant a lot in the Rupt, and I was suddenly furious that Dominic had *had* one, only for it to be thrown aside.

"I was named by an orderly," I tell him. "He liked birds, so everyone in my ward got a bird name. I got Sparrow. It's not the same as a family, but it was kind of cool as we grew up to run into a stranger and know that we'd been together and taken care of by the same person. I even met him once."

"My first name is my mother's name from before she was married," Dominic says. "So I guess it's kind of cool that I have both family names."

It probably seemed nice when he was young, like his parents were making extra sure to let him know that he was their family. Now, I imagine it feels like a pair of weights tied around his neck.

"Did you get pulled out of school for a gifted program?"

Dominic asks. "Is that how you and Ren ended up here? Dr. Jeffers mentioned something about that at the departure."

He's so painfully genuine in his questions that they don't feel intrusive. Usually, people want to know about my childhood because they have an agenda and a little box to slam me into. Dominic is just curious.

"No, I was in a government school," I tell him. "I was supposed to go into commercial manufacturing. Factory work, assembly line stuff. I took short contracts in high school, which sucked in terms of making money, but it gave me a bit of free time to study on my own. I wanted to go to college to be a mechanic originally, but when it was time to apply, *Titan* applications were open. That's when Dr. Jeffers stepped in with hiring bonuses for the construction companies. We're her tax write-offs, basically. The ones she saved from drudgery by recognizing our brilliance and potential."

"Ugh," Dominic says. "That definitely sounds like something a Jeffers would say. So, you wanted to leave Earth?"

"Yes," I say. "I wanted to get out of the Rupt, and that's . . . hard."

I hope that Dominic has overheard enough of his mother's policy debates to understand everything I haven't said, because I don't really want to get into it. Rebuilding a country after a massive disaster requires people to do the jobs that no one wants to do, and it helps a great deal if all of those people are already on location and have no other options.

"I feel bad for Ren," I say. "She's leaving behind people she actually cares about. She pretends it's fine, but I know she misses her family."

"Did she come for you, then?" Dominic asks.

He says it so simply, and yet I'm too surprised to answer him. It never crossed my mind that Ren would give up her family to stay with me, no matter how good the opportunities on Mars are going to be. My mind races as I remember everything we talked about while we were deciding and chasing down our goal. I feel like a selfish idiot. I hadn't done it on purpose, but I'd pushed the most important person in my life into giving up the one thing that every single kid from the Rupt knows is irreplaceable.

"Shit," I say when the moment drags on for too long.

"I'm sorry," Dominic says. "I didn't mean to . . ."

He trails off, and I don't blame him. This isn't exactly "by the way, there are aliens" in terms of revelations, but it's pretty damn close in my book.

"I'm going to kill her," I say. I want to jump up and do . . . something, but I have no idea what. "She has parents who actually *like* her."

"She clearly thought you were worth it," Dominic points out. "And she's getting all the same benefits you are. That must have been part of her decision-making process, right?"

"I can't talk about this right now," I say, desperate to change the subject. "Please ask other intrusive questions about my terrible childhood."

The gallery door opens and both of us tense, but it's only one of Dr. Ripley's archaeologists. He smiles when he sees us.

"Please, keep talking," he tells us. "I'll come back later."

We thank him and he leaves us to it. For a moment, there's a weight of awkward silence between Dominic and me, but then he seems to have a hundred thoughts at the same time and starts asking questions again.

He keeps me talking, and I find myself telling him stories about events I haven't thought of in years. From making the most of what little was available to me in the dorms, to my efforts scraping by after I was old enough that I had to live on my own, I tell him about all the ugly parts of living in the Rupt. There's good stuff, of course, but as I say the words out loud in this gilded room, I'm struck by how paltry the good parts were. Dominic listens to everything with a thoughtful concentration. Both of us occasionally find our focus drifting to the display case. It's hard to forget about the aliens, and once I start looking at them, it's even harder to stop. It's nicer to focus on the warm body beside me.

"I know that people have said this to you a lot, and always in a terrible sort of way, but it really is incredible that you're here," Dominic says, worrying his pencil between his fingers. "I don't know if there's a nice way to say that, but you're pretty awesome."

"Thanks," I say. His words don't sting the way those kinds of comments usually do. Maybe it's because I feel like he genuinely believes them.

"Judging people is too complicated," Dominic says. He looks down at his drawings, his face closing off from the open way he'd been speaking to me. It's sad to watch him shut himself down. No one should have to do that.

"Except Adam," I say, suddenly desperate to make him smile. "That boy is an asshole."

Dominic snorts, suddenly just a boy again instead of a wounded animal.

"Is he making it bad?" I ask. "I get the feeling he's the type who doesn't mind a dramatic breakup, but only if he's the one doing it."

"Oh, he's mad," Dominic says, taking the bait. "And he's definitely trying to take it out on me. Which is why I'm in here."

"Dominic Reubens," I say, pressing my hand to my chest like he's wounded me. "I thought you were here to see me!"

This time, Dominic truly laughs. It's infectious, and I join him, both of us giggling until we're loose-limbed and punch-drunk. I surreptitiously check my wrist comm, but no one has given me a new task yet. Swing shift has a few upsides, it turns out.

"Can I ask a favour?" he asks when he catches his breath.

"Sure," I say, even though I can't imagine what I could possibly do for him.

"I know you probably don't have a lot of space in your quarters, but I was wondering if you could keep these for me?" He gestures to his drawings. "My valet had to scrounge the paper because my father threw out everything I had packed."

"Of course," I agree. I start to collect the papers. "Can they be folded?"

"I'd prefer if you rolled them," Dominic says, gathering the drawings that are closest to him. "But I know I'm not really in a position to be precious about it."

"Rolling it is," I say. "I can slide them in the top of my storage compartment or something."

We finish getting all the drawings together just as the chime for after-dinner activities sounds. Dominic has an elastic tie that will hold them for now. There's a tube in my quarters that has some ship specs rolled up in it. I can add them to that.

"Tonight's a movie or a bowling tournament," Dominic says. "So we're good here, if you want to stay."

I hesitate. I want to spend time with him, but I know it's just a matter of time before I'm missed belowdecks, and, even with Ren and Dominic to cover for me, I feel a little exposed.

"I didn't even tell you about the aliens," Dominic says, reminding me why I came up here in the first place. "I spent all our time badgering you about your childhood."

"I didn't mind," I say, and it's true. I check my watch, even though I know what time it is. Surely an hour up here won't be too bad. I worked extra hard all afternoon to make up for this unscheduled break. "But I do want to hear about the aliens."

Dominic stands up, placing the rolled-up drawings on the chair behind him, and then extends a hand to pull me up. He bows gallantly and I blush in spite of myself as he helps me to my feet. Boys have flirted with me before, and I'm not actually sure that Dominic knows he's flirting, but just as himself, he is quickly climbing my short list of favourite people. That certainly hadn't been something I thought about when I'd been plotting how to network on *Titan*. I expected connections, not an actual friendship.

"Then please step right this way," he says, guiding me towards the cases, "and I will tell you everything I remember."

With his hand at the small of my back, I look into the case with the largest alien. For the first time, its gaping maw doesn't seem so intimidating. I reach out a hand and brush my fingers against the barrier over the display. This time, the weird buzzing feeling doesn't irritate me. It sings.

twelve

DOMINIC

I don't remember the last time I was able to spend an hour in conversation with a person and be this unguarded. It's almost frightening. I've built walls around myself for years, defence mechanisms to protect me during conversations. I can keep my face from showing emotion when I'm actually bursting with it. I can keep my voice steady when what I really want to do is to cry. I can hold myself still and straight, and look for all the world like I'm calm, collected, and completely rational.

Talking with Celeste isn't like that. All of my pretenses are gone. I feel free for the first time in years. As I pass my drawings into her hands, I realize that it's the first time I've ever truly trusted another person with my self-expression. It's a gift she doesn't even know she's giving me, and I revel in it. I'd never felt like this with Adam, even in the beginning, when it was a thrill from the adrenaline of rule-breaking and a rush of hormones I could finally act on.

There are still a few sticking points, of course. I did just break up with my boyfriend while we're both stuck on the same spaceship for the next week. I don't want to rush into anything new. Even though Adam and I always had a tempestuous relationship, I'd still given a small part of my heart— or something—to that jackass. Adam is terrible, but for a while he'd let me be terrible too, and I used that as both a shield and a battering ram. Without the weight, my heart felt lighter, but I know better than to immediately transfer my feelings to the first person who's nice to me, but it's much harder to execute that restraint in practice than it is to think about it. Friendship first. I can do that.

Celeste listens to everything I say about the aliens, nodding when I get to the part about the big one being called the queen. She doesn't hang on my words like a sycophant; I can spot that sort of thing a kilometre away. She shows me genuine interest, like she did when I talked about my art. It's so refreshing, I barely know how to deal with it.

I had just gotten to the part of Dr. Ripley's lecture where she talked about the permafrost when Celeste yawns.

"I am so sorry," she says. Her hand is over her mouth in embarrassment, but she speaks clearly. "I promise you're not boring. It's just late."

"Oh, I didn't mean to keep you," I say. Of course I *would* do something selfish the moment I have access to someone who isn't trying to use me or make fun of me. She isn't going back to plush quarters. She has a job to do. "You're still on shift, and I'm prattling on."

"I don't mind," Celeste says. She smiles, and I believe her. "I mean, I stayed up here because I wanted to hear what you were saying, even though I know I have to get up for work tomorrow. Don't worry about it."

"We've pretty much covered everything anyway," I say. "The permafrost stuff was more about mining and environmentalism than it was about the aliens. There's a couple articles in *Titan's* entertainment database. Do you have access to that?"

"Yes," Celeste says. "We can access it on our crew tablets. There's a common room if you're all watching the same thing, but I usually just read in my bunk."

I turn a truly ridiculous colour when she says the word "bunk," but am saved from having to reply by the worst possible set of circumstances.

"Of course you'd hide in here." Adam's voice cuts through the pleasant quiet of the gallery as he clomps down the stairs from the upper deck to reach the floor. "Hiding in the dark like a coward."

Of all the people who had to notice my absence. Adam would have skipped a group activity anyway, but I didn't think he'd track me down. I know he's going to be vicious, but I won't let him take it out on Celeste.

As I turn to face him, Celeste steps behind one of the cases. At first, I think she's trying to hide, but then I realize that what she's actually doing is concealing the roll of papers she picked up from where I set them. My heart sings. It's such a kind thing for her to do, and she did it so fluidly, like it didn't take any consideration. I definitely need better friends—or, to be honest, any friends at all—if basic kindness is enough to get me feeling like this.

"I suppose your evening of VR sports car racing was better?" I say. Adam likes the driving programs because he can speed, crash, and hit things without consequences.

"At least I'm not—wait, are you slumming it without me?" Adam steps close enough to make out Celeste's face. Even if he doesn't remember her from the party and the tour, it's clear she's a crew member, not a guest.

"I'm not doing that either," I say, bristling. "This is the scientific discovery of a lifetime, and we're discussing it."

"I'm sure she's very interested in your discussion." Adam leers. The grin on his face holds no humour at all.

"I should go," Celeste says, taking half a step towards the hatch.

I reach for her reflexively, trying to stop her from stepping far enough away that Adam will see my drawings in her hand. She blinks at him and then stills, understanding my dilemma. The ball is in my court, and she's trusting me with it.

"You don't have to leave," I say, over-enunciating for Adam's benefit. "I know it's an extra challenge to work around your schedule. Take your time looking at everything. It's really fascinating."

I'm not sure I even make sense, but I have to say something.

"Jesus, how did you ever land me?" Adam muses. "Your game is terrible, even for someone who will obviously take everything you give her. And we all know you're a giver."

Celeste flinches, but her eyes flame. I don't even think to

be offended. Adam's barbs are so customary now. They still hook me, but the hurt is less. I just want him gone so that Celeste is free of his menace.

"What do you want, Adam?" I ask, turning to face him directly.

"My mother wants you for euchre, God knows why," Adam says. "Probably so she can watch your parents squirm while you disappoint them."

A whole ship full of people and Sylvie Jeffers needs *me* for cards? It's just ridiculous enough to be true. Everything that had relaxed in me as I talked with Celeste snaps back to attention, reinforcing my weak spots.

"I won't keep her waiting, then," I say. "I know you're lousy at cards."

"Only the ones you play in teams," Adam says. "I prefer to go it alone."

"That's fortunate," I say. "Considering."

It isn't often that I land a hit with Adam, but it was an opening, and I'm not in the mood to play nice right now. His eyes narrow, and I know I'll pay for it later, but if it gets us both out of the room right now, it'll be worth it.

"Come on," Adam says. "Wouldn't want your new girl to miss out on her full museum experience."

Until this morning, Adam would have taken my hand to show ownership, or because he likes pulling me along, but this time he keeps his distance. I decide I like him better that way. Not much, but better than up close.

"Good night, Celeste," I say. There's no reason to be rude just because Adam's a dick.

"Good night," Celeste says. She places her free hand on the case, her fingers splayed wide just above the alien queen's sharp mouth. I like that she's confronting her discomfort and getting close up.

I leave the gallery, turning to make sure that Adam is behind me. There's a small chance he'll stay to hassle Celeste, but usually Dr. Jeffers requires her assignments to be reported on in person. Plus, the card room has the best bar on *Titan*, in that it's out of sight of the card tables and Adam can drink as much as he wants without his mother's disapproving glare.

A hesitation before the door shuts and the sound of footsteps let me know that Adam has taken the bait. Celeste will be able to make her escape now. Or stay at the display for a bit longer, if that's what she'd rather do. She should be able to stay and learn in peace as much as I can.

The card room is the reading room during the day. In the evening, tables are brought out from concealed spots behind bulkheads. Since the reading room is my other escape, I'm a bit annoyed to see it full of other people and completely repurposed from my usual quiet sanctuary, but I can't really register a complaint. It's a short walk, but I can feel Adam breathing down my neck the whole time. At least there are only four seats at every table. If Adam's not playing, he won't be able to sit near me.

I'm surprised to see that Adelaide Connor is my father's partner for the evening, and Dr. Jeffers has the third seat. My mother is nowhere to be seen, but that doesn't mean much. She's been distant since *Titan* got underway. Alodia Reubens would never suffer from something as common as space sickness, of course, and no one would ever suggest it. She has only been taking her time adjusting to news of alien life on Earth, my father had told our server this morning when she missed breakfast. The politics are complicated, and she's been in contact with Earth at all hours. Everyone pretends to believe it, no matter how green she looks when she does make an appearance.

"Dominic, how wonderful to see you," Adelaide says as I take my seat across from Dr. Jeffers. "I was just telling your father how wonderful it is to have young people on board. It speaks well for the future of Mars to have a young population. A lot of the miners are in their mid-twenties, of course, but it's important to have youth in all demographics."

She speaks lightly, like she's half kidding, but I know that population dynamics are something that the mine tycoon is always thinking of. She has to plan for workers in a place where no replacements can be brought in without substantial lead time, and it's just as serious for mine management as it is for the actual miners. She can't for a moment expect that I would work for her, but small talk is always rife with inanity of that sort.

"Yes, well," my father says, "Dominic doesn't always set the best example. You'd be better off looking at those engineers belowdecks. And not just because I don't want you poaching my software engineers."

The adults laugh, but I catch the undercurrents. The miners are all locked into contracts, but the other workers have more options and can be lured to a position with the right incentive. Even Celeste and Ren will be able to be selective, if they play their cards right. It is going to get very competitive when we land.

Dr. Jeffers deals while our drinks are delivered, and I reach for my cards without thinking about it.

"What's this?" My father grabs my hand and turns it over to expose my palm and fingertips. They're stained with charcoal. I thrash myself internally. It's like I *want* to get caught.

"I was just—" I start, but my father is having none of it.

"Is this what you've been doing when you disappear?" he demands. "I thought you were moping because of that boy, but you have been sneaking off to draw."

He says the word with such venom that I flinch. Dr. Jeffers pretends nothing is happening, but Adelaide Connor watches with only slightly veiled concern.

"I've been sketching the aliens," I say, as calmly as possible.

"Oh, that's wonderful!" Adelaide intercedes before my father can react. She's clearly trying to cheer me up, but it's only going to make everything worse. "Are you an artist?"

"He is a spoiled child," my father says.

"I don't imagine there has been a lot of art done about the aliens yet," Sylvie drawls. She's clearly enjoying the spectacle quite a bit. She hasn't even bothered to pick up her hand.

"You could set all kind of trends," Adelaide says. "Imagine being the artist who first develops the style needed to make evocative representations of them. They name that sort of thing after people, you know. And I'm sure Dr. Ripley has technical drawings, but art is one of the things that makes us human. I think it's important we extend that to the aliens as soon as possible."

My father looks angry enough to spit nails, and Dr. Jeffers fiddles with her drink. I look at my cards and try to focus on the rules.

"Yes," Dr. Jeffers says, almost sounding like she means it. "And how poetic: the father designs the display case and the son translates it into different media. You're mostly pencils and watercolours, right, Dominic?"

Adelaide is watching me with great curiosity.

"Yes," I admit slowly. "It's my preference, though I have been using graphite lately. I can draft as well, for technical work. It's how you learn perspective, and it's a good exercise for muscle control."

"A computer can produce a draft," my father grits through his teeth. "And you were supposed to be focusing on real work for when you arrive on Mars."

"Oh, Benedict, there's no harm in a hobby," Adelaide says. She looks like she'd pat his shoulder if he wasn't across from her, and murder flashes in his eyes. I have no doubt at all who the target is.

Sylvie Jeffers finally picks up her hand and looks at the cards she's been dealt. She smiles, but I know it isn't because of the game. It isn't even because she's getting vengeance for me dumping her son. I know she didn't care about our relationship in the slightest. If anything, it had been an inconvenience she no longer has to deal with. It's because she's watching Benedict Reubens be embarrassed in public. Again. And my father knows it.

Adelaide turns her attention to her cards and the game proceeds. It's strained, but that doesn't keep Adelaide from maintaining a constant stream of chatter. I'm grateful, because the idea of sitting here in silence while this plays out is intolerable. Thank goodness my mother is a no-show.

By the time the midnight chime sounds, I'm exhausted. I know better than to leave the table first, but I'm profoundly glad when Adelaide stands up and excuses herself.

"Thank you so much for the game," she says. Then she winks at me. "And let me know if you want a drafting job. I'm sure we can find you something."

I mutter something polite while Dr. Jeffers covers a mean burst of laughter with an excessive cough. Then she gets up and leaves without saying anything at all, which is a mercy, since any gloating would really seal my fate.

The card games around us are winding down, and players are consolidating at a few tables as the bulk of the passengers retire for the evening. I want to be anywhere else. I want to talk about aliens with Celeste, or see if Dr. Ripley really *is* interested in artwork of her discovery. I'd even take a job interview with Adelaide Connor. At least as a company drafter I'd make a good wage and be able to leave my job at work. I could do my own art in the evening. It's a dream I've been building as we played, even though I know my parents will refuse. There's no way I'll contribute to anyone's legacy but theirs.

Instead, I'm sitting in the reading room, a place where I usually find sanctuary, and I'm alone at the table with my father.

the hum stops

and for a moment

we fill the metal, searching

she reaches out

she finds

she takes

and now

we are ready

READY ROOM

Captain Bernard stares into the fish tank. Silver swirls in the water, everything so churned up that it's hard to see anything beyond the flashing of scales. He hasn't fed them yet today, but when he opens the lid, yesterday's food is still floating in the water. He turns off the water cyclers, but the sediment doesn't settle.

Something is in the tank.

And it's had all the herring it can eat.

MEDICAL BAY

Alodia Reubens is furious with everyone. Her overbearing husband, who talked her into early retirement. Her idiot son, who seems determined to throw away every gift she ever gave him. Sylvie fucking Jeffers, for existing. Space, for making her feel like this. Herself, for letting it get to her. The engineer who is being tended to ahead of her—again—because the little cow had given up a kidney or something.

When she finally gets up on the examination table, she's so angry she can barely speak. The medic, at least, knows better than to bother her with stupid questions. She's guided down onto the pillow, and as the IV needle pricks her skin, all she can think about is how welcome oblivion will be.

DOMINIC'S QUARTERS

Benedict Reubens paces back and forth outside the suite he had so graciously paid for his son to inhabit. He's drunk, but that doesn't dull any of the anger in his mind. He took that boy into his house, gave him his *name*, and now it's starting to look like it will all be for nothing. He's so close to over-shadowing his wife, and no little brat is going to stop him.

That display during the card game had been the last straw. Benedict had been forced to stay polite while there were other guests around, but the moment father and son were left alone, he brought the hammer down. Dominic's newfound spine had all but disintegrated as his father berated him before escorting him roughly back to his room. Now, with the boy inside, Benedict's anger recedes enough that he can make a plan.

Hacking into the door codes, he activates the emergency lock on Dominic's door. There's water in there, and the little prick probably has some snacks secreted away somewhere. But a few days in lock-up will show him some perspective.

Benedict strides off with his shoulders square, only a slight weave to his step. He'll let the boy out when he deserves it.

ADELAIDE'S SITTING ROOM

Mars has forty extra minutes every day, and her company would love to exploit them. Adelaide doesn't want to. Her father's indenture policies are something she'd inherited along with his office, and the whole concept makes her skin crawl. She's hoping that being on Mars herself will make a difference. Maybe she can steal her own mine before the board back on Earth decides to fire her.

She wants to go and visit them, the people in the hold. Everyone tells her it's a bad idea. That they'll riot once they realize who she is, but she's not afraid. Still, she's not about to make a big deal about it, either, so she waits until an evening when she's alone before she packs a bag and makes her way to their section.

The guards don't want to let her in. They're not sure they'll be able to get her out if something happens. There are only eight of them, and they're only armed with stun rods. Adelaide Connor leans in, the only good lesson she ever learned from her father, and makes them do what she wants. When the door seals behind her, she doesn't flinch. She'll arrive on Mars with humane contracts or she won't arrive at all.

CELESTE'S QUARTERS

Ren snores, which is something Celeste always finds hilarious, because both of them have spent their entire lives in shared rooms, trying to be quiet, only Ren can't help what she does when she's asleep. After all this time, Celeste has no problem tuning it out. It's almost a comfort. So many things have changed lately. Sometimes she feels like her insides are being rearranged. But Ren is always there, even when she isn't sure she deserves such a good friend.

Titan's hum has sharpened, like something's going to happen. But that's ridiculous. That's not how engines work. That's Celeste, too tired to think clearly and too distracted by aliens to really try. She tucks the cylinder she found for

Dominic's sketches into a cubby under her bunk and then climbs under the thin—but—efficient blanket.

She sleeps, and it's finally quiet.

THE ENGINE ROOM

Michael does not get paid enough for this. He does his job, and he does it well, even when it's another goddamn night shift and the coffee is rationed.

But he does *not* get paid enough.

BRIDGE

The first officer taps on the screen, zooming in and out as she hovers over *Titan*'s course projections. Something isn't right.

She never figures out what it is.

THE GALLERY

No one has turned up the lights. Shadowy figures circle the display cases. Some of them walk strangely, like they're pulling along limbs they don't quite know what to do with. Some of them move fluidly, swift like fishes cutting through clear water. All are drawn to the same goal and to the peace and guidance it will bring.

They place a device on the top of the largest case. It whines, then screams.

Then

she commands

thirteen

CELESTE

I wake up to an alarm so shrill it makes my ears hurt. It's the ship alarm, but it never used to feel like I could hear it in my teeth. It's probably because I'd been out cold. I roll off my bunk instinctively, the first order during the earthquake drills that peppered my childhood. Ren is on her feet quickly too, though she's not as affected by the sound as I am.

"Fire?" I ask. It's so loud I can't determine which alarm it is. My comm says it's 1:00 in the morning. I've been asleep less than two hours.

"Containment breach!" Ren replies.

Any kind of emergency on board a spaceship is heightened, and *Titan* is no exception, no matter what Dr. Jeffers says about the ship's design. We will have to be at our best to deal with whatever's happening, even though it feels hard to think with all the noise.

The alarm ceases suddenly, cut off mid-wail. I can still feel it in my teeth like an itch I can't reach. It takes me a moment to realize that the sound has actually been stopped, but I'm relieved that it has. Ren doesn't look comforted.

"It's not a drill," she says. "Drills have accompanying instructions. So it was either a malfunction, or it was real."

I know better than to stop Ren from catastrophizing. It's how she copes. Even if I don't want to hear all the options, Ren has to say them.

"If it was a malfunction, we'd have the error alert on our comms," Ren continues, looking at her wrist. "But we don't, so that means it was real."

It isn't entirely solid logic, but it's a good start. Ren is a worst-case-scenario planner by nature, and her survival skills have been honed by her dads. They aren't preppers, exactly, but they hadn't adopted multiple Rupt survivors lightly. They do everything they can to make sure that all of the kids they'd raised can take care of themselves in dire situations.

"My therapist says it's the only way they can deal with sending us into an uncertain future," Ren had told me once, halfway through a camping trip that I'd regretted going on almost immediately. I'd learned a lot, though.

Now I watch as Ren mentally catalogues everything in the room, weighing usefulness and portability against practicality and potential.

"Why aren't they telling us what's happening?" I ask.

The alarms are to make sure everyone is paying attention, but the wrist comms are supposed to receive information about what's happening in the case of an emergency. To have one without the other is against procedure, indicative of a larger problem that the system hasn't been designed for. That's enough to make anyone nervous, even if they aren't already hyper-aware that they're isolated in the middle of nowhere, surrounded by the black vacuum of space.

"I don't know," Ren says. "Get dressed and let's go to the mess. It's where we're supposed to report if there's no other instruction."

I get into my uniform mechanically, muscle memory making sure all the zippers and buttons are done up. Even though I'm moving just fine, it feels like my body belongs to someone else. I can't stop thinking about Ren's first instinct: containment breach. That could mean almost anything, from the hull to the sewage recyclers. I hope there are a few senior officers heading to the mess too. I want answers.

Ren is filling her pockets with every tool she has squirrelled away in her trunk. She pauses when her fingers touch her hairbrush, and I know she's mentally calculating its worth. Does she need to do her hair? What if it gets in her eyes because it's not done? That kind of thinking would drive me crazy, and it's one of the many reasons I've always kept my hair short.

"I can fix your braid later," I tell her, hoping that it'll give her the momentum she needs to keep moving. "I don't need a brush for that."

"Thanks," she says, and grabs the few ration bars that she has stashed in our room for when we're hungry at a weird time and too tired to go to the mess.

"Got everything?" I ask. I pat my own pockets down as I think about it. I don't have as many things in the room as Ren does, but I still keep a few useful tools on hand. Nothing that's going to help us if there's a hull breach or an engine malfunction, but definitely a few things that'll get us through deck plates if needed. I grab what I can and tuck them away.

"No," Ren says. She grabs a hair elastic and wraps her braid into a knot on the back of her head. "But I have as much as I can carry right now."

Ren is a great person to have near you in a crisis. She's good at planning ahead.

"Great," I say. "Let's get going."

The corridor outside our room is quiet, the lights low for the night shift. Nothing is flashing or banging or actively decompressing, which is good. It also gives us no indication as to what has happened, which is frustrating. Ren sticks to the wall as she walks, and I follow her, another holdover of earthquake drills. She'll pull herself out of it in a moment and remember that we're in space, but the important thing is that we're moving.

We make it to the first bulkhead with no incident and without seeing anyone else. That's weird, but not completely unlikely. Our room is quite close to the bulkhead, and even though we should have seen Wendy or David by now, it's possible that they left their rooms faster than we left ours. The bulkhead is shut but not sealed, which means all we have to do to get through it is open the door.

I don't tell a lot of lies as a general rule, but the one that I have maintained for most of my life is that I don't remember anything about the earthquake that killed my family and wiped a chunk of Canada off the map. I remember exactly one thing: the smell of blood. And that's what I smell as soon as the bulkhead slides open in front of us.

"What is that?" Ren asks, but I know she'll know it too as soon as she thinks about it. "Why is there blood?"

"Maybe someone tripped and cut themselves?" I say hopefully. Neither of us believe it. It's too strong for a scraped knee.

The smell gets stronger the closer we get to the ladder to the mess. By the time we get to the hatch, we're both extremely nervous as to what we'll find on the other side. Logically I know that smell can't travel between decks if the hatches are shut, but nothing is doing what it's supposed to be doing right now. There should be people. There should be noise. There should be some kind of announcement. The silence is terrifying.

Ren stops under the hatch that'll lead us straight up to deck three. It's the most direct route without walking any farther around when we could be climbing. I understand why Ren has paused. She's wondering if the direct route is the best or if we should be more circumspect.

"Ren," I say. "The important thing here is speed."

"Right," she replies.

We open the hatch to total darkness but begin to climb anyway. We turn on our headlamps, but it's not enough light to see much in the way of details. We have our gloves on, but I can still feel the rungs of the ladder are slippery. I keep my eyes—and light—firmly on Ren, climbing above me, and do my best to not think about it.

"Shit," she says, to herself as much as to me. She must have looked at her hands. "Keep climbing."

We pass through deck two without contact and finally make it to the hatch that will bring us out onto deck three. Neither of us is in a hurry to open it, even though we know we have to. Suddenly the quiet and the ignorance isn't so bad. When we open the door, it'll be all over. We'll know for sure what's happening and if we're going to survive it.

"On three?" Ren asks, her hand on the latch.

"One." I nod.

"Two," she says.

"Three!" we say, pushing the hatch open and jumping onto the deck as quickly as possible.

The mess hall is in shambles. The tables and benches are bolted to the floor, but there are trays and food everywhere. A streak of something dark and red that I don't want to think about leads towards the doors to the galley. No one's here, but there's undeniable evidence that a bunch of people had left in a hurry, and it hadn't been the alarm that caused the exodus. If Ren hadn't been so thorough in preparing herself, we could have been here when it happened. I'm glad she took her time.

"What now?" Ren asks. "This is where we're supposed to meet."

I don't know anything more than she does, and she knows it, but she can't help asking. Wendy and David should have beaten us here. They wouldn't have packed before they left their quarters. We should have seen them on the ladders. We should have seen *someone* on the ladders.

"Ren?" a voice whispers from below a table in the back. "Ren, is that you?"

We both jump, and I see the top of Michael's head as he peeks out from beneath the table he's hiding under. He shouldn't be here at all. He was on duty, so he should have reported to the engine room if he hadn't already been there.

"What are you doing?" Ren asks. "Where is everyone?"

"Get under here," Michael insists. "And turn your damn lights off."

Ren and I exchange a glance and I shrug, reaching up to switch off my headlamp. We get down on our hands and knees and crawl through the wreckage of the mess towards where Michael is hiding. I look up and down the rows of tables as we crawl through them, but there's no one else in here besides him.

"What's happening?" Ren demands, stopping two tables from Michael's hiding spot.

"We're under attack," Michael says.

"By what?" I ask. The very idea is ridiculous. Space pirates are completely impossible and aliens are—

"I don't know," Michael says. "Anthony came into the engine room a few minutes after the alarms started. He ordered me to meet up with everyone here. When I came in, the room was crowded, but then the lights went out before I could get a good look around. Someone screamed—I mean, *really* screamed, like they were dying—and then it was chaos.

When the emergency power finally flipped on, everyone was gone and that giant streak of blood was on the floor. I decided to stay here because . . ."

I don't really blame him. I don't know what I'd do if I was alone either. Still, being pinned down in one place isn't ideal. This isn't going to be like an earthquake. There's no search and recovery. We're going to have to make it out of here on our own.

"Right," I say. "We have to move."

"And go where?" Michael demands.

"Back to the engine room," Ren says, following my train of thought. "That's where Anthony was when this started. And if he's still there, maybe we can help."

"What part of *under attack* did you not understand?" Michael says, his voice rising in disbelief. "We barely have security on this ship, and they don't have real weapons. I am *not* going back out there until I know what the hell is going on."

I don't know what Ren was going to say to him to convince him to come with us because she never says it. Instead, Wendy appears in the galley door. She's got a medical technician with her—a man I don't know well but recognize by his uniform—and they're both carrying hypodermic needles. I'm about to call out to her when she takes a step forwards, and then I clamp my mouth shut and grab on to Ren. Everything about how Wendy and the med tech move is wrong. They jerk and shuffle, like their own hands and feet are unfamiliar to them. Their gait is so uneven it looks like they'll fall over, but it's like they're being held up by strings. The med tech disappears from my view and I hold my breath. I have no idea what's happening, but every single one of my instincts is telling me that it's extremely bad.

Wendy drops out of sight and I hear an awkward shuffle on the floor. Ren must be holding her breath too, but I can hear Michael panting from his hiding spot across from us. I look in his direction, hoping there will be just enough light that he'll see me and realize he has to shut up. Instead, as soon as I lock eyes with him, Michael's body jerks once, and then, before he can grab on to the table or a bench leg, he's pulled away from us so violently I hear snapping sounds as every tendon and bone in his lower half rips apart. He makes a horrible sound like he's trying to scream and vomit at the same time, and then the noise cuts out way too abruptly. Two slumped figures, carrying something between them, lurch back towards the galley door, and it slams shut behind them.

"What the f—" Ren squeals, and I tackle her under the table to shut her up.

"Go!" I hiss directly into her ear, and the two of us crawl desperately towards the back door of the mess.

It's the longest few seconds of my life, not knowing if I'll feel something coil around my ankles or if Ren will simply disappear from beside me. There are tears running down my cheeks that I don't recall crying, and I can hear Ren trying to keep her own whimpers quiet as she moves. We come out from under the tables and push ourselves up, running hunched over towards the door as quickly as we can. Nothing is chasing us, and somehow that's worse.

We spill into the corridor and don't stop running until we're through a bulkhead and have it shut behind us. I finally look at Ren. Her chest is heaving, as mine must be, and I can't think of what to say.

"It has to be the aliens," Ren says. Her face is streaked with sweat and tears. I know mine must be too. "It *has* to be the aliens."

It's such a ridiculous thing to say that I want to laugh, but my body betrays me, and I end up vomiting all over the deck plating instead.

fourteen

DOMINIC

I'm far too keyed up to sleep after I finally manage to get rid of my father. Nothing about this evening has gone the way I wanted. My chat with Celeste was interrupted by Adam, and then it had been that hellish game of cards with only slight breaks in personal mortification thanks to Adelaide Connor, of all people, and her interest in my art-work. The Connors have more money than just about anyone so my father has to be polite to her, but there have been all sorts of rumours since the family patriarch died a few months ago. My parents sold their shares in the company, even though my mother's access to trading information hasn't indicated there's a problem in the company yet. It's too much of a mystery for me to figure out, even with my mind racing as it is right now. I need to calm down.

I get the paper and charcoal pencils out of their hiding places. Celeste has all of my finished works now, but I can't resist the impulse to keep going. My hands won't rest until I do, and that means my brain definitely won't. It's strange how quickly the aliens went from being something I couldn't wrap my brain around to being something I can't get out of my mind. All I want to do is draw them. Their horrible shapes are what I see when I close my eyes, and even though I don't think I'll ever be able to find the particular shade, and I don't have anything other than a pencil right now, I want to see how close I can get to their off-putting purple.

The charcoal scratches against the paper and I feel immediately soothed. The drawing that takes shape under my fingers is of the nest, the one that's tucked into the corner of the display case. I can see it clearly when I close my eyes, and it's easy to duplicate since it's the least alien thing about the exhibit. I draw the outline and then fill it with eggs. When I'm adding the eighth one, I stop. I've drawn the nest full of eggs, but that isn't how it looks in the display. There are only five eggs, with space left around them, like the alien queen wasn't finished laying them yet when she froze. I wish I could have seen the original site photographs. I want to know if my father just built the wrong nest or if there really was that much space. I'll have to ask Dr. Ripley when I see her next.

A shrill alarm breaks through my reverie and I scrape the charcoal across the paper in surprise. The sketch is ruined now. You can erase charcoal a bit, but not when it's pressed in as darkly as I just did it. The alarm takes a few moments to fully register after my initial shock, and I actually spend several seconds trying to figure out if there's any way to save my picture, before common sense takes over.

I check my wrist comm, only to find that there's no message. There's a screen on my desk, but there's no information there either. Just the over-loud jangle of the alarm that blots out every other sound *Titan* is making. I don't know what I'm supposed to do. I know there are different alarms for different emergencies, but I can't remember what exactly this one is.

After a few moments, the noise mercifully stops and I can hear myself think again. I don't think the emergency is over, so I roll up my pages and hide them away before putting my shoes back on. I should go check on my mother. She must have gone up to the Medical bay since she hadn't been in the card room. Even though I'm a bit frustrated with her, she's still my mum. The other choice, obviously, is checking on my father, but I'm not feeling that generous yet. He'd deposited me in my room with barely masked anger, and I'm in no hurry to expose myself to that again. I can check on Peters too. He has a room of his own in the inner cabins on deck six.

I wave my hand near the door handle and nothing happens. *Titan*'s doors are keyed to motion on the passenger levels so that no one has to physically open the door or even scan their comm. I should still be able to open my own door from the inside without touching it. I wave my hand again, with the same result.

There is a handle, of course, if only for aesthetics. I grab the brass knob and turn it, and then I try pulling it, and then I try pushing it, but the door refuses to budge. I try again with both hands, but the door remains shut and I remain inside.

I remember my father, standing in the corridor after escorting me back here like I was an infant who couldn't find his own room without help. An infant, or maybe a *delinquent*. My father has locked me in. I don't know how he did it. He might have reprogrammed the door to his own voice, or maybe shut off the opening functions entirely, but either way, the message is clear: I'm on lockdown because I have misbehaved. Only he can get me out, and he'll do so when he feels like I've earned it.

I lean my forehead against the door and sigh. Maybe it was a false alarm. There still hasn't been an update on my wrist comm. I should go to bed and hope that my father has calmed down by morning. Or that Peters discovers a way to bring me breakfast, if he doesn't. I don't have anything to eat stored in here. Until right now, I didn't have a reason to.

I pace for a few minutes, which feels like hours, even though my comm says it's been less than half an hour since the alarm started. Finally, I sit down on the little bench near my door and reach for my shoelaces.

"ATTENTION CREW AND PASSENGERS. ATTENTION." The voice recording that comes over the loudspeaker catches me off guard and I almost fall off the bench. "THERE HAS BEEN A CRITICAL FAILURE WITH A SHIP SYSTEM. EVACUATE IMMEDIATELY TO YOUR ASSIGNED ESCAPE POD."

In the seconds it takes for my brain to catch up with what the announcement is actually saying, I have time to think about how they could have chosen a more reassuring voice for this kind of thing. Captain Bernard has a great voice. It would feel way calmer if it was him. Instead, it's this weird mechanical voice, like the computer that announces the subway stops has been dialled up to mass disaster without any change in inflection.

Then I realize that I'm supposed to evacuate, except I'm locked in my room.

There's a list of supplies we're supposed to take with us in case of an evacuation. Peters has a go bag packed for me, and I put it in the bathroom because it seemed like the most logical place. But I don't go for the bag like I'm supposed to. I head straight to the door, hoping like hell that whatever evac protocols have been activated have overridden my father's changes.

They haven't.

I'm locked in my room during an evacuation, and my only hope is that my father remembers before it's too late.

I feel tears rise, the kind that fill your throat with a furious lump that makes it hard to breathe. The evacuation message repeats, and this time my wrist comm chimes with it as well, but I barely hear it over the rush of blood that anger pumps through me. My fucking father and his fucking pride, and now I'm going to fucking miss my escape pod. I can't even call someone with the wrist comm because they're not designed for two-way communications, but for *aesthetics*.

I throw my shoulder against the door, knowing it won't do me any good, and the pain of bouncing off the metal clears my head a little bit. I can at least get the go bag. That way, if my father comes here, I'll be ready.

I'd shoved the bag under the bathroom sink, so I can retrieve it quickly. I also take the opportunity to use the toilet, because who knows when I'll have that chance again, and I grab the two water bottles I have somehow accumulated. I fill them and pack them away in the bag. It seems very light, even with the added water, to carry everything I'm going to need if we have to leave *Titan* behind. Space is vast and help is far, far away, and suddenly the bag makes me feel like I'm trying to empty a bathtub with a measuring spoon.

I get a sweater. I change into better shoes. I pace back and forth some more. The evacuation alert repeats three more times. It's on auto-play, so I can't even imagine that hearing it means there's anyone left on board. For all I know, the pods launched five minutes ago, and I'm going to hear that message every three minutes until I run out of air. Or starve. Or however the actual thing that kills me gets around to doing it.

Just as I'm about to give up hope entirely, I hear a sound at my door. Someone is trying to get in. For a moment, I forgive my father for every insult he's given me over the past few days. He's remembered me. Then I realize that my father would just open the door. Whoever is out there now is taking too long to get in to be the original hacker. My delusion of parental goodwill vanishes between one breath and the next. He didn't come for me.

I squash that feeling before it makes me tear up again. It's not important right now. What's important is that *someone* is on the other side of that door, trying to get me out, and it doesn't really matter who it is.

The door finally slides open, and my rescuer is not at all who I had been expecting.

"Dr. Ripley?" I ask.

"Mr. Peters said your father had done something to your door," she says, waving me out into the corridor. I follow her quickly, ready to never see these rooms again. "He was going to leave it until the morning, because it would slightly take the edge off your father, but when the alert sounded, he was frantic."

The doctors, scientists, programmers, and so on are all on deck six. I hadn't thought about it, but it makes sense that Dr. Ripley and Peters would be neighbours. Peters's room is right below mine so that he can get back and forth easily, though I know he doesn't like the ladders, so I try not to ask too much of him.

"Where is Peters?" I ask.

"He's in the pod already," Dr. Ripley says. "I can climb faster."

"Thank you," I say. "Do you know what's happening?"

"No," Dr. Ripley tells me. "Though I heard whisperings that there was some kind of explosion."

We reach the ladder that will take us to the outer hull and our designated pod. Everyone in this section of *Titan*, regardless of the deck they're on, is assigned to the pod "above" them. We only have to climb through decks eight and nine. Someone like Celeste will have to climb all the way up from deck one in the centre of the ship.

We reach the top of deck seven and the hatch that will take us through eight and beyond to our pod when Dr. Ripley pauses. I know immediately what she's thinking. The alien specimens are on this deck, just to our right and through one bulkhead. The greatest discovery of human history, and we're evacuating the ship without it.

"Fuck," says Dr. Ripley.

She'll have notes, of course. And photographs. And who knows what other kinds of records. And maybe the display will be salvageable, eventually. My father is very good at his job, and the cases should be as good at keeping things out as they are at keeping things in. The cases have their own power system in case of emergency. They're the one thing on *Titan* that might outlast us all.

"Fuck," says Dr. Ripley again, and then she keeps climbing.

we are stronger now

our words flow like theirs

we could communicate if we wanted

that is not our way

these beings gorge themselves while others starve

they are worthy only to be our shells

fifteen

CELESTE

By the time I've finished throwing up, an announcement finally comes over the main address system.

"ATTENTION CREW AND PASSENGERS. ATTENTION." The automated voice grates at my ears. It's better than the alarm, but only just. "THERE HAS BEEN A CRITICAL FAILURE WITH A SHIP SYSTEM. EVACUATE IMMEDIATELY TO YOUR ASSIGNED ESCAPE POD."

Ren is bent over, her arms braced on her knees while she tries to catch her breath. I guess that while I'd been puking, she'd been hyperventilating. I reach out cautiously to touch her shoulder. I'm not sure how she's going to react, so I murmur her name just before I make contact. She doesn't lean into my hand, but she doesn't flinch away from it either.

"I'll be fine," she wheezes. "I can climb."

At least we're already on deck three, and we're still in the same section we started out in. Our pod is right above our heads, more or less. We just have to climb through five decks to get there.

"A critical failure in a ship system," Ren says. "How would the display—"

"It doesn't matter," I tell her. I know she'll panic if she thinks about the aliens too much, so I head that right off at the pass. "A critical failure is a critical failure. We have to get to the pod."

If it hadn't been taking all of her concentration to breathe normally, I know she would have argued that it *did* matter which system. Sewage, we had time. Air, we had considerably less. Something flammable, and who knows. But I don't want to think about it, and I don't want her to think about it, either, so I herd both of us towards the ladder and we begin our ascent.

The space between the decks increases dramatically after three, because decks four and five are for cargo. *Titan* is carrying luggage, of course, and no one would dare call the ship anything less than luxury transport, but you don't just send a ship to Mars without loading it to the gunwales with things people on Mars need. There are machine parts and seed crops and a truly unfathomable amount of chocolate, because people always have weird priorities. There are also, though I am trying not to think about them, a few compartments full of people. They do have escape pods, technically, because they legally have to, but I'm not sure I like their chances.

Right now, none of those things are my problem. My problem is getting Ren and myself up the ladders as quickly as possible.

We're pretty good at climbing around *Titan* now, so it doesn't take us too long to cross both cargo decks and finally break out onto deck six. We still don't meet anyone, which is deeply unsettling. The ladders should be full of people from our section and the one beside it climbing to their pods. It's possible, I suppose, that they're using the other ladders—*Titan*'s design means that each section has direct access to two ladders, as much for redundancy as anything else—but it strikes me as mathematically impossible. We can't be that far behind.

The emergency call repeats as we climb, never getting less aggravating, but it sounds strangely muted on deck six. Maybe it's because this is a passenger deck, so there are more things like rugs and sofas and brass fucking knobs to absorb the sound. We don't slow down, but by the time we get to deck seven, Ren's breathing is out of control again and we have to stop.

"I'm sorry," she wheezes. "You can keep going."

"Are you stupid?" I ask. "I am not leaving you here. Besides, they'll do last calls and all that stuff before the pods launch. We're close now and we've still got time."

I watch her employ every technique she can think of to control her breathing, short of sitting down and crossing her legs to meditate. As she calms, I feel my own heartbeat slow down a bit too. It had been racing ever since we woke up to the alarm, and then after what happened with Michael—no.

I feel my stomach heave again and refuse to think about him any more right now. My heartbeat. That's where my focus is.

"Celeste, the gallery is twenty metres away from where we are," Ren says.

"And?" I ask. I know *Titan*'s layout as well as she does, and for some reason, ever since the big dramatic reveal, I feel like I always know how much space there is between me and those alien display cases.

"We should look," Ren says.

"Are you kidding?" I ask. "We have some time, but we don't have that kind of time. What good would it do?"

"I have to know," she says. "Please."

Ren asks for so little from me. She left her family on Earth so I wouldn't have to make this trip alone. She always includes me, even if what I get will come out of her own portion. The last thing I want in the whole universe right now is to go out and look at the gallery, but I can't say no to her.

"We're going up one more deck," I tell her. "We'll look down from the top of the stairwell on deck eight."

"Right," she says. "That's very smart."

I think of several things to say about what would be smart right now, and swallow all of them.

"Let's go," I say, and once again, we climb.

I always thought the design of the upper passenger decks was foolish. There's so much wasted space. We could have taken so many more supplies or building materials with us, except they get to have fancy staircases and two-storey galleries and gaming halls instead of anything remotely practical. Now, however, I'm extremely glad about the staircase, because it means I don't have to actually stand on the same level as the display cases. I can look down on them, the way that people like Dominic's father look down on me.

We reach deck eight and make a dash for the bulkhead. There are bodies on the floor. Most of them are wearing pyjamas, not uniforms. One of them is somehow still clutching a stuffed dinosaur. All of them look like something tried to shake them apart and then cast them aside when they were broken. We can't stop to look too closely, and I'm *glad*.

On the other side of the bulkhead, we can see the open space where the top of the stairs is. There's an emergency seal between the two decks but it hasn't activated, so we can see the soft glow from the gallery below. We crawl forwards to the railing at the top of the stairs and look through the gilt-covered spindles.

"Oh my God," Ren says.

The gallery is in ruins. The display cases are shattered, glass and whatever high-tech polymers Benedict Reubens had used to build them strewn around the floor. The chairs are all pushed aside like something swiped them all at once.

In the middle of the wreckage lies the alien queen. She's almost iridescent in the low gallery lights, her purple shine intoxicating to look at. I find myself leaning forwards even though the bars of the railing are in the way, as though I could touch her. There's no sign she's alive—no breathing or noise—and for one irrational moment, that makes me sad.

"Look," Ren hisses, and my chest freezes.

There are at least four figures down there, standing like humans but not moving like them. One of them is Wendy.

Another is the med tech. They're both covered in gore and don't seem to care. The other two are archaeologists from Dr. Ripley's team. They hadn't been introduced by name at the launch party, but I remember them sitting in the crowd and eating dinner in the crew mess because it was less pretentious. They shamble around sorting through the damaged cases and pulling things out of the broken displays. I don't have to see other shapes to know what they're doing. They're retrieving the alien eggs.

"Why—" Ren begins, but I put my hand over her mouth.

"Not now." I mouth the words at her. I jerk my head back the way we came and Ren nods.

The most important thing right now is getting the fuck out of here, so we scramble back towards the bulkhead, standing up taller as we run. We get through easily enough, but when Ren tries to shut it, the latch doesn't click. She tries again. I look down the corridor and realize that all the doors have opened, even the floor hatches.

"Ren, we have to go!" I say, pushing her towards the ladder.

She climbs and I follow her, and just before we reach the next hatch, I see movement below us. It could be a passenger, making a last-minute break for their escape pod, but I'm not about to stick around to find out. The doors won't shut. We can't protect ourselves at all.

We climb through deck nine frantically. The open hatch at the top is less of a welcome and more of a threat, but we don't have time to waste. We dash down the corridor, the last usable space between *Titan*'s command deck and the void, and finally make it to the airlock and our escape pod.

"Ren!" David screams when he sees us. "Celeste! Thank God."

He's by himself, of course. I haven't seen him without Wendy very often since they found each other. They even shared a recovery room at the hospital, even though the nurses wanted to divide the floor by gender. I wonder what it's like to find a person who's so close to you after so long apart, literally give them a piece of yourself, and then lose them. I don't want to ask.

"Strap in," says the officer in charge of our pod. He's not a senior officer. I look around and realize he's the only other *Titan* crew member to have made it on board. Over half the seats in the pod are empty, so it's easy to spot Benedict Reubens and Adam Jeffers, through neither has family members with him. The whole section can fit in here, one hundred people at least. How many bodies did we pass in this section? How many people are still alive in the others?

"The auto-launch is locked. You've got about five minutes."

"We don't have five minutes," Ren says. "There was something behind us on the ladder."

"Was it Dr. Ripley?" A man I don't recognize asks the question, voice wildly hopeful. "She went to get Dominic when, uh . . ."

"When what?" I ask. This must be the valet who tried to help Dominic hide his art supplies.

"When his asshole father sealed him in his room," he says, glaring at his employer.

"What?" I shriek.

"Wait, what do you mean *behind* you?" Adam demands. I grind my teeth. There are six other pods. Why did he have to have quarters in *my* section? "What's going on?"

There is a pause longer than any of us can afford to take, and I realize that no one besides us knows that it's the aliens. The passenger decks were just told to leave, and they hadn't made the detours we did.

"The aliens," David says, his voice on the edge of hysterical. "Those fucking aliens got out, and my sister is missing, and—"

His voice rises as tears take over and he can no longer speak. The engineer next to him tries to take his hand, but the straps limit her reach, and David just bats her away. The noises he's making aren't grief, not yet, but they're going to be.

"That's not possible," says Benedict. His wife is missing too. He doesn't look concerned about her, and why would he? "The system is contained. Even an explosion wouldn't affect my cases."

"Unless the explosion *was* your cases," Ren says.

"Where," my voice is cold and loud, and everyone except David shuts up, "the fuck is Dominic?"

"I left him in his room," Benedict says. "I locked him in."

I can't waste time thinking about all the ways in which Benedict Reubens is a horrible human being, but somehow, I will make sure he pays for this.

"Time?" I ask the officer.

"Four minutes," he says.

"Let me go over and check the ladders," I say, gesturing to where the other ladder terminates. "Just in case."

I'm not senior enough to give orders, but he doesn't hesitate to follow my lead. If anything, he looks relieved. He's not supposed to be in charge either.

"All right," he says.

As I make my way down the corridor, I hear a scuffle behind me. I turn just in time to see Adam Jeffers punch the officer in the face, dropping him to the floor of the pod. Ren jumps towards him, but she's too late. He's already reached the launch control. The emergency launch button is pretty damn obvious, on account of it being a giant flashing light. It overrides the countdown. Everyone will remember that from their safety briefing.

"Fuck Dominic," Adam says. "We're going."

"No!" Ren screams as his hand comes down.

Then, because my best friend is too good for me, she jumps back into the airlock just as the door seals behind her. She lands hard, rolling to a stop as the launch sequence continues.

"You fucking prick!" I yell at Adam, even though he can't hear me, as I drag Ren through the shipside airlock door.

It shuts, and the pre-launch decompressions begin.

Whatever is causing all the death and mayhem on *Titan*, we now have one less way to escape from it.

sixteen

DOMINIC

I know something is wrong the moment I haul myself through the hatch and into the little walkway that should lead to our escape pod. I mean, a *lot* of things are wrong, but as soon as my feet hit the deck plating, I know we're about to find something else. It's too quiet. It's been horribly quiet all the way up, but there are several decks' worth of people in that pod and there's no way none of them are saying anything.

As I look up, I see Ren and Celeste standing in front of me, and for a moment I think I'm going to be okay. Then I realize that they're both staring at the airlock, which is empty.

"We missed it?" I hear Dr. Ripley ask. "My team knew we were coming. So did Peters."

"They left without us," Ren says. She rubs her knee like she's bruised it, but it's hard to tell because the uniforms the engineers wear are basically indestructible.

"Adam left without us." There's so much venom in Celeste's voice that I recoil. Even Ren seems surprised.

"What?" I ask, even though I'm honestly unsurprised to find out Adam would do something like this.

"He panicked," Ren said. "There were five minutes until launch and he couldn't wait, so he punched the officer in charge and hit the emergency override."

"While you were standing here?" Dr. Ripley demands.

"I was going to check the ladder for you," Celeste admits. "Ren jumped out when she realized I wouldn't be able to get back on board in time."

"Can we make it to another pod before the general launch?" Dr. Ripley asks.

I can see Ren and Celeste do the calculation in their heads automatically. Even if we all ran at top speed, this level of the ship has the biggest circumference. We all know the answer.

"No," Celeste says.

The airlock has a view port, and Ren presses her face up to it. She won't be able to see the other pods unless she gets really lucky, but we have no other way of telling right now. There's no console up here, and we won't hear the airlocks, even with the bulkheads open. The timer above our airlock is still counting down. There isn't really any point in sticking around until it reaches zero, but I have no idea where we'll go.

"I'm sorry," I say. All of them are stuck here because they were worried about me.

"It's not your fault Adam's an asshole," Ren says. "And your dad is no prize, either."

A loud scraping noise comes from the ladder that Celeste and Ren would have climbed up to get here. They clearly know what it is we're hearing and are afraid of it. I'm still hung up on Adam fucking Jeffers leaving us to die, so my brain feels like mashed potatoes. I watch as Ren leaps forwards and tries to shut the hatch, but for whatever reason, the hatches still aren't sealing properly.

"We have to go," Celeste says. "Now."

"Is that—" Dr. Ripley starts to ask, then cuts herself off.

No, it can't be. My brain rejects the possibility even as it starts to reason it through. The scraping noise coming from the ladder shaft cannot possibly be—

"Now!" Celeste insists, and she runs towards the next section of the ship.

Titan's design is supposed to be revolutionary, and maybe it is if you're just on a normal voyage, but when you're abandoned and being chased by God knows what, the layout is a little inconvenient. I follow Celeste and Ren as they run along the corridor. It's not exactly easy going, because there's never supposed to be anyone all the way out here. The bulkheads are sunk into the flooring on the passenger decks. Up here, they're raised, like we're on an old-fashioned sea vessel, and jumping over them is awkward because the roof is so low.

If we'd gone the other direction, we would have ended up in the Medical bay, which is at the top of section C. The way we're going now, we'll be crossing over Navigation, and the next ladder down will be between Nav and the flight deck. It's a smart choice. Even though the Medical bay would probably be safer if someone got injured, you can scan the whole ship from the flight deck. Plus, if we went to Medical, we'd have to go in the direction those noises were coming from.

"Here!" Ren stops dead, pointing sideways at a small ladder.

"What is that?" Dr. Ripley asks.

"It goes to the captain's ready room," Ren says. "It might be safer than just jumping out onto the bridge."

"It's them, somehow, isn't it?" Dr. Ripley's voice is full of dread. "They're here."

"Not now," says Celeste.

This hatch is entirely manual, so we'll be able to shut it behind us. Celeste and Ren struggle to lift it open. There isn't enough room for me to help them, even if I could—my hands are shaking as all of the facts start to land on me. Finally, they get it open, and Celeste leads the way down. She makes a surprised noise—not a scream, but definitely not the good kind of surprised noise.

"It's fine," she calls up. "It'll be safer. Get down here."

Dr. Ripley goes down the ladder, and I follow when Ren indicates that she'll go last to shut the hatch. Before I get to the bottom, I already wish I could be somewhere else. But Celeste is right. This place is the safest for now.

Captain Bernard is at his desk. Somehow, he is still sitting upright. He's even wearing his hat. But it's immediately apparent why all the ship-wide announcements were automated and not made by him. Where his chest used to be is a giant gaping hole, all the way through the back of his chair to the smashed glass of what I assume used to be a fish tank behind him. The water is all over the floor, but the little fake corals are still standing. I don't want to turn my head but I force myself to look, following the path of destruction towards the door.

The water has washed some of the blood off the deck plating, but there's no mistaking the splash of gore where whatever came through the captain landed on the floor. There's a trail that looks like a drag mark towards the door, but then I realize that it's probably from something slithering like a snake.

"Tell me everything," Dr. Ripley says hoarsely. "Everything you saw."

I listen with growing horror while Celeste and Ren describe their flight from the lowest deck. They take turns, usually when one of them has to stop and gag. Dr. Ripley turns paler and paler as they describe what happened to Michael, what they saw in the gallery, and what they heard before they reached the escape pod. If we had diverted into the gallery, we might have walked right into whatever scene they disturbed, and seen the strangely moving figures for ourselves.

"Why did you think the specimens were dead?" Celeste asks as Ren finishes bringing us up to date. She sounds accusatory, but Dr. Ripley doesn't seem to mind.

"There were no signs of anything like what we'd call life," Dr. Ripley replies. "And it has been thousands of years. *Millions.*"

"Do we really need to know how they survived?" Ren asks.

It's terrifying to think about something that old.

"Yes," Celeste says. "Because we might have to kill them."

The inquisitive girl who volunteered to hide my sketches is gone. Celeste is all hard lines now. My mother would call her "mission-oriented."

Shit.

"Was my mother in the pod?" I ask. "She was in Medical before."

"No," Ren says. "Your dad didn't seem worried, though. There's a pod there too."

She's too nice to tell me what the other option is.

"Okay," Dr. Ripley says. "We need to know who is on board, and we need to find out if the aliens show up on scans."

"And find out who blew up the display cases," Ren says. "They didn't just fail. From what we saw, there had been an explosion. Someone outside the cases did it."

The implications of that make my head spin, and then I can't stop spinning. All I can think about is that my dad had locked me in my room and then evacuated without me, and Adam had intentionally launched the escape pod even though he knew I was on my way and could *actively see* two of the people he was leaving behind. They've both been frustrated by me so much lately, but I never for a moment imagined they'd just leave me to die. And yet these three people, who I barely know, had come back for me.

"Dominic!" Ren calls out, and she catches me before I can slide onto the floor, which is very nice of her because the floor is disgusting. My stomach heaves.

"We can't stay here," Dr. Ripley says. "Even if there are dead people on the flight deck, it'll be a bigger room."

No one has anything to say to that, but we all follow her out of the ready room. Ren has my arm over her shoulder until I take a few strong steps on my own, then she lets go with a reassuring squeeze.

There *are* dead people on the flight deck. Unlike Captain Bernard, they had time to run. Their bodies are all over the place, but mercifully away from their workstations, which we'll have to use. Celeste makes her way over to where the first officer would be standing under normal circumstances, if the first officer wasn't in a pile of her own sludge on the floor.

She sits down, a bit gingerly, and taps at the console. Ren goes to stand behind her and Dr. Ripley does a circuit of the room, looking at the carnage in a detached way I'm extremely jealous of. There is nowhere I'm in a hurry to sit, but at least I can lean on one of the consoles without accidentally pressing any buttons, and that helps me calm down a bit.

A thought occurs to me, and now is as good a time to ask as any.

"Dr. Ripley," I say. By some miracle my voice doesn't crack. "How many eggs did you put in the display case?"

She looks at me like I'm insane.

"Five," she says.

"I was drawing the aliens," I tell her. "I couldn't stop thinking about them, and drawing is how I deal with stuff. I noticed when I was sketching the nest that it was much bigger than it needed to be. I wondered if the nest was just really big, or if you'd built it differently for some reason, or if there were more than five eggs."

"Do you have an original picture?" Ren asks.

Dr. Ripley pulls her tablet out from one of her pockets and we watch her flip through her dig site photos.

"I know I took pictures of the eggs," she says. "I took pictures of everything. But they're not here."

"Could someone have erased them?" Celeste asks without looking up from her console.

"No one on my team would erase our data," Dr. Ripley says. "They'd have to be out of their minds."

There's a horrible pause.

"Fuck," says Dr. Ripley. "I'm going to look through my personal photos. I wasn't supposed to take anything too revealing, because it was so highly classified, but I know I had a few candid shots that CSIS let me keep."

We wait while she looks. I can tell the girls are trying to stay calm as all the implications sink in. I can barely manage, but they're helping me focus.

"Here," says Dr. Ripley. She makes the photo take up the full tablet screen and then zooms in when Ren and I move closer for a better look.

It's a picture of two archaeologists smiling up from the semi-frozen dirt they're excavating. Behind them, in the corner of the shot, is the nest. There are eleven eggs.

"I didn't set up the display," Dr. Ripley says mechanically. "I was so busy preparing for all the lectures and writing articles for publication back home that I let my assistants do it."

"We saw those two in the gallery with Wendy and the med tech," Ren says quietly.

I don't even know how to describe the feeling that creeps through me. The aliens had always been off-putting, but they'd also been weirdly compelling. Now it's the total opposite. I'm so repulsed that I want to put *myself* out that airlock, even though the pod is long gone.

Eggs can't walk. Something has to carry them. And I'm pretty sure someone would have noticed if the aliens had been out of the case *before* the explosion, which means a human had definitely done it. And the only reason to move an egg is to hatch it. I can tell by the expression on Dr. Ripley's face that she's reached the same conclusions I have. Suddenly, those lurching figures the girls described take on a whole new level of menacing. Six eggs are unaccounted for.

Dr. Ripley presses a hand to her sternum like there's a weight in her chest. I hope it's metaphorical, like the one in mine, because if this is how I find out that these damn aliens hatch out of people, I will never recover. Well, I'll probably also be its first target, but that's definitely not the last thing I want to experience.

"I've got it!" Celeste says from her spot at the computer.

"We'll solve one problem at a time," Dr. Ripley tells me and moves towards her.

It's another entry on the growing list of things that are going to keep us from getting off of *Titan* alive.

they skitter, they flee

they risk the void rather than face us

we watch

they don't know where we are

they don't know who we are

but soon they will

we grow so well inside of them

seventeen

CELESTE

I'm scrolling through *Titan*'s automatic ship's log when Dr. Ripley comes back over. The implications of six missing eggs are too much of a distraction while I'm working on something else. I've made a list. Why and how this is happening are not as critical as us finding out who is still here, if they can help us, and where we can hide. And even all of those things are not as important as the issue I've just uncovered in the log.

"The autopilot has been disengaged," I tell her, while Dr. Ripley takes a moment to breathe. "Right before the explosion. It was taken offline, reprogrammed, and then turned back on. It happened so quickly that the log barely registered it, but we're definitely not flying on our original course."

There's a viewscreen on the wall that pretends to be a window most of the time but can be used for projections.

I do that now and the map of our new course appears on it. I try to avoid looking at the shadows at the bottom of the projection. I don't want to think about what's casting them. I do my best to remember the flight deck as it had been: shiny and professional, with a reassuring hum.

"We're not going to Mars," Ren says, her eyes tracing the plotted line. "There's no destination, but we're going to go right past Mars."

"Can you fix it?" Dr. Ripley asks.

"I can't," I admit. "There were optional courses about ship operations, but all of the ones I did were for engineering."

"I took the flight modules," Ren says quietly. "I didn't tell anyone because I knew it was silly, but if I ever wanted to go back to Earth, I'd need skills that would make it worth hiring me for a return flight."

She looks at me apologetically, and for a long moment I don't understand. Then it clicks: Ren *had* given up her family for me, but she hadn't given them up entirely, and she was worried I'd see that as a betrayal.

"Of course you might want to go home, Ren," I say softly. "You'd make sure I was okay, because that's who you are, and then you'd decide. It's completely fine. Don't worry about it."

"But you can fix the autopilot?" Dr. Ripley asks.

Right. Priorities.

"I can try," Ren says. "Let me get to the pilot's console."

The pilot who had been on duty had time to run before he was taken out through the chest, so the seat is clear and the console is mostly gore-free. I don't think there's anything on the flight deck that's not a little bit bloody, but Dr. Ripley had been correct about it being easier to manage in a bigger space. Ren slides into the chair and hovers her fingers over the controls before beginning to push her way into the system. Dr. Ripley goes over to watch.

"The captain changed course," Ren reports. "But he didn't lock it in with his codes. I should be able to get around it and recalculate."

"Why would he do that?" Dr. Ripley asks. Then she laughs—not because anything's funny—at herself. "The same reason my assistant made sure I never looked closely at the nest."

There's nothing any of us can add that's much better than wild speculation at this point. We'll have to put it all together eventually, but it's like my brain shies away from thinking about the aliens too much.

"Hey," Dominic says to me. I welcome the distraction. "Are you okay? I notice Ren has some scrapes and bruises. There's got to be a med kit somewhere around here."

"I'm fine, thank you," I tell him shortly. Then I look up and try to smile at him. He's doing his best. "But the kit is a good idea. You should find it so we can take it with us if we have to go somewhere else."

He wanders off to look, and I turn my attention back to the screen in front of me for a moment before Ren interrupts.

"I'm plotting a course back to Mars," she says. "We'll have to do an engine burn to correct us, but we're well inside the safety window."

"Good," I say. Then something occurs to me. "How long is the window?"

"Why?" she asks.

"Because something wants us to not go to Mars," I remind her. "And presumably, if we start the course correction, it'll come back up here and try to take control again."

Ren's fingers freeze on the console. I can see her turning the problem over in her mind.

"Well," she says, "I can lay it all out and save all the activations for the end. That avoids a few safety checks, but those protocols assume we're starting from zero. The fact that we're already in motion should mean that it's fine to correct without doing all the checks."

"That sounds good to me," I say. "I'll make sure I don't undo anything in the other systems while I'm in here. We don't want to attract attention."

"What is the situation with life signs?" Dr. Ripley asks.

"The personal ID scanners didn't work properly on the escape pods, which means I know how many people are left on board but not necessarily who they are," I report. "I can also tell you where the life signs are registering on the ship, but I can't tell what kind of life signs they are."

"So we have no idea how many of the . . . lives on board are aliens?" Dominic clarifies, returning with the medical kit.

"We know of at least four. We also know that whatever was in the captain isn't there any longer, and we don't know where it is. That's five," I say. "Aside from that, I can get a basic readout from all of *Titan*'s systems. That's how I knew about the autopilot."

"I'll need to know how the engine is doing before I can schedule the burn," Ren says, talking while she types.

"On it," I say, and switch over to the engineering screen.

It takes its sweet time to load, which I suppose is only fair since the whole of *Titan* is currently in crisis mode. It wants an ID with clearance higher than I have, so I have to reach into what's left of the first officer for her security chips. Dominic watches me with a look of horrified fascination on his face, but instead of freezing, he's immediately ready with the sanitary wipes from the med kit.

"Thanks," I say, cleaning my hands. I really need a nail brush, but that will have to wait.

I insert the new chips and try to access the engine room scans again. This time they show up a bit faster.

"The engines look fine," I say. "They're not stressed by the original course change and they should be good to go. The lines through sections D and E to the fuel recirculation tanks are all intact."

"The aliens must need the ship," Dr. Ripley says. "They survived being frozen on Earth for millennia, but then they made sure to be on board when we left orbit. Maybe they can survive a vacuum, but they need a way to travel through it."

"Small mercies." I say it under my breath, but Dominic hears me. He smiles a bit.

"I'm sorry about Michael and Wendy," he says. "At least you know David's okay. Even if he's stuck in an enclosed space with, well, you know."

I snort in spite of myself, but neither of us finishes the joke. It's not better to be here and in danger when the other option is safety, no matter whose company you're in.

"I didn't really know Michael that well before we came on board," I say. "But I've known the twins since the kidney operation. They managed to stay out of the spotlight somehow. Usually, kids from the Rupt with heartwarming stories get plastered all over the news."

"It was too embarrassing," Dominic says, then corrects himself. "I mean, not for them—for the government. My mother talked about it a bit. Basically, they were worried that the news would focus on the 'separated' part, which would be more evidence that they hadn't done enough after the quake."

I feel something rankle in me, angry about the harm done to my friends, even if it was years ago. The government *hadn't* done enough. But no one liked to think about that part. It was easier to bloviate about moving on from "this horrible loss" and pepper it with a few stories about Rupt kids raising money for something the government should have paid for, framed as "feel good" news. Most of us went out of our way to avoid becoming that kind of story. No one who experiences a tragedy wants to be famous for something they did because of it. And Dominic is the original poster child.

"Every time I say something like that out loud, I get angrier with my parents," Dominic admits. "They shut me off from most news surrounding the Rupt, but even I knew that the government could have done a lot more."

He's quiet for a moment, but I see a whole host of memories play across his face.

"They used to take me to fundraising dinners and I'd have to speak to whole rooms full of people about how lucky I was to have been adopted, but how there were so many other kids who were in dire need," he says. "Then there would be donations to some foundation, and most of the money would go to the foundation itself. My mother would write or sponsor bills in Parliament, but they were always focused on making sure the Rupt kids got jobs."

I make an extremely rude noise. Alodia Reubens had been the architect of so many social programs for Rupt survivors, and most of us had devoted large amounts of time to never getting caught up in one of them.

"I actually thought they were doing the right thing when I was little," Dominic admits. "It wasn't until a couple of years ago that I realized what my mother was really doing, and who she was really helping."

"Preaching to the choir," I say, though I do feel a little sorry for him. He's caught in the impossible position of having been spared a hard childhood, while also feeling like he's betraying all the kids who weren't selected. It's not his fault his mother tried her best to indenture an entire generation of inconvenient children.

Despite my best intentions, my mind is wandering while I scroll through the system log. It's like my brain has decided to replay my greatest hits. I keep getting sideswiped by old memories, like the first time Ren took my hand, and new ones, like the expression on Dominic's face when he handed me that roll of his sketches. I couldn't get Ren off the ship *or* protect those drawings, in the end. We're all on our own.

"I can only imagine what they're going to be saying about *Titan*," Dominic says, pulling my attention back into focus. Right: the extremely hostile alien takeover and our reaction to it. "Right now, I mean, not historically. Like, the news on Earth is mostly about aliens and conspiracy theories currently. What will they say when they find out their cutting-edge spaceship is lost?"

That is an excellent question, and one that I should probably look into while I'm at the console. I tell him as much as I switch to a search window and look up a few news serials. They don't have word of the explosion yet, which makes sense. The reports probably have to be filtered through some kind of transportation security office first. I close the window of hockey scores and minor celebrity scandals that newsfeeds use as filler while they wait for a bigger story and go looking for the official reports instead—thanks to the first officer's ID.

"Oh, shit," I say, much more loudly than I mean to.

"What now?" Ren looks up from her console.

"Earth has been informed of our incident," I say. "Both by *Titan*'s alert system and by someone in an escape pod who guessed what the containment breach actually was, so probably the pod we didn't make it into. There was an emergency meeting right away, and they must have just decided what to do, because the internal memos are going out and the first officer has clearance to see them."

"What are they going to do?" Dr. Ripley asks.

"They're speaking in code," I tell her. "I guess they really don't want to use the word 'alien' in official documentation.

But it says that they're working on a permanent solution."

"That doesn't sound like it's going to be very good for us," Ren says.

"It's not," I tell her. I keep scanning and my heart sinks as I read.

"How bad?" Dominic asks.

"They've fired rockets," I say. "Two nuclear missiles. They're going to blow *Titan* to smithereens."

eighteen

DOMINIC

The worst part is that I can imagine my father making the call to Earth with the escape pod's emergency transponder. It just sounds like something he'd do. If he makes the call, he can control the outcome. I doubt he'd let someone else make history by revealing the aliens are *alive*.

The transponder is primarily programmed to be a beacon so that the pods can be located and tracked while they travel to safety, but my father is great at rewriting things to make them suit him better. Also, there's a distinct chance that *Titan*'s parent company would just ignore the pod's beacon, or not accept it as proof of life. Space travel is expensive, and no one wants to launch a rescue mission if they don't have to. Part of our ticket price had been an insurance payment, but the payout for the search would be so massive that it would be hard to get another vessel funded. Until they heard my father on the comm, they at least had a little bit of plausible deniability.

But he didn't do it to save anyone other than himself. And he probably suspected what the other part of Earth's reaction would be. Somewhere, deep behind security clearance, possibly even deeper than *Titan*'s owners could look, there would have been a last-ditch plan to deal with a worst-case scenario. There always is, when the people who make the money aren't on board.

Dr. Ripley has a much more animated reaction to Celeste's news, and stumbles across the flight deck to look over her shoulder instead of Ren's.

"Will the course alteration let the missiles pass us?" she asks.

I'm extremely fuzzy on the exact physics of it, but the general idea is that the missiles travel much, much faster than we do for two reasons. First, they don't have any people on board to keep alive during the flight, and second, they can keep accelerating the whole time because they don't have to worry about slowing down for a safe entry and landing. Their speed also means they can't change direction once they're fired. The alien course correction might save our lives from that, at least.

"Yes," Celeste says. She adds the missile flight projection to her map of *Titan*'s route. It shows the missiles going right past us and continuing on to Mars. "We'll have to hope they have a manual override for the explosion, and that they realize they haven't hit us in time to stop the missiles from hitting Mars."

It feels extremely mercenary to gamble with that many lives, but I can tell from Celeste's face that she has already done the math. Learning we're alive will not make Earth destroy the missiles. Learning that they're about to destroy the Mars compounds will definitely make them do it. There's too much money on the surface of that planet.

"They'll have an override," I say, even though I don't a hundred percent believe it. Things can always go wrong. But we're still going to choose ourselves, and this gives us the best chance.

"Ren, can you figure out the last possible moment to make the course correction?" Celeste asks. "We need to be sure we can avoid the missiles without missing the landing window."

"On it," Ren says. "I can make a countdown, if you like?"

"Just to our wrist comms," Dr. Ripley says. "The four of us, I mean. I don't think a ship-wide announcement is a good idea."

"Right," says Ren, her fingers flying. "We're going to have one last problem, though."

"What?" Celeste says.

"Well, a problem and a half," Ren says. "You'll say I'm catastrophizing, but I think it's being prepared."

It's clearly a joke between them because something in Celeste's face relaxes a bit.

"In this case, I'm okay with a bit of paranoia," she says. "What are you thinking?"

"We need a person to stay on the flight deck," Ren says. "Not out in the open, necessarily. There are plenty of places to hide up here, especially if you can access the count-down on your comm. But we know the aliens changed the course once. If they check, they'll see my calculations and erase them."

"She's right," Dr. Ripley says. She sounds exhausted, and I realize that while we've been up here, our adrenaline has started to wear off. We're all going to crash at the same time if we're not careful. "What's the second part?"

"We need to go to the engine room and make absolutely sure everything is working," Ren says. "We can't trust our only hope of getting out of this to the system readouts. We have time, though I don't know if we'll be able to come back up here."

Splitting up is the last thing I want to do. They'll make me stay up here because I don't really have that many skills, and I'll have to wait while they risk their lives to make sure we're safe. It'll be just like how I left the Rupt: something to be grateful for, even when it makes me feel ashamed.

"I'll stay here," Dr. Ripley says. "Show me what I need to do. You three can go together. I'll be safe enough up here, and you'll have more chances to succeed."

There's a brief moment of quiet while everyone considers it.

"Dominic, you don't have to come," Ren says softly. Beside me, Celeste nods.

"I know," I say. "And I realize I don't really understand enough about the engine to be useful down there, but Dr. Ripley is right. We only need one person up here, and we have no idea what we'll run into down there."

It almost sticks in my throat, but I'm glad that I can say it. I won't be randomly saved again. I'll earn it this time.

"Okay," Celeste says. "Go through every drawer you can find to see if there's anything to take with us. Light sources, food, medical supplies. We'll leave some of it here for Dr. Ripley and take the rest."

I nod and move away to start looking. Ren is walking Dr. Ripley through the systems she'll need. Dr. Ripley is making notes on her comm to make sure she doesn't let anything slide. Celeste is still looking through system logs, I assume double-checking to make sure we haven't missed anything. Whatever commands she's typing, I know they're for *Titan*'s safety and preservation.

I move around the flight deck opening any compartment I can. There isn't much in the way of useful gear, aside from the med kit that I already found. There's food, though. Apparently, the bridge crew kept a lot of snacks around, which makes sense, I guess. It's a long way to the crew mess from here. The navigators had a drawer full of off-brand chocolate bars, the kind you buy when you just need sugar. The first officer was more of a pretzel woman. And so on. I didn't really know any of these people, and I feel like learning about them from their snacking habits after they're dead is unfair to all of us. The operations officers have a stash of cheese puffs and licorice, but one of them seems to be a bit more practical and has a tin of jerky and dried fruit packed away.

I add all the food to the pile and then steel myself to go back into Captain Bernard's ready room. I breathe through my mouth—which helps as long as I don't think about what I'm inhaling—and check the drawers that run along one wall. They turn out to be mostly filing cabinets that contain paper copies of *Titan*'s design. They're wrapped in plastic that says "In Case of Emergency," and I almost laugh. I'll tell the girls that they're here, but I don't think they're going to be very useful in *this* emergency.

I turn to the captain's desk. I've left it for last because I've been trying not to look at what's left of him, but now I can't put it off anymore. I rifle through each drawer quickly and come up with a flashlight, another headlamp, and an emergency toolkit. At least it was worth my while. I manage to make it out of the room without touching anything else, and when I get back to my little pile of supplies, Celeste is sorting through it.

"I should have gone into navigation," she muses, holding up a bag of dill pickle chips. "We get breaks, but we don't get snacks like this."

"Right now, I'm very glad you're an engineer," I say.

"Because that's the most useful?" she asks with a grimace.

"No," I say, alarmed that she could interpret what I said that way. I want to be better than what she expects of other people. "Because everyone up here died."

"Oh," she says. That clearly hadn't crossed her mind. "Thanks, I guess."

She does her best to smile at me and then goes back to packing everything up. The food she leaves for Dr. Ripley is, for lack of a better word, the puffiest packages, like the chips and the little cakes I found under the communications panel. We still have almost a week until we get to Mars, and it's going to be thin rations, but Dr. Ripley should be fine with what we're leaving her, and we'll be moving through the ship and possibly able to resupply. Celeste stuffs the medical bag with as much of it as will fit and then starts filling her pockets.

I sling my own go bag off my back and pass it over. It was packed for the escape pod, so there are some things in it that we don't need, like changes of clothing. Celeste pulls those out without comment and replaces them with the tool kit and some of the chocolate.

"Ren, are you almost ready?" she asks.

"I'd like one or two of those stun rods the security officers have," she says. "But they're not on our way to the engine room, if they're even still on board, and I'm not about to go looking for them."

"I think I've learned all I can, Ren," Dr. Ripley says, which is the answer I think Celeste was actually after. "You've thought of multiple scenarios and walked me through all of them. If something else comes up, I'll have to improvise."

"Can you do that?" Ren asks.

"It would be easier if the wrist comms were remotely useful." She waves her wrist. "But I'm an archaeologist. That's what I do best."

"I thought you were an ethnobiologist," I say without thinking.

"Well, yes," she says. "But all of that traces back to archaeology, and archaeology almost never gets enough funding. You learn to get creative."

A cloud passes over her face as she thinks about the ramifications of the one time she *did* get funding, but she shakes her head as if to dismiss it and takes Ren's seat at the console.

Ren makes some additions to her own pack and then looks at me critically.

"What?" asks Celeste.

"He doesn't have anywhere to attach carabiners," Ren says. "I have my spares, same as you, but they won't do him any good with those clothes."

I look down self-consciously. This is my most utilitarian outfit and it barely has pockets. There's no way my belt loops will support my weight if I slip while attached to the ladder with a safety line.

"Um," I say, unsure. Maybe they'll make me stay after all. The girls exchange a look and manage to come to a decision without speaking.

"We can worry about health and safety later," Ren says, mostly for my benefit, although it's not exactly reassuring.

"Or you can find him a uniform when we get belowdecks again," Celeste offers.

I hadn't thought of that. Though I would prefer a more particular definition of "find." There are bound to be bodies down there.

"All right, then," Ren says, checking her pockets out of habit. "Let's get a move on."

We head for the hatch at the opposite end of the flight deck from the one we came in. It's an unspoken agreement— a bit because none of us wants to take our chances with whatever had been on the ladders behind Ren and Celeste, but also because that ladder will keep all of section A between us and the alien gallery. We'll have enough on our hands without getting too close to that room again.

At the same time, *not* knowing exactly where the aliens are is creepy too. Celeste hadn't been able to get the life-form search to differentiate between them and us, so we won't know until we see them with our own eyes. This ladder was clear of everything when Celeste had scanned it, but the interference in the engine room made it difficult to scan accurately. We'd just have to get down there.

Titan had promised adventure, but I doubt this is what anyone had in mind.

here I am

I am here

here am I

I have never been alone before, in my thoughts

I have taken this mind and it has taught me how

someday I will no longer need my shell,
and then I will crack it open

but not yet

this one has much to give

nineteen

CELESTE

I would like to punch whoever decided that *Titan* should have so many ladders. I spend the whole of the descent through decks nine and eight imagining the hypothetical before I realize that I *know* who decided *Titan* should have so many ladders. Or at least I know who had final approval of the ship's design. I imagine punching her specifically through all of deck seven, and then I realize that I don't remember seeing her in the escape pod. I actually don't know where her quarters were, or if she had a suite near Adam's, or if Adam was even in the correct pod. I don't know if she got off the ship. Adam would absolutely have launched without knowing where his mother was. There's no excusing him. He's just a dick.

We stop for a breather at the top of deck six and I vaguely listen while Ren explains that the next two decks will be the longest climb on account of the cargo space. I can't remember what was stored in the two sections we'll be climbing between, but it doesn't really matter. We don't have time to go through the bays right now and they're way too exposed anyway, since there are fewer bulkheads and compartments.

I shake my head against the headache forming behind my eyes. It feels like someone has cracked my skull open. I don't get migraines, but I've been awake for longer than I slept last night—still *this* night? I check my comm and wince when I see that it's only 4:00 a.m. I'm probably dehydrated too, even though I don't feel hungry or thirsty. We should make sure we eat something before we make the final descent to the engine room.

Ren is apparently having the same thoughts, because she gets a package of powdered electrolytes out of the med kit. She pours some into her water bottle, then Dominic's, and then passes them to me. I trust Ren to keep track of things like this. She always knows how much is left and how long we need to make it last. Her rationing is strangely comforting, in a way. At least I know I'm with someone who has a timeline.

The countdown on our comms still has a while to go, so we take our chance to rest while we can. It's still unnerving not to meet anyone on the ladders. I hope the crew got off, obviously, but I also hope we're not alone with a bunch of corpses and monsters. My headache flares when I think about it, so I redirect my thoughts.

"You doing okay?" I ask Ren. She'd banged her knee pretty hard when she jumped into the airlock. Climbing can't feel good.

"It's fine," Ren says. "I put some analgesic on it before we left the flight deck, so it's okay unless I bang it against a rung, and that would hurt anyway."

I know she'll have made a note of how much analgesic is left and how much she thinks she'll need. I'm lucky that none of my bruises need treatment. It'll save supplies.

"All right," I say. "Let's keep going."

Dominic hasn't said much since we started down. I know he feels bad about at least twelve different things right now, and I know he's absurdly grateful we didn't leave him in slightly better safety on the bridge. I don't know why I wanted him to come with us so much. Maybe it's because having one person I trust nearby is good, but having two is better. I know Dominic will do whatever he can, even if it isn't much. And I appreciate that he's genuinely wanting to help us. So often, the people from his echelon that I meet just want to use my tragic backstory for something and they don't actually care about me at all.

The headache stabs through me again. Maybe I should stop thinking about anything at all. It's easy enough to limit my focus to the rungs below me. You'd think climbing down a ladder would be easier because gravity's on your side, and that's true, but even if you trust yourself, you still look down a lot for the next place to put your foot . . . and that strains your neck.

We get all the way down to deck one without incident. From here, it's a matter of getting to a hatch and climbing through.

"Have you ever been in zero-g?" I ask Dominic. "It can be really disorienting if you haven't."

"A few times," Dominic says. "I didn't get sick or anything, but I had lines to follow if I started drifting."

"Right," says Ren. "Then I think, when we get inside, it'll be best if you stay near the hatch."

Dominic makes a face, and I know what he's thinking.

"Hey, it's not a bad thing," I say. "Both Ren and I will be busy dealing with whatever is in there. It'll be nice to know someone's holding a door for us."

"Thanks," Dominic says dryly. He doesn't entirely believe me, but I'm not just buttering him up. If there's something dangerous in the engine room, I'm going to want to know I have an exit ready.

Ren passes around the electrolytes again. I add my share to my water bottle, but it's not helping much with the headache. Usually, electrolytes clear that up within seconds. That's why they're in the med kit. Michael uses them when he has a hangover. Used them? Fuck, now I feel bad *and* I have a headache.

I shove all of my useless thoughts away and carefully open the hatch. Doors on this level are sealing, apparently, so it's nice to know that my little trip into the systems log helped. I'd much rather know the way behind me is secure than know the way forwards is open right now. I stick my head out into the corridor and it's still empty. The lights are flickering, which I feel is a needless addition to the creepiness of the scene, but no one asked me.

The others follow me as I step into the hall and we make our way to the last hatch, the one that leads down to the engine room.

"Hold on to something all the time," Ren reminds Dominic. "At least one hand. No matter what. It is the most important thing. Do you understand?"

"What if one of you needs me?" he protests. He wants to be needed so badly that it shows on his face.

"If you're unsecured, you could end up in the engine," I tell him gently. "You stay by the door and you hold on, so that when we need a way out, you've got it for us."

He nods. I only feel a little guilty. What I told him is true, it just feels like crass manipulation. I want to be genuine with him. I want him to be himself and comfortable when he's with me. We have absolutely met under the wrong circumstances for *that*.

Ren and I lift the hatch and then do the safety checks automatically while Dominic stands waiting for us. Then Ren clips on to the ladder and climbs down. I wait for her to be clear before I follow.

"Hold on," I remind Dominic, hoping that the repetition shows how serious we are and isn't just annoying as hell. "Both hands whenever possible, and at least one all the time."

He nods, and I climb down the last ladder to *Titan's* heart. Ren is waiting on the platform below, but I can't see anything past her. The engine is bright, but none of the other lights are on, even the emergency ones. We all have headlamps now, but we don't want to use them until we know who, or what, is in here with us. All the same, we should have left Dominic on the deck. He won't be able to see the handholds. But I hear him step onto the platform and I know it's too late. He'll just have to stay where he is.

"Who was on duty?" Ren whispers. "Besides Michael, I mean."

"I don't remember the night shift," I say. "But Michael said Anthony showed up and ordered him to the mess, so I guess that's who we're looking for."

He hadn't been in the pod either, but he could have chosen any section to climb through when he evacuated. *If* he evacuated. He might have been cut off after the alarms sounded, though once all the hatches were open, he had a chance.

"Everything looks fine," Ren says. "And the hum is normal. The console is on the next platform over, though."

Usually she'd just jump, but in the dark, even Ren uses her safety lines. I quietly tell Dominic where we're going, pointing his head in the right direction with my hands even though he can't see it clearly.

"Be careful." He cuts me off before I can remind him to keep his hands on the railing.

Ren plots her jump carefully and goes first, because even in the dark she's better at this than I am. When she tugs on her line to signal that she's landed safely, I follow. She hasn't moved very far from where she landed and I crash into her accidentally.

"Ooof," I gasp as all the air is driven out of me. Then I see why Ren hasn't moved.

Anthony is standing there, clipped on to the platform and holding one of the jump cables we use to kickstart the backup systems if something goes wrong. They pack quite the punch and would definitely fry all of us if Anthony panics and drops them on the platform.

"What's happening?" he asks. His voice is calm, which only makes me more nervous.

"There was an incident," I say. "An explosion in the alien cases. They're still alive. Someone sabotaged the display cases and took the eggs, and they're somewhere on the ship. Didn't you hear the evacuation call?"

"The hatches all sealed," Anthony says. He lowers the cable, but doesn't turn it off. Ren takes a step forwards so we're not on top of each other anymore. "I couldn't get out."

"Every other hatch on the ship was open," Ren says, confused.

"Maybe these ones somehow missed the glitch," I suggest.

"Why aren't you two evacuated?" Anthony asks.

"We didn't make it to the pod in time," Ren says. It's not the whole truth, and I notice that she doesn't mention Dominic, but I don't add anything to her explanation. "Look, we came down here because we need to make sure the engines are working properly. I wanted to see it with my own eyes."

Anthony knows her well enough to accept this as normal Ren behaviour and motions her towards the console. I step up beside her. I climbed all the way down here and I'm going to damn well look myself.

"How many others are still on board?" Anthony asks.

"I don't know," I tell him. "And I don't know how many aliens are running around, either."

It's the second time I've mentioned that the aliens are, in fact, alive, and Anthony still hasn't reacted. I admire his compartmentalization, but I'd expected some kind of reaction.

"Why are the lights off?" I ask. "Are you hiding something?"

"I turned them off," Anthony says. "I heard the alarm and then the call to evacuate, and then there was nothing. At the very least, turning off the lights will save power. But then there were strange noises on the other side of the hatches, and I decided I didn't want it to be easy to see in here."

"Which hatches?" I ask.

"The ones under the indenture holds," he says grimly.

I don't have to see his face to guess his expression. It's possible they all got off just fine. There had been time to evacuate, and since the secondary water tanks in those sections of *Titan* double as extra pods, there is enough space to accommodate them. But knowing what I know about human nature, I have my doubts that everyone made it out okay. At least the seals on those decks are reinforced. If the doors are shut, maybe the aliens can't get in. It'll buy them some time while we figure out what the hell to do with the rest of *Titan*.

"Ren, are you satisfied with the engines?" I ask. I had focused on the connections between the engines and ship's systems, because I knew more about that than the actual engines themselves, but Ren knows the engines better.

"Yes," she says. "There's no strain and they seem to be running steadily. The connections are all good?"

"Everything is running smoothly," I tell her. "All of the systems are doing what they're meant to. There's a blip in Medical, but that might just be because someone left a machine running. It's probably not something we have to worry about right now."

"You're right," says Ren. "Anthony, are you going to stay here or come with us?"

"I wasn't planning to leave," Anthony says. He's moving normally, but there's something off about him that I can't place. Maybe this is just what he's like under stress. "I assume all the escape pods launched when yours did?"

"Yes," I tell him. "All the pods are gone."

"Good," he says, a strange gurgling noise coming into his voice.

And then, in a horrible flash of purple and gore, an alien bursts out of his chest.

twenty

DOMINIC

My hips and shoulders are aching by the time we reach *Titan*'s lowest deck. I'm not completely unaccustomed to physical activity. I had played lacrosse on Earth because my mother thought it was more suitable than hockey, and the kids at my high school all played cricket because we were pretentious private-schoolers. *Titan* had issued a manual to all passengers aboard, and there was a whole section about making sure your muscles don't atrophy while you're in space. Admittedly, we hadn't been travelling for long before the aliens took over, but I had done my recommended workouts, though not enthusiastically because I hate being in the gym with other people. I had even swum lengths in the little pool.

None of that was particularly helpful as I climb down ladder after ladder, the bag I'm carrying getting heavier with each rung. The girls are affected too, though not as much as I am. They had a whole workday before this started, and only a couple hours of sleep, but they still manage to be steady as they climb. We stop twice, once above the cargo holds and again just before we emerge onto deck one, but my legs still feel like limp noodles as I walk on the deck plating.

The engine room is zero-g, which I remember from the tour. We hadn't gone inside, because it's not a place for tourists, but we had looked down through one of the hatches. I liked watching the engineers push themselves around, leaping from platform to platform with the engine thrumming beneath them. All of them wore safety lines, but that didn't make them any less graceful. I'm not going to be that good. The girls tell me to hold on a million times and I try not to resent it. I know people can do stupid things when they're distracted or startled, and I have no desire to end up in the engine. It got a bit annoying after the fourteenth or fifteenth time, though.

In the end, it doesn't matter that much. The lines can't attach to me, so I'm stuck on the first platform. On a normal day, that would be kind of fun. Once upon a time, my parents had gotten me a bouncy castle for my birthday. My whole class had been invited to the party, and we'd spent a sunny afternoon in the yard of our Alberta house, flinging ourselves down without worrying about what would happen when we hit the ground. It was the last birthday I had in Alberta. After that, we were always in Ottawa, in my mother's government suite. Those parties are much less fun to remember. My birthday was just another time for my parents to network and figure out new ways to take advantage of poor people.

The engine room is kind of like the bouncy castle, only in reverse. If I don't pay attention, my feet start to come off the platform. I can push them back down by bracing my hands on the railing, but it's not a natural movement. It's way too dark to see much, and the engines are so loud that I won't be able to hear what the girls are saying. I feel isolated, and for the first time since I came on board *Titan* it truly feels like I'm in space. My stomach threatens to turn over, and I understand my mother's discomfort over the past few days.

A headlamp comes on, illuminating Ren and Anthony. I'd recognize him from the tour if I was close enough, but in this lighting I only know who he is because I was expecting it to be him. I breathe out in relief. Anthony isn't the most senior engineer on *Titan*, but he is one of the higher-ranking ones, and he'll know what's what with the engines. From the movement of Celeste's headlamp, I can tell they're talking, and eventually Celeste and Ren both move to consoles and start working. I leave my light off because it's battery-powered and I don't need it to see them.

There's no console on my platform. My eyes have adjusted to the dim light a bit, so I can make out more details. There are lines extending off my platform in the direction the girls went. That's how they'll get back. If I had been able to go with them, they could have just climbed out whichever hatch was closest. I try not to feel sorry for myself for being so much dead weight on this expedition, even though I wouldn't have been much more use to Dr. Ripley. But it's hard to think positive thoughts about myself when there's nothing immediately apparent to focus on.

They don't need an artist. They don't need money. They don't need the mediocre social connections I have. If I'd listened to my father when he started harping on about my future a few years ago, I'd at least be a semi-decent programmer. I don't know what Celeste sees in me and why she keeps being so kind. And I don't know why it matters, why I want there to be something for her to see.

I know what a crush feels like. Before the Adam disaster, I had them on all kinds of people—my schoolmates, sports stars, the occasional trombone player. Adam had been a calculated choice, a mercenary decision to get what I thought I wanted. He had seemed fine with everything, even though I knew he didn't like me all that much either. We definitely didn't have good examples of relationships to follow from our home lives. He was more into sex than I was, but he'd only really started to make me uncomfortable towards the end, when I was thinking about breaking up with him.

It's too early to have a crush on Celeste. I barely know her, for starters, and I had literally broken up with my boyfriend a few hours before aliens took over our ship and forced us to do . . . whatever we're doing. But she *had* come looking for me when she realized I was missing from the escape pod. I don't have a lot of examples of human decency to follow from home either, so maybe that's just a normal thing people do, but in a very private part of my heart, I hope she came back for me because she cares.

I shake my head, trying to dislodge these juvenile, unimportant thoughts. There are much bigger things to worry about right now. But this is the first quiet moment I've had, and I have to think about *something* or I'll think about how my father and my ex knowingly left me behind on a ship and then made a call to Earth that prompted them to launch missiles at us. I don't really like that as an option either. I need something real to focus on. Something that will help us.

To that end, I check over my shoulder to make sure the hatch hasn't magically closed itself or something. My only job right now is making sure our exit is clear, so I'm definitely going to do it. The hatch is fine, obviously, but my body is starting to turn in response to my torque, so I straighten up and make sure my feet are where I want them to be. I take one hand off the railing to flex my fingers, and then repeat the motion with the other hand. No sense cramping, either.

The light on the other platform moves, and I surmise that Celeste and Ren have seen what they need to on the consoles. I check my comm—carefully, as it involves moving a hand—and see that we have plenty of time until the countdown runs out. I don't know what we're going to do for the rest of the time. The flight deck is the obvious choice, but it would be much more comfortable to wait in a place that has fewer exploded corpses in it.

Celeste's light is bobbing, like she's nodding in agreement with whatever they're talking about. They must be making a plan. I stave off my feelings of self-pity before they can overcome me. They'll tell me when they get back to the platform. I'm holding the door open. I'm not completely useless.

I would feel *more* useful if the door was in any danger of closing.

The safety line ripples, indicating that whoever is attached to it must have come near the edge of the platform, but Celeste's light isn't facing me. It's like she'd taken a step back, a hesitant one, but I have no idea what she would be worried about.

It happens so quickly that I almost miss it. I only see it because I'm already looking in the right direction. If I had been looking away, even a metre or so, it would have been over before I realized that anything was happening at all.

My eyes are overwhelmed by the flash of purple light that seems to tear through Anthony's body. In the time it takes me to blink, I remember what that shade of purple means and why it's an extremely bad sign. I manage to force my eyelids open, bringing up a hand reflexively to shield my face even though I'm far away. The light is so bright after the dimness of the engine room that it hurts to look at, but I see the shape that leaps out of Anthony's chest with all the stark clarity that backlighting can provide.

The display cases really hadn't done them justice. Frozen into a curated exhibition, the aliens had been off-puttingly *other*, and disturbing. In movement, they are blood-curdlingly horrifying, each tentacle reaching out to grasp whatever it can, the maw gaping in a way that suggests everything is food. And they're fast—like ravenous purple lightning projected from Anthony's chest, hungry beyond human measure and willing to blow straight through everyone else's torso if it can.

The alien leaps towards the girls as Anthony's body slumps down on the platform. I want to shut my eyes. I want to be on the flight deck. I wouldn't even mind being stuck in an escape pod with Adam, but I don't look away.

I can't help them. I never could. So I watch.

And I scream.

the frozen ground was a poor incubator,
but my children endured

they rose when they were uncovered,
and grew in new hosts

they took control when they were ready

they were so patient

now they can take that final step and
become themselves in their own form

they wait for me again; their patience
means that I can take my time

my rebirth awaits, but my cocoon is so, so warm

twenty-one

CELESTE

The thing about zero gravity is that your instinctive reaction to something determines your movement, until you run into something that stops you. This is what saves my life, and Ren's, when the alien jumps out of Anthony's rib cage, impossibly big, maw flaring, and heading straight for us. We're both screaming, and I can hear Dominic screaming too. I have half a moment to hope he's still holding on to the rail, and then my own self-preservation takes over.

The good news is that the alien can't change direction. It's barrelling towards the platform where we were standing, but since Anthony is tall, it's going to fly right overtop of us. The bad news is that we can't change direction easily either, and neither of us had time to think before we moved. I can't see Ren while my eyes recover from the flash of light, but I hit a surface above me a few seconds after my reflexes pushed me off the platform. I put my hands up, not to break my "fall" but to help me pick a direction to ricochet off in. The last thing I want is to run headfirst into that *thing*.

The safety line is coiling around my leg and I don't have time to shake it free, so I do my best to push off and head straight down to the platform again. I'm pretty sure Ren had jumped sideways, but she's so good at navigating in here that she could have chosen to land anywhere, so I don't know where she might have ended up.

I land on the platform and hook my foot over the lowest part of the railing to keep my hands free. I look around desperately for the iridescence that will give the alien away, but it must be close enough to the engine that I can't see it separately from the mechanical glow. I want to yell for Ren and Dominic, but I know they won't understand me. It's too loud to hear anything but screaming. I'm on my own for now.

Movement catches the edge of my vision and I whip my head around to follow it. It's Ren, thank God, gracefully moving along the wall. She's trying to get back to the platform, but right before she launches herself towards me a cable of what looks like tar and viscera comes flying across the platform between us and attaches itself to the ladder at the back. It's not one of the thing's tentacles. It's something the alien projected from its gelatinous body mass. It smells awful, and I know without looking that there are pieces of Anthony in it. I don't wait for the alien to haul itself back onto the platform before I jump away again. It's more of a dive, honestly, as I push myself off and down, angling for the platform under the one where Dominic is supposed to be. It's the most uncontrolled jump I have ever made in here, and I hate every moment of it, but I make it to the platform without being attacked again, so I count it as a win.

As soon as I'm steady, I look up, but it's no good. Ren has the flashlight, but she'll need both hands to stay manoeuvreable. The headlamps we're wearing are more of a beacon than anything else, giving away our positions, so I reach up and turn mine off. Thankfully, Dominic never turned his on. The alien might not know he's here. Now the only lights in the room are the engine and the alien, and neither of them are things I want to end up close to.

I feel a tug on the safety line and bend over to uncoil it from my leg. Nothing attacks me while I'm doing it, so I gently tug back. If Dominic is at the other end, he'll know I'm okay. If the alien is on the other end, I'm in a lot of trouble. The line goes taut, and then I feel little pulls on it, like someone is climbing hand over hand. I don't think the alien would do that, but I still retreat to the far side of the platform I'm on and prepare to unclip. I'd hate to abandon Dominic, but I'm no good to him if the alien is on top of me.

Two feet hit the platform, and I exhale.

"Celeste?" Dominic says. We're close enough that I can hear him over the engine. "I saw what happened. Where's Ren?"

He must have unclipped my line from the platform where we left him and followed it over here like a fishing line reeled in in reverse. It means our exit isn't secure, but I can't really blame him for moving away from danger if he felt it, and I'm glad he didn't leave the line as a trail. He carefully collects the safety line as he comes towards me, so there's not a lot of slack between us. This is good news, because a few seconds after he asks the question, a pair of hands slam into the railing behind me and I jump again. I don't go very far before Dominic pulls me back down.

"I'm sorry!" Ren says, trying to stabilize herself. She's lost her line when she jumped, but I don't know if she'd used the emergency detach on purpose or by accident. Somehow she can still concentrate enough to do this. I'd be toast for sure.

"We have to go," Dominic says. "The alien was heading towards me when I climbed down here. It'll figure out where we are."

Ren and I exchange a glance. There's no way to make sure Ren's jump is safe, and it makes it hard for me to follow. But we don't have time to change everything around, and Dominic has actually tied his line around his waist anyway because he doesn't have clips. If we had time and light, we'd probably be fine, but without those two things, there's no way to be sure.

"I can do it," Ren says.

"I don't know if I can follow you," I admit.

"We have to go somewhere," she says.

"Right," I say. "Let's go up and over one, so we'll be one platform away from where we came in, but back on the top level."

I don't know what "Anthony" might have done to the doors down here, and despite his normal-sized chest, the alien is already as big as he . . . was. It's certainly not a fragile new-born, freshly hatched. It's more like a vicious, demonic monarch butterfly: right out of the cocoon and ready to fly to Mexico. We have to assume it's strong. It might have already closed the hatch Dominic had been watching, but we don't have a lot of options, and given the choice, I'd rather be closer to a way out.

"Okay," Ren says. "Give me ten seconds to get clear."

Usually she only needs five, but she can barely see where she's going. I count off in my head while Dominic comes to stand beside me. He hands over the looped safety line and I get ready to spool it out behind me when I jump.

"Wait until I pull," I tell him. "If you jump before that, we'll both miss the landing."

That's the main reason I don't want to jump towards the engine.

Dominic nods and I get ready to go. I push off just as something purple appears above the platform. I swear loudly, even though no one can hear me, and pull the safety line as hard as I can. I haven't let much of it uncoil yet, so I get Dominic off his feet and moving towards me without too much effort. He sails past and I see the panic on his face, but he manages to land on the platform a few seconds before I crash into him and we both go sprawling.

"Again!" Ren calls out, already prepared to go.

We get to our feet. The next jump goes more according to plan, and I land securely on the platform before Dominic does. We're under section H now, the markings on the wall helpfully keeping me oriented as we jump.

Ren has moved to the ladder to climb up to deck one where we can hopefully get a hatch and a few bulkheads between us and the alien, but before we can follow her, a shrieking noise and a streak of coloured light indicates that the alien had the same idea. It has forgone the platforms altogether and just jumped straight onto the ladder Ren is about to climb.

Once again, we all react instinctively and inertia takes care of the rest. Ren flies off the platform in the direction we were going, Dominic jumps back the way we came, and I jump straight towards the engine. I have just enough time to register the alien following Ren before I panic and frantically start to pull the safety line in. I can't do it too fast or I'll just pull Dominic with me. My only hope is that he gets himself anchored before I pass the point of no return.

I've collected as much line as I dare, holding it loosely in my hand in case I haven't given Dominic enough space. The engine gets louder and brighter as I get closer to it. I'm not even moving that fast because my jump hadn't been particularly intentional, but I can't stop myself either, so it doesn't matter. Isaac Newton, seeing me straight into annihilation.

The line slips between my fingers, scraping over my skin in a way that will hurt if I'm still alive after my adrenaline wears off, and then goes tight. I pull as hard as I can, hoping that Dominic is anchored and I haven't just doomed us both. I feel an answering pull and I know he's reeling me in like I'm a fish instead of an engineer who came this close to frying herself in her own engine.

There are tears running down my face when I hit the platform. I don't know why I'm crying, except that I was scared I was going to die, and now I'm pretty sure I'll live for at least a few more minutes. Dominic catches me, one arm looped through the ladder and the other holding on tight until I can put my feet down.

"I can't see Ren," Dominic says as soon as he has me steady. His eyes are wide.

"We have to climb," I tell him. I don't want to leave her, but we don't have a choice. Staying in the engine room is too dangerous. I can only hope she'll reach the same conclusion and save herself.

Dominic doesn't look happy, but he nods and starts to climb. We make it to the hatch without any further incident, and then pull ourselves through it to stand in the blessed quiet of deck one. As soon as we're through, I slam the hatch shut and turn the manual lock. I hesitate, because this means there's one less door that Ren can use if she needs to, but then I set my shoulders and finish the seal. She had been going in the opposite direction, and the alien had been right on her tail. She'll be lucky if she *needs* a door to escape from.

It's a terrible thought and I feel terrible for having it, but it's my only option.

"Where are we?" Dominic asks. "I lost track."

"That was your door," I tell him. I feel a bubble of laughter coming up through my stomach, but I know if I let it out it'll turn to hysteria. "We're back where we started."

"We can't stay here," Dominic says. "We're both too wound up, and you haven't slept properly in God knows how long. We have to hide."

He's right. My adrenaline is waning, so I expect my hands will start to sting, and I'm too exhausted to feel hungry even though we should all eat. Ren will be the same, only with her bad knee. She had her own food and water with her. If she can get out of the engine room, she'll be fine. I will myself to believe it. I have to think about Dominic and me, but it's hard. I'm so used to thinking about Ren. She's always been with me, even when she could have been somewhere else.

"Our quarters," I say shortly. I'm not angry at him and I hope he knows that. "They're not too far away, in section B."

He pulls me to my feet, holding my wrist to avoid the scrapes on my hand, and we make our way down the corridor. We're still tied together by the safety line, which strikes me as hilarious for some reason. It's probably the aforementioned hysteria. I want to sit down so badly, I wouldn't mind if the chair was the dead alien queen, upcycled into furniture.

I palm the door open and wave Dominic inside. I look up and down the corridor, desperate to see Ren and terrified I might see something else, and then I follow him. Once the door is shut and locked behind me, I drop my bag and slide to the floor. I slump over to my bunk. Dominic stands awkwardly in the middle of the room and I point to Ren's bed.

"You might as well sit down," I tell him. "We're going to be here for a while."

twenty-two

DOMINIC

The thing about a countdown is that it makes you feel like you're rushing headlong towards something. No matter how high the number starts, there's a sense of inevitability. The ball will drop. The rocket will launch. That kind of thing. Up until now, the whole time our countdown had been running I had been on the move. It had felt like everything is going to work out fine because I didn't have enough breathing space to think of everything that could go wrong.

Now I'm locked in a small room with a girl I, well, let's just go with "like," and even though I'm relatively safe and have access to a private toilet, time has slowed right back down again. Celeste is taking a quick shower, so I don't even have someone to talk to right now. I'm alone with my thoughts, and they're spiralling downward pretty quickly.

I notice a tube in a compartment under Celeste's bed and recognize it as the one I'd given her. Everything on *Titan* was falling apart, but my sketches had been safe. For no particular reason I take them out and flatten them on the deck. They curl up at the edges, but they haven't been in the tube long enough to roll back up as soon as I set them down.

The aliens had been awful in the truest sense when they were static in my father's display cases, but they had been mesmerizing too. Even now that I've seen them come alive, the images I'd made of them are still hypnotic. I could look at the drawing and imagine one of these creatures bursting out of someone's chest, but it doesn't make me as nauseated when it's just on paper. I'm not sure what that says about me. Probably that I'm compartmentalizing my trauma.

The door to the bathroom opens and Celeste comes out. She's wearing a fresh uniform and her short hair is wet, but she looks like she feels better. She has a tube of analgesic cream in her hands, and now that she's clean and dressed, she takes the time to tend to her abrasions. I thought I would feel bad about hurting her, but I know that pulling the line saved her life.

"It doesn't hurt," she says. "I'm just making sure they're sterile."

I feel better instantly.

"You can shower, if you want," Celeste says. "There's a spare uniform you can put on."

It's a bit late. If I'd had a uniform in the engine room, we might not have been separated from Ren. At the same time, I have no idea where we'll end up, and the uniform is much more resilient than my own clothes, so I agree.

"All right," I say.

I shower as quickly as possible. I know I don't actually have alien bits on me, but it feels like I do. A miasma, or whatever the word is. Scrubbing them off my skin might be more metaphorical, but it still makes me feel better. I towel off and put on the uniform. It's not a great fit, but it covers me from wrist to ankle, with a bit of a turtleneck because *Titan* can get cold without warning.

When I come out of the bathroom, Celeste has emptied both of our bags onto the floor. She hasn't disturbed my sketches, which I find weirdly touching for some reason.

"Sorry to go through your stuff," she says apologetically. "I just wanted to do an inventory and I forgot to ask before you got in the shower."

"It's not a problem," I say. "Do you need me to do anything?"

"No," she says. "But may I borrow your tablet?"

I don't remember putting that in my go bag, so Peters must have. I spare him a thought. I hope he's okay in the pod. The pods have enough thruster power to make it to Mars eventually—a failsafe in case some insurance adjuster on Earth decides it's not cost effective to come pick them up—but it's not going to be very pleasant the longer it takes. *Titan* will reach the planet before the pods do, assuming the missiles don't catch up with us first.

"Sure," I say.

Celeste scoops up the tablet and lies down on her bunk. I sit gingerly on the edge of Ren's. It feels like I'm intruding.

"You can sleep, if you like," Celeste says. "I'll be awake."

"I don't know if I can," I tell her. I lie down anyway, and even though my heart is still beating a bit fast, I do feel better. "What are you doing?"

"I still have the first officer's security codes," she says, holding up the chips she'd used on the flight deck. "Your tablet will have passenger access, but I think I can get to the main system through it. There's a console in the hallway if I can't, but I'd rather stay in here."

She hums a little to herself while she works. I want to ask if she's okay, except that would be stupid because I know she's not. She just had to leave her best friend behind to an unknown fate, and all she got in the bargain was me. I can't ask if there's anything I can do, either. I roll onto my side and stare at my sketches some more.

"Tell me a story about something from your childhood," Celeste says after a few minutes. I look up at her. The tablet is resting on her chest and she has her hands over her eyes. "Something that doesn't end with either of your parents being dick bags."

I snort.

"That really limits my options," I tell her. But I know there has to be something. My parents kept me close, but I still have some memories that don't include them.

"Just try," she says.

I want nothing more than to make her feel better, and if that means a distraction, then I'll distract.

"I went to an art gallery in Toronto once," I say, after a few more minutes to think about it. "Not any of the famous ones—just a little private studio thing. One of my friends from school had parents who loved art and had enough money to show off about it. They were nice, though, so it wasn't terrible."

"Nice people with money were never a good sign when I was growing up," Celeste admits. "But I guess they weren't really nice, they were just pretending, so maybe that's the difference."

"Probably," I say. "Anyway, it was a school trip or something, and the gallery had some pieces that their friends owned on display."

"We definitely moved in different social circles," Celeste says.

"It had its moments," I admit. "Anyway, we get to the gallery and most of the art is post-Rupt, which is annoying because I don't like brutalism, but there's this little room off to the side. I wander into it and there on a wall, just hanging there, is a van Gogh." My voices catches a little bit just thinking about it.

"He's the sunflower one, right?" Celeste asks. "Who died?"

"Yes," I tell her. "It was the first time I had ever seen one of his paintings in real life. It wasn't even that big. But I must have stared at it for an hour. Our teacher had to come and get me after everyone was on the bus and she realized I wasn't there after the head count."

"How old were you?" Celeste asks.

"Eleven," I say. "I already did a bit doodling, but after that, I started to get serious about art. I took classes and extra credit stuff at school."

"Then what happened?" she says.

"You said you didn't want a story where my parents were dick bags," I remind her. "If I keep going, they will be."

"Right," she says. "I'm sorry."

"It's not your fault," I say. "Do you have any stories that don't end with some rich guy trying to screw you over?"

She looks over at me and my heart skips.

"Maybe," she says.

We lie facing each other, separated by a space that would feel infinite if I didn't have recent, extremely personal experience with how infinite space really is. I should change the subject, ask about the tablet or the countdown or literally anything else, but instead I ask a question I've been wondering about for a while.

"Why did you leave the pod?" I ask. "You were in the clear, you and Ren, but you got off to come look for me."

"Well, I didn't think Adam would launch it," she says with a huff. "I don't know if that would have changed my decision-making process."

"Fair enough," I say. "But you still got off. Why?"

"Honestly," she says, like she thinks her answer isn't going to be the one I want, "I was angry with your father. It was his fault you weren't on board, and he didn't look like he was sorry about it. It was like he had gotten everything he needed from you, the kid he saved from squalor in the Rupt, and now you were on your own. It made me mad because I grew up in the Rupt and I never had people who were *supposed* to care about me. I just had people who *did*."

I'd wanted her to say it was because she cared about me, but somehow this is better. I want to reach for her hand, but it'll be too far if she doesn't reach back, and I can't handle any more complicated feelings right now, no matter what my heart thinks it can deal with.

"I think I might have a different reason now, though," she muses. "If it happened again."

"It had better not happen again," I say. I want to cheer. "One alien takeover is enough. I'm never going back into space if we get out of this."

"I meant that now I like you more, idiot," she says. "You didn't have to come down here with us, and I know you thought you were useless the whole time, but if you hadn't been there, I would be engine exhaust right now."

I hadn't thought of it like that. I had only seen the dead weight, when it had been that exact thing that was strong enough to pull her back. I reach out and try not to grin like a fool when her knuckle brushes mine.

"I thought you'd be some little rich tourist," Celeste admits, her fingertips against my palm. "That you'd want to know all about the Rupt because you thought you'd missed something, but when you had enough stories, you'd go your merry way and never think about me again. But I know better now. Even if everything had stayed normal, you would have gone out of your way to see me, me and Ren, after we landed."

"Yeah," I say. Suddenly her hand isn't enough. I curse the space between us, even as I'm grateful that it's keeping me from doing something impulsive. It's too soon to rush into anything new, no matter how much I want to. And that's not even taking into account the aliens and her worry over Ren. "I did want to know all that stuff because I felt like I was missing something, but I wouldn't have left you behind any more than you left me."

"Also to piss off your father," Celeste laughs.

I can't help it—I join in. "That's a side benefit, yes," I say.

"Are you worried about them?" Celeste asks. "Your parents, I mean? I know they're awful, but they still raised you."

"It's complicated," I say. "I don't want them to die, and I certainly don't want an alien to eat them, or whatever it is the aliens do to get inside a person's chest, but I don't want to live with them again. That's for sure."

"That makes sense," Celeste says.

She picks up the tablet and goes back to work. I try not to think about my parents or the countdown, and so my thoughts crash right into something else.

"Ren had most of the food," I say. I hate how mercenary I sound, but it's true. We have water, at least as long as *Titan*'s systems last, but the engine room proved we need to eat enough that we can run if we need to.

"Fuck," Celeste says. It's quiet, and I can tell from her face that her thoughts are a variation of my own. She's worried about Ren, but we also need food.

"I've lost track of where we are," I admit. Everything on this level of the ship is closer together than things in the outer rings, and it's like looking at a sketch with forced perspective. My brain sees it but has trouble processing the differences. "Is the mess nearby?"

"Yes," Celeste says. She grimaces. "Going there is going to be uncomfortable. And dangerous."

"I think those are our only two options at this point," I say. She starts to speak and I cut her off. "And you can't go alone. I'll stay out of your way, but if you leave me here alone and something happens, I'll . . ."

I can't finish saying it, but she nods.

"We have about one hundred hours until we're scheduled to get to Mars," Celeste says after a brief check of her wrist comm. "We should be back on the flight deck by hour ninety-five, at the latest, just in case. Who knows what will change between now and then, but I think we're safest here."

"We left Dr. Ripley enough food, if she rations it," I say, mostly to remind myself. I don't say that Ren will also be fine if she's still alive and managed to find her own safe place to hide.

Celeste has been rummaging through the bag, even though I know she has memorized its contents.

"We have enough for four small meals each," she reports. "And we should eat one of them now."

"I think we should go to the mess now," I say. "The longer we wait, the more variables there will be."

"I agree," Celeste says. She stands up and slings the bag across her back. "Let's get this over with."

we forgot this part

the waiting

the part where everything is set,
yet nothing is complete

we don't like it

our children are spread out

hunting, hiding

they are waiting too

we travel through the void, each of us alone

soon we will be together

twenty-three

CELESTE

The very last place in the universe that I want to be right now is the mess hall. Admittedly, the list of places I don't want to be is quite long at this moment, but after what Ren and I witnessed in there, the mess is definitely notable. I wouldn't even mind being on board *Titan* so long as I never have to go into the mess hall again.

But that's where the food is. Ren had taken all of her supplies with her when we left the first time. We hadn't anticipated being split up, any more than we'd anticipated being attacked by aliens. I hope she's still alive so that when I find her she can laugh and tell me that she told me so. All her catastrophizing, and I told her she was being ridiculous.

Dominic follows me closely as we make our way down the corridor. We're both moving as quietly as we can, but I can hear him breathing behind me. It's actually kind of reassuring. If he's not possessed, it's nice to have him close by. If he *is* possessed, I'll be dead before I can turn around. I roll my head on my neck and feel the stress in my shoulders. Stretching isn't going to fix this, but it'll help for a moment. I've never been in a spa, but I can imagine what a massage therapist would say if they got their hands on me right now. The knot between my shoulder blades is annoying, like an itch I can't scratch. I do my best to ignore it. We have much bigger problems.

The service corridor is still empty, and we don't have far to go before we get to the ladder we'll need. We get to deck three without running into any problems, but I pause before I lead us out into the hall again.

"It's bad in there, Dominic," I say. "When the alarms sounded, that's where Ren and I went first. It's procedure for the crew to assemble in the mess hall. But the aliens had already arrived."

"Was it like Anthony?" he asks.

"No," I tell him. "The aliens were in the galley, but there was blood all over the floor."

I try to tell him about Michael, but the words stick in my throat. His screams have echoed in my head more and more loudly as we get closer to our destination. I don't want to see whatever he ended up as, but I have a terrible certainty that we will.

"It's bad," I repeat, taking Dominic's hand and making sure that he's paying attention to me. He meets my eyes and sees how serious I am.

"Okay," he says, because sometimes you need to say something. "I'll be right behind you."

He says it sardonically, but it is a genuine comfort. He doesn't let go of my hand, but it's easy enough to open the hatch. We step out and continue to make our way towards the mess. I pause again at the door and take a deep breath before the final push. As he promised, Dominic follows half a step after me.

The smell has not improved. The hours are hard to track, so it feels like both forever and a moment ago that I was here with Ren. Back then, we were still confident. *Titan* was the best ship Earth had ever made. The redundancies had redundancies. Short of a catastrophic systems failure, there would always be time to make it to a pod. The designs were impeccable. Until you accounted for human nature, of course—the hubris to bring an alien life form on board, and the asshattery that made Adam Jeffers launch the pod early. That's where *Titan* failed, and no engineer could have prepared for that.

I hear Dominic gag as the stench hits him. It's impossible to think about food in this moment, even though that's why we took the risk. His grip on my hand never falters, though, and when I step forwards, he does too.

"Breathe through your mouth," I tell him. "It'll help."

"I'm more grossed out by the fact that the air in this room is entering my body at all," Dominic says, but I hear the shift in his breathing, and he seems a little more steady for it.

"Come on," I say, pulling him towards the galley doors.

There is some food on the tables, left when people evacuated or abandoned when the aliens killed everyone in the room. I don't even think about stopping for it. Maybe if we were desperate, but unless we're in dire straits, I'm not going to eat this stuff. What Dominic said about the air in this room is true. I haven't seen the inside of the galley, but I hope it's better.

When we get closer to the door, it becomes impossible to avoid stepping in the blood. I resolutely don't look down. I want to remember Michael as he was, not as so much paste on the mess hall floor. I can tell the exact moment Dominic looks down, though, because he checks his next step and almost trips.

"How many crew members would have come here?" he asks.

"Most of them," I say. "Unless they were close to another rally point or on shift. At least seventy-five."

He gags again, and I reach for the galley door.

"Be quiet," I say. "The aliens went in here after they took Michael."

"You saw it?" he hisses, managing to keep quiet despite his horror. "You saw them take your friend?"

"We didn't know for sure what it was," I say, even though I'm sure Ren had already started thinking about it. "I'm sorry I didn't tell you the details. It was—"

"Bad," he finishes. "I understand."

I push the door controls and the galley is revealed. The emergency lights are stronger in here, so I wince a bit at the new brightness. We have our headlamps with us, but not on. After Anthony, we definitely don't want to make it easier for anything to spot us.

The lights reveal nothing, except that the floor in here is covered in blood and viscera too. In an uncontrolled moment of imagining, my brain starts listing options for what could have happened to Michael's bones, which are not visible. Mashed into the sludge beneath our feet, eaten for some reason, displayed in some new shrine the aliens built on another deck. I force myself not to keep going down that rabbit hole. Nothing good can come of it. Maybe they just shoved him out an airlock.

"The refrigeration units are at the back," I say, still whispering even though we might not be in active danger at the moment. I think I'll probably whisper for the rest of my life.

"Lead on," Dominic says.

I look back at him and see that his eyes are firmly fixed on the wall in front of us.

We reach the units, and it occurs to me that what we should actually be looking for are the shelf-stable supplies like ration bars and other things that are easy to carry. *Titan* carried a variety of luxury foods, and there was even room for the crew meals to be well-provisioned, but there were always fast options, things that could be eaten during shift break or saved until they were needed.

Dominic follows me when I divert to the nearby shelves without asking questions. He has his bag unzipped by the time I pass him the first few ration packs. We fill each pocket and then I do the same with my bag. None of the food we're getting is interesting or fun. This isn't like the snacks that the flight crew had tucked away for when they got peckish. These are meal replacements, and they won't be delicious, but they'll get the job done.

"That's good," I say, closing my bag. Dominic does the same. "I just want to check the fridge really quickly in case there's something that will be useful immediately."

Dominic nods and stands behind me while I open the first heavy metal door.

For the rest of my life, I'll wish that I had just settled for the dry rations.

twenty-four

DOMINIC

I don't know if Celeste can tell, but as we make our way through the mess hall towards the galley I am barely keeping it together. She told me it was bad, and I believed her, but I didn't really understand what she meant. Celeste has seen *bad* on a far grander scale than I have. She grew up in it, had it hovering over her as a threat for her entire life. I only ever saw it on television or thought about it in absent daydreams. At worst, I thought of it as something along the lines of moderate inconveniences. I'm both grateful and deeply embarrassed.

So yes, the mess hall is bad. Celeste seems to be blocking it out, thanks to the low light and her determination, but I'm seeing everything for the first time, and it's a lot to process. It smells like a slaughterhouse (which I know because once upon a time my mother visited places like that to pretend she cared about the people who worked there, for her own political gain), and it's only at Celeste's reminding that I remember to breathe through my mouth. Blood hangs in the air, it seems, and tasting it is worse, but at least the sensation is *less*.

We're following a streak of blood towards the galley doors, and I realize that it's Michael on the floor beneath my shoes. I almost trip, but Celeste keeps me focused. That focus lasts while we cross the galley and load up our bags with non-perishable rations, but shatters absolutely when Celeste opens the fridge.

There are—or, were, I suppose—more than two thousand people on board *Titan*, and it's not like we can just stop at the local store for milk. Yes, we grow some stuff in hydroponics, but mostly we rely on what we've brought with us. Accordingly, the refrigerators are large, and there are several of them along the back of the galley. Celeste has opened the one closest to us.

I'm honestly not sure which one of us screams. It might have been both. I can't smell it, probably because I'm in shock, but there is no mistaking the contents of the fridge for anything besides what they are.

The slaughterhouse my mother had dragged me to had cold rooms for after the cows were killed and dressed. They had rows and rows of hooks hanging from the ceiling so that meat could be hung up for butchering. The meat cutters could turn the portion they were working on easily and access all the parts of the heavy whole without too much strain. *Titan* does not have meathooks like the slaughterhouse did, but that hadn't stopped the aliens.

Michael and several crew members I don't recognize hang from the ceiling of the fridge, suspended by the same sort of gelatinous tentacles Anthony had excreted to grab the walls of the engine room. The bodies seem extended somehow, beyond just gravity pulling them towards the floor. It's like the only thing keeping them together is their skin, every bone and muscle and tendon shredded and dragging down.

Celeste's breath comes in pants as she freezes, unable to look away from the carnage. I pull her backwards towards my chest, turning her around so that she's facing me. She fights me, panic drowning out the rational explanation that I'm helping her and replacing me with an alien come to drag her away. Her fist connects with my jaw and she steps on my boot as hard as she can before she comes back to herself. Then she lets me pull her close, shielding her from the scene before us. The door slams shut as she releases it, and for a moment she clings to me, her arms wrapping around me just as tightly as mine are wrapped around her.

"I'm sorry," she says, finally staggering away from me. She rests her hands on one of the prep counters, leaning hard.

"It's okay," I say. I move my jaw back and forth. There doesn't seem to be any real damage. She does hit like a pro, though. "I surprised you."

Obviously, that hadn't been the way I'd imagined touching her, but my brain is entirely unhelpful and replays the moment in deliberate detail. I can feel my face flushing, but in the emergency lights it's possible she won't notice.

"Thank you," she says. "For pulling me away, I mean. I am not sure how long I would have been stuck there."

"No problem," I say, and then wince at how inane it sounds.

"It was comforting," she continues. "I forgot that hugs are like that."

It's not like there have been a lot of hugs in my life, but I'm not a stranger to them, and it hurts to know that Celeste has had so few that she forgets what they feel like. No one should be that alone. She's had Ren, but Ren had a family. Celeste had no one else, and now Ren is gone, and all she has left is me. Who is apparently good at one thing, after all.

"I can hug you again," I say. Then my brain catches up with me and I realize how stupid that sounds. "I mean, if you want. If you wanted to, uh, hug."

Despite everything, she almost laughs.

"Maybe when we get back to the room," she says.

Right. Getting to the mess hall was only half of the trip. Now that we have what we came for, we have to get back. It feels like our luck is going to run out, but that might just be because the bodies hanging in the fridge were a stark reminder of our circumstances.

Celeste takes a deep breath and cracks her neck, the vulnerability disappearing again.

"Come on," she says. "The sooner I'm behind a door that locks, the better."

We leave the galley and mess hall behind us, the blood all over the floor somehow easier to deal with now that we've seen worse. Celeste opens the door to the hallway and her eyes widen as she hears the noise of something coming down the corridor. It's between us and the hatch we came up. We'll have to go the other way and trust that all the hatches have been unsealed. Hiding in here is too risky because a methodical search would reveal us. We need a door that we control, and that means the crew quarters.

Celeste squeezes my hand and points down the hall in the direction we'll take. I see her mouth the word "Run" and count down from three with her other hand. On "one," we make a break for it. I have never been much of a runner and the bag slaps against me uncomfortably, but I find the speed I need to keep up with Celeste as she bolts down the corridor. The noise behind us is heavy, not the skittering of tentacles but the step of boots or shoes. Either it's one of the possessed crew we've identified or it's someone else and we have no way of determining if they're possessed. We can't take the chance.

The hatch is open, and Celeste pulls it down behind us after she gets me safely through. The locking mechanism is inactive, but it'll buy us some time. I wonder for a moment about climbing to deck two and then doubling back or something, but the truth is that we don't have time for that kind of creativity. The only predictable safety is the locked door of Celeste's quarters. We descend so quickly I'm afraid of bashing my chin on the rungs, and then, before I can fully catch up, we're back in front of Celeste's room. She opens the door and we both dive through. There's a sound in the hall, like one of the hatches is opening, and Celeste closes the door, locking it with her wrist comm. Even I won't be able to open it now.

"Fuck," she says, stumbling towards her bunk. She drops her bag on the floor as she moves through the small space and comes to rest next to her bed. She doesn't collapse onto it yet.

"Are you okay?" I ask. It's a stupid question, but she'll know what I mean.

"Yeah," she says. "You?"

"For now," I say.

We can't hear anything from outside the room, which is a comfort. I wonder if Celeste really will let me hug her again. I think I might need one.

"We're both going to crash when the adrenaline wears off," Celeste says. "We should lie down."

She holds out her hand again, and I let her pull me towards her.

"We could," she says, sitting down on the edge of her bed. "I mean, if you want."

I do. For all the right reasons, but also all the wrong ones.

"It's a lot," I say.

"It's a mess," she says. "But it might help."

We lie down. It's awkward and uncomfortable, and much too tight a fit, but my heart starts to beat more slowly almost immediately.

"Ninety-eight hours," Celeste says. She sighs and shifts closer to me, still holding my hand.

Time passes, as one hundred hours march on. It's hazy and repetitive and blessedly dull. We eat. We shower. We change clothes. We do as many of the things you're supposed to do as part of your daily routine as we can without leaving the room. Every time we lie down, it feels like we are closer together, even though the size of the room has not altered. Space travel is absolute, but humanity always makes it work for it. It's quiet, and I don't even think too much, because every time I do, I get closer to a question I don't want to ask. Finally, after hours I can only track because of the countdown on my wrist comm, I can't avoid asking it any longer.

"How *do* the aliens get inside a person's chest?" I ask. I'm not really expecting an answer, but now that I've said it, I can't stop talking. "I mean, Anthony was far away from the gallery, and the eggs can't walk anywhere. You saw those lumbering figures, but you said there was nothing off about Anthony until the last minute."

"The alien wasn't, you know, small or unsure of itself," Celeste says. "What if it used Anthony as some kind of incubator to get from hatchling to . . . that?"

"The archaeologists were infected on the original dig, somehow," I say, mostly just thinking out loud. "They infected the med tech and Wendy, and maybe someone else before the explosion. Anthony could have been infected after that. It's possible that incubation takes however long the aliens decide it takes."

As soon as I say it, my brain reels from the horrifying implications. If my conclusion is correct, that means a possessed person might not even—

Celeste sets the tablet down again and looks at me. She opens her mouth, either to answer or ask another question, and that's when the alarms go off again.

the others have taught me about fear

we do not feel it

there is only hatching and hunger

but the beings we've taken feel so much more

the fear gives the bodies strength and speed,
a rush of chemicals

we have gorged ourselves on it,
though we can never have our fill

it makes me crave other feelings my shell might have

I will stay

I am getting stronger every moment

twenty-five

CELESTE

I sit up quickly, the tablet falling to the mattress beside me and my feet crashing to the floor. Dominic is a fraction of a second behind me.

"What's that one?" he asks.

I check my wrist comm, which has only been working sporadically since we left the flight deck. The countdown has been intact the whole time, but the other functions have been in and out.

"A section breach," I say. "But that doesn't make any sense at all. None of the sections were closed off, except—"

I trail off as I put the pieces together. Dominic is leaning forwards like if he gets close enough my thoughts will transfer to him.

"Except the indenture holds," I finish. "Decks two through five in sections E and F. They were shut to keep the workers in isolation. Wouldn't want them mixing with the paying passengers."

I sound venomous, but the truth is that I'm mostly angry at myself. For most of the voyage, I haven't thought about those people. They've been out of sight, out of mind, and I've been focusing on my own future. It seems hypocritical of me, given that one of the reasons I hate Dominic's parents so much is their willingness to exploit desperate people. I didn't even wonder how they've been doing this whole time, even after "Anthony" brought them up, although the part where he immediately tried to kill us might be a decent excuse.

The alarm cuts out, either turned off or resolved.

"Anthony said he heard strange noises coming from those decks," I say. "But deck one is clear the whole way around. He would have had to be outside the engine room to hear it."

I can tell Dominic is trying to keep up, but I push on anyway.

"He must have tried to go to the mess hall when the first alarm sounded," I say. "And then one of the shamblers we saw caught him and infected him with one of the missing eggs. Then he went back to the engine room to send Michael to his death."

Dominic looks down at his drawings and then back at me.

"Okay, then I need a minute or two to think out loud," he says. "The aliens got out of the case and then somehow, I don't know, infected people like Anthony. But that doesn't make sense, because the explosion that destroyed the display cases came from outside of them, which means it had to have been caused by someone who was on board *Titan*."

His gaze drops to the floor and fixates on one of his pictures.

"Okay, we know there were missing eggs," he says. "I drew the five that were in the display case, but Dr. Ripley said there were originally six more."

"And someone erased the official photos," I say. "And kept Dr. Ripley too busy to notice."

"Yes," Dominic says. "So one of the original archaeologists was infected or whatever by an egg, and then took the eggs to use on other people, and that's how all of this started, before we ever took off?"

It's not the worst theory. Dr. Ripley said that none of the alien specimens had shown any signs of life, but it's possible they had been so deep in hibernation or stasis that nothing registered while the scientists were examining them. Then whatever was in the eggs just had to wait.

"So at least one . . . human-alien thing brought the eggs when they boarded *Titan*," I say. "And there were five more of them in the cases before the explosion. But all the cases were in pieces when Ren and I saw them. Why blow all the display cases if they just needed the eggs?"

"I have no idea," Dominic says. "I do have another question, though."

I flop back onto the bed and gesture at him to keep talking.

"The captain makes sense as one of the original five, right?" he says. "And then the alien burst out of him when he wasn't needed anymore and killed all of the people on the bridge. That's why they had a moment to run. The alien had to get from the captain's chest to all of them one at a time."

"Gross," I say, shuddering at the memory of the captain sitting at his desk with his rib cage missing. "But it does explain who changed our course."

"Yeah, but *where is it?*" Dominic asks. "Where are any of them? And why did Anthony seem so normal while you were talking to him?"

"That's three questions," I say automatically. It's not funny, but I don't have a real answer or even a guess yet.

"Fine, ignore the first two," Dominic says. "If the captain was infected the whole time, that means the aliens can control people well enough to pass as human for a while. The shamblers are just a stage, or maybe they have different jobs, like a drone instead of a worker or something."

I take a moment to consider it. Anthony had seemed genuinely glad to see us, and it felt like he'd been telling the truth when he said he hadn't left the engine room. The captain had been normal the whole time. And the archaeologists also acted perfectly human for an extended period. I'd had dinner with Wendy and didn't notice anything wrong.

"Okay, so shamblers and talkers," I say. "And for the talkers, the person doesn't know. Anthony blacked out when he was infected, and when he woke up, he didn't realize he was missing time *or* that he'd locked himself in? The alien could just wait and, like, pupate because Anthony wasn't doing anything the aliens didn't want. Until he talked to us. And then it—"

I can't bring myself to relive those memories.

"So the captain didn't even know?" Dominic asks. "That's terrifying."

"It also means that Dr. Ripley might be infected," I point out. "And we left her on the bridge as our only method of enacting the course correction."

That hits him hard. He likes Dr. Ripley a lot, in addition to wanting to survive all of this.

"No alien has burst out of her yet. Or at least it hadn't the last time we saw her . . . and the countdown is still going," I tell him. I don't think it's entirely encouraging, but it's the best I can do. "I mean, Dr. Ripley knows our whole plan, and the alien in the captain took out the whole bridge crew. If she was infected, she could have already taken us out."

"Celeste," Dominic says gently, "this means *anyone* might be infected."

"What?" I ask.

"I was alone in my room before Dr. Ripley got there," he says. "You and Ren have spent most of your time together, but not all of it, and Ren's on her own right now. If she's alive, it might be *because* she's infected."

"No," I say. "This is exactly the kind of bonkers paranoia that Ren's dads would buy into, and then we'll all end up separated and no one will survive because we're not working together. We need each other to get through this, so we can't be against each other now."

"I'm not turning on you," Dominic says. "I just want you to be aware. Prepared, like Ren says, not paranoid."

"Fuck," I say, rubbing a hand over my eyes. "I'm really not cut out for this sort of thing."

"I would be more surprised if you were," Dominic says. He reaches down to the floor for a bag of pretzels and tears the package open.

I look at his drawing and a cold wave creeps over me.

"What about the queen?" I ask.

Dominic freezes mid-pretzel.

"They must need one," he says. "The eggs in Dr. Ripley's pictures weren't clear enough to do anything besides count shapes, but none of the ones in the display were different from one another."

"We still have to assume one of the aliens on board is a queen," I say. "And since the shamblers and the talkers are different, maybe the queen is different too."

Both of us sit in silence, unable to really deal with everything.

"We have to keep going," Dominic says. "Did you hack the tablet?"

"You're right," I say, pulling my brain back from scary thoughts. "And yes, I did. I just wanted to make sure that the readings from the engine were still good, and they are. That probably means neither Ren nor the alien ended up getting fried. There was a blip in Medical that I want to look at, but with the sections breached, I'm not in a hurry to go all the way up there."

Dominic winces, and that's when I remember that Medical was the last location he knows his mother was at.

Wendy also spent a lot of time there. They could have infected her while running one of her kidney tests. I wonder why they didn't pick David, but we don't know enough about the aliens to guess how they pick their prey.

"Anyway, we're all on track for the course change, but knowing what we know about how the aliens infect people, maybe we should head back up?" I don't really want to leave this room, but I'd be lying if I said I wasn't extremely nervous about leaving everything unsupervised. If Dominic is right, I can't even trust myself, so the more of us who are on the bridge, the better.

"Yeah," he says. "You're probably right."

We start repacking the bags, distributing weight evenly to make up for the things we've eaten or used. I put more of the cream on my hands when they start to sting again. Climbing is going to suck. It doesn't take us very long to get ready, and I'm putting my boots back on when the absolute last thing I was expecting happens. There's a knock at the door.

Both of us jump. It was such a polite knock, not a desperate hammering or a mindless pounding. It's like the person outside knows we're here and knows we'll be happy to see them.

I pick up the biggest blunt object from the toolkit and gesture at Dominic to open the door. Our only advantage is that whoever is outside can't tell when we're going to open it. It's a small sliver, the slightest element of surprise, but it's all we've got. I can tell this is against his better judgement, but he does it anyway. The door slides open to reveal at least a dozen people, and every nerve I have lights itself on fire until I hear someone saying my name.

"Celeste!" Ren says, sounding relieved and excited at the same time. "I wasn't sure you'd be here, but then the door was locked and I figured that meant you *had* to be here. I am *really* glad to see you."

She throws herself into my arms and I hug her back as enthusiastically as I can, given my surprise and the topic Dominic and I had been discussing. She squeezes me and it feels so much like Ren that I want to let my whole guard down and just enjoy the fact that we're both alive . . . but I can't. Ren pulls away and points behind her.

"I came out of the engine room below the indenture decks," she says. "I didn't have time to run to another section, so I just broke in. You will not believe who I found. My dads are going to kill literally all of us if we get out of this alive."

I look over Ren's shoulder and see two familiar faces. Chels and Glory—who had argued so hard to come on board *Titan* and were absolutely forbidden to do so—are standing in the corridor.

"What the hell?" I exclaim. "Do you have any idea how hard it was to keep you all out of indentures when we were kids, and now you *volunteer*?"

Dominic stands awkwardly beside me, clearly unsure what to say. This is a part of the Rupt he didn't experience and will never truly understand, no matter how many questions he asks about it.

"We read the contracts, Celeste," Chels says. "We're not stupid."

"So you say," I snap. Indenture contracts are *full* of hidden traps.

"So I say," comes a new voice, and Adelaide Connor pushes to the front of the group.

"How did you—" Dominic starts to ask a question and then just fizzles out halfway through, throwing up his hands.

"After talking with your father, I realized that I needed to straighten out a few things *before* we got to Mars," Adelaide says. "So I made the guards let me into the decks. I wanted to meet these people, to talk with them and come to some kind of solution that wouldn't destroy their lives, while still allowing me to maintain control of the company so that I can eventually unionize the whole damn thing."

"What happened to your pods?" Dominic asks. Several people in the corridor make rude noises. "There were supposed to be extra ones on that side."

"They weren't big enough," Adelaide says darkly. "And two of them malfunctioned. I promised that anyone who stayed behind would have a clear *employment* contract if we eventually got to Mars, and these fifteen volunteered. We had no idea what was going on, but I sent a copy of my will along with the pod, and then the volunteers and I went back to the decks, because we knew the seals down there are good for us to make it to the planet even if the rest of the ship is depressurized. Ren has filled us in since we found her."

"You stayed." I say it like a challenge, even though I meant it as a rhetorical question.

"I am not my father," Adelaide says. "If I'd gone, it would have undone everything I am trying to build within my family business."

"The dads are still going to kill you," I say to Ren's sisters. They have the decency to look slightly abashed. "Why are all of you here now? Like, in this hallway, I mean."

"The deck with the air-recirculation system is the most secure part of the ship, even better than the indenture decks," Ren says. "If we have a landing without a pilot, deck nine of section H will be the best place to be."

I haven't even thought ahead to landing yet.

"Let's make sure we're clear of the missiles first," I say.

"The what?" asks Adelaide.

Ren and I exchange a look.

"Come on," says Ren. "We have some more catching up to do."

twenty-six

DOMINIC

I'm worried about Celeste's hands. I'm worried about a lot of things, actually, like if travelling in this large a group is a good idea, or what we'll do if Dr. Ripley is an alien, but at the moment, my main concern is Celeste's hands. I know she scraped off a lot of skin on the safety line, and even though she says it doesn't hurt, she has to wrap her fingers around rung after rung as we climb, and that can't be fun. For about half a second, I wonder if I should suggest that she, and a couple of people from the indenture decks who are injured, should take the lift to Medical, even though that's almost the complete opposite of where we're going, but then common sense reasserts itself. We don't want to split up again.

Instead, I take a page out of Adelaide Connor's book and try retraining my brain to drop the word "indenture" when I talk or think about my current climbing companions. Legally, they aren't indentured anymore, but I noticed how Adelaide spoke about the decks they'd been staying on, and I respect her for what she's trying to do. I didn't know her father was a terrible person. To be honest, I hadn't really spent that much time thinking about her at all, even though I did appreciate what she'd said about my sketches. I can understand wanting to be better than your parents, and I'm not stuck in their footsteps like she is. Maybe that's why she's been so nice to me. I have a chance she doesn't. I can do something new. She's stuck trying to fix something that was broken when it was built, and even though she could walk away, she's not going to. It's another kind of bravery.

We take the same pauses we had taken on the way down. First at the bottom of deck four to get ready for the cargo decks, and then again at the bottom of deck six to recover. The breaks are a bit staggered due to the length of our climbing line. There are nineteen of us. Celeste is already rubbing her hands together by the time I get to the stopping point, but it looks more nervous than medical. She flexes her fingers and winces, but it doesn't seem to slow her down while she's climbing.

She'd filled Ren in before we left. She hadn't mentioned the part where we thought people might be taken over by aliens without realizing it, and by the way she caught my eye as she skipped that part of the story, I knew it was on purpose. On one hand, I hate keeping secrets. On the other hand, there's no point in worrying everyone with the idea that the person next to them, or even they themselves, might crack open at the sternum at any moment. It does make me flinch a bit every time someone talks to me. It's silly: these people have been together the whole time. Ren and I—and Adelaide, I guess—are still the best suspects.

It's a tense moment at the top of the ladder, before we exit onto deck nine, because no one wants to go first or make someone else go first. We get through the hatch without incident, and I'm suddenly not in any hurry. On the other side of the bulkhead is air-recirculation, the best-sealed part of the ship, and once we're there we'll have to make some decisions.

There's no stopping Celeste, though. She's moving forwards like a machine operated by someone with a higher purpose, her determination pushing her on. She and Ren have armed themselves with various tools that we found on the cargo deck, and the others have similarly prepared themselves. I'm at the back of the boarding party, such as it is.

I see Celeste nod to Ren, and then they open the bulkhead.

At first glance, you wouldn't think anything is wrong with air-recirculation at all, but when I look closer, I realize that the giant tanks are all disturbed, like someone tried to pull them out of their casings. I remember the lines of sinew the alien in the engine room had utilized. Maybe this is where the alien who was in the captain came after it finished killing everyone on the bridge. The lights are extremely bright after all the time we've spent in cramped passageways, and most of us are blinking rapidly as we try to adjust.

"Dominic?" My mother crawls out from behind a tank. "What is going on? Who are these people?"

Of all the people I might have expected to run into, my mother wasn't even on the list. Medical is three sections over, past the flight deck and Navigation. When she sees the rest of the crowd, she stands up quickly and tries to make herself look like she would never hide or crawl. I step forwards to talk to her.

"Have you been here the whole time?" I ask. "From the time you skipped the card game until now?"

"Of course not, dear," she says. Her eyes are darting around furiously. They land on Adelaide, but that doesn't seem to make her feel any better. "I took a sedative, in Medical, and I was supposed to sleep until *Titan*'s morning, but some alarms woke me up . . . something about a section breach. Everyone was gone, and the pod had launched without me, but I remembered Sylvia saying that this place was the most secure on the ship, so I took all the emergency supplies I could carry and came here."

"Through the flight deck?" Celeste asks. We look at each other: she would have seen Dr. Ripley if she did.

"Through the corridor where the pods are." My mother sneers at her. "There's no point in me running around in populated areas when I don't know what's happening. The doctor's computer told me what the alarm was and that it was stopped. There was no point in me adding to the problem. It was already a mess when I got here, in case you were going to accuse me of vandalism."

We exchange a glance. Ren and her sisters clearly just think my mother is insane, but Celeste and I share a slightly different concern. If my mother has been asleep and then alone, anything could have happened to her. And the doctors surely had the means to evacuate patients. Even unconscious, she should have been taken into the escape pod with them. It might be another situation like what happened with Anthony.

"Where is everyone, anyway?" my mother asks. "The computer locked me out when I didn't have security codes, so I couldn't get any news from my comm."

"The ship has been almost fully evacuated, Mrs. Reubens," Adelaide says. I'm glad she's taking care of it, because my mother will only argue with me and actively disbelieve Celeste and Ren. If it comes from someone she views as something remotely like her equal, she might accept it.

"What? Why wasn't I taken to the pod?" She sounds genuinely surprised and outraged.

"We don't know," Adelaide tells her. "There might have been a problem with the evacuation process itself. The alien display case exploded, and it turns out the aliens aren't as dead as Dr. Ripley and her team thought. They are infiltrating the ship, and they are very dangerous."

My mother just stares at her. I suppose it does sound ridiculous if you haven't seen the bodies or the aliens themselves, but we don't have time for her incredulity.

"Mother, we have to prep this section," I tell her. "We're going to use it as a bonus escape pod."

"All of us?" My mother eyes some of my companions with great distaste and speaks quietly, like that makes it better.

"Yes," I say firmly.

"Fine," my mother says. "But I need to run down to our rooms first. There are a few things I need to pick up. And I'll probably need at least one of these people to carry them back up here."

"Absolutely not," Celeste says. She has better hearing than I thought. "I don't care if you want to go out there on your own—even though I think you'll be alien food before you get to deck seven—but there's no way you're making any of these people go with you."

"How dare you!" my mother exclaims. She's attracting attention, but she doesn't seem to care.

"Shut up, Mother," I say. "You can go on your own, you can stay here and sulk, or you can work with us. I don't care which, and we don't have time for any bullshit."

My mother turns red as I speak, and both Celeste and I recoil, like we're expecting an alien to jump out of her any moment. But it's just her stupid human selfishness. I turn away and walk back to where Ren and Adelaide are waiting for us. Celeste is quivering with rage, but she also looks proud of me. To be honest, I'm a little bit proud of myself.

"Let's go, then," Ren says, and leads the way to the bulkhead that will take us into the most secure part of air-recirculation.

This is the trickiest part, because every entry to this section of deck nine has a bio-seal—a mini airlock that you step into with a decontamination program running on a timer. On the climb up, Celeste and Ren argued about how to deactivate it so we could all pass through it quickly, but they agreed that would only render the seal useless, thereby negating the reason we came here in the first place. The only option is to go through bio-seal decontamination in three small groups.

Celeste, Adelaide, my mother, two of the workers, and I go first. There's no argument, because Ren wants to stay in the same group as her sisters for as long as she can. We step into the mini airlock and start the timer. My ears pop immediately, and I feel like every hair on my body stands up straight and tingles. I don't know if it's because I took a shower shortly before we climbed up here, and no one else in my group is too bloody, but the process seems to go fairly smoothly, and we're out the other side before the tingling gets uncomfortable.

There are a few moments of downtime while Ren, her sisters, and four others step into the mini airlock, and then it kicks up again. Unlike the flight deck, where all the equipment is at desk level and therefore you can see around yourself pretty well, air-recirculation is all pipes and machinery. Anything could be hiding in here. We stay close to the door until the third group has cycled through, and then we start toward the other side, where our exit is located.

It's a nervous walk, but we make it across the deck without anything happening. We're stalled for a few moments because there finally *is* an argument as Ren tries to convince her sisters to stay behind.

"You'll make it more dangerous if you come," Celeste finally says flatly. "If we're lucky, there will be five of us coming back through the seal, and we might be in a hurry.

The airlock will clear faster if there are fewer of us in it. It's how spaceships work, even ones like *Titan*. Sometimes there are just limits. You can't come."

They're not happy, but they accept the ultimatum. Ren says her goodbyes quickly. My mother doesn't even look at me. Adelaide and Celeste step into the next airlock, and just as Ren is about to follow them, the other shoe finally drops.

"What are you all doing in here?" Unbelievably, it's the voice of Sylvie Jeffers, shipwright for the stars. "You'll contaminate the air supply."

"Are you kidding?" says one of the men who climbed up with us. I rebuke myself for not learning their names, but no one was in any state to think about introductions. I only know the names of Ren's sisters because she and Celeste yelled at them. "Lady, we're just trying to survive. Who the hell are you?"

"Well, you can't stay here," Sylvie says. Her gaze falls on my mother, and her lip curls. "Benedict left you, I see? I know the feeling. I doubt my son even considered coming to rescue me, so I've been up here trying to rescue myself."

"You've been here the whole time?" my mother demands.

"I just got here a few hours ago," Sylvie says disparagingly. "I've been hiding in hydroponics because there's food, and the water there is clean. I came through the upper corridor now that we're close to Mars. Would you have wanted to be alone with me anyway? I would have been bad enough in the pod."

"Your son is the one who launched the pod ahead of schedule," Celeste says, coming to the edge of the airlock.

She stays inside it, like the door that's not there anymore will shield her from Sylvie while she insults Adam.

"Good for him," Sylvie says. "Space is hard, little girl, and I raised a survivor."

"Nothing about Adam's life is hard," I tell her. "And you raised an asshole."

She starts to laugh, her head thrown back and her arms held out wide. I still have questions for her. Why hadn't she made it to an escape pod in the first place? What had she seen when she was alone on the ship? Were there any secrets she'd built into *Titan* that could help us now? But all of my questions are immediately rendered moot as her laughter reaches an almost painfully high pitch and her body shifts, like her skin is too small for her bones.

I was too far away to see the change with Anthony, but there's no missing it with Sylvie Jeffers. Her body stiffens, moving like she's under rictus, and her mouth seems to open wider and wider, well past the possibility of a human jaw. Celeste and Ren also realize what's happening and start to move, but, for once in my life, I'm faster. I push Ren into the airlock with Celeste and activate the seal behind her.

it's a balancing act, growing

how much can I learn before I must
break my shell and move on?

the others have broken out

I can feel them all, now

they have taken what they need

so have I

but I think I'll stay

just a little longer

twenty-seven

CELESTE

I'd like to be able to say that I threw myself against the glass and pounded on the window, trying hard to get to Dominic after he sealed us in, but the truth is that he pushed Ren straight at me and we both went down when we collided.

By the time I get back on my feet, there's absolute chaos in the room behind us. Everyone from the workers' decks already knew, at least in theory, what the aliens can do—they saw a few corpses that backed up what we'd told them—but there's really nothing like seeing it yourself for the first time.

Adelaide was in the sterile room, completely sealed off, and she still screamed and tried to open a door that was going to stay closed for the next four minutes. Ren's sisters manage to hold their ground, though, to be quite honest, I almost wish they'd hidden safely somewhere instead.

Dominic's mother collapses, but even if it makes me a slightly terrible person, I don't give a shit about her.

I know Dominic better than to imagine he would have followed us in here, but I'm still furious with him. He has the smallest wrench, for starters. He brandishes it anyway, like an idiot, and I have to watch as the alien that used to be Sylvie Jeffers launches itself at him. Like Anthony, the body on the floor is shredded beyond recognition. The alien is even bigger than the one in the engine room, and it propels itself through the air by reaching out with its tentacles, grabbing whatever it can, and pulling. Dominic ducks and it goes flying over his head, but it catches itself on the pipes with the same precision that "Anthony" used to move around the platforms in the engine room, and gets ready for another pass.

The extremely petty part of me wishes it would just target Alodia Reubens, because she's not a moving target, but I'm not so lucky.

"Two minutes," Ren says.

I don't know whether she's letting me know that in two minutes we can go back towards Dominic, go forwards and take our chances, or that in two minutes the alien might be able to get in here with us, but I think at this point it's six of one, half a dozen of the other. Adelaide has finished vomiting, which I'd think would *add* time to the decon, but apparently the system can cope with that sort of thing.

Back in air-recirculation, the alien has swung around and is aiming for the man who all but cursed Sylvie out. I don't know if aliens hold grudges or if it's just a proximity thing.

He and some of the others have stun rods—it's what the guards outside the workers' decks were armed with in case of incidents—and he swings his like a baseball bat. We can't hear the sound it makes when the electricity connects, but the way everyone grabs for their ears indicates that it must be pretty loud.

The first hit just seems to make the alien angry. It extends three of its tentacles to grab at the rod, but the weapon is still charged, so it can't get a grip. The worker doesn't waste any time, and he hits it again. Two of his comrades join him, and electricity arcs into the alien's body. It finally gets one tentacle around the first worker, who goes down screaming, but the damage is already done. The combined force has knocked it down on the deck.

The other two workers manage to keep their rods on top of it, pinning it down. The injured man rolls away and Glory leaps to his side, med kit in hand. I see Chels grit her teeth, activate her own stun rod, and head over to help him. Even without being able to hear, it's still terrible to watch. The alien writhes, sending out tendrils in a vain attempt to shake itself free, but its movements get more and more convulsive and uncontrolled. It lands a few blows, but the fighters are able to keep going. After way too long, it finally stops moving, and Chels and her companion slowly remove their rods.

The alien isn't moving, but we all thought it was dead before and that proved to be a mistake, so no one is letting their guard down.

The timer ends and we're released towards the flight deck. I look back at Dominic, who waves us forwards. I point at the alien and he makes some kind of gesture about making sure it's dead, and then hastens us on again.

"Come on," says Adelaide. "There's nothing we can do that he can't except keep going."

It's true, but I don't have to like it.

We head onto the flight deck. I look around fearfully, afraid of what might have happened to Dr. Ripley since we left.

"Celeste?" she calls out. I don't see her yet. "Ren?"

"It's us, Dr. Ripley," Ren says.

"You're safe!" Dr. Ripley appears in the doorway of Captain Bernard's ready room. I'm not sure if she's glad to see us or glad that she doesn't have to keep hiding in there. "Adelaide?"

"It's a long story," Adelaide says. "We don't have time right now. Where are the missiles?"

"They're still on target, but they haven't crossed the point of no return yet," Dr. Ripley says. She looks at her wrist comm. "We still have some time on the countdown."

"I think we should do it now," Ren says. "The aliens know we're here, and it's not that hard to figure out what we're doing. I'd rather check the missiles off our list than keep dealing with all the problems at once."

"Agreed," said Adelaide.

I watch them all very closely. We're coming up to a point where one of them, if possessed, is going to show signs of it. I didn't tell Ren that Dominic thinks people can have an alien in them and not know. She'd have a million questions, starting with "How would the egg even get in?" and none of us know the answers. Anyway, it would just make her worry, and we all need to focus.

"Okay," Dr. Ripley says. "Ren, since you're here anyway, do you want to help?"

The math hasn't changed in the time we've been away from the flight deck, but I appreciate Dr. Ripley not wanting to be alone anymore. Ren steps over to help, and I step behind her in case one of them turns into soup from the inside out while an alien tries to kill the rest of us. I'm not sure what I'll do, mind you, except maybe buy time to run.

Ren inputs the course change and presses the button to activate the autopilot. I wonder what it would be like, having *Titan* move because I made her. I've never wanted to fly a ship until this very moment, but watching Ren, a smile on her face in spite of everything, makes me understand the draw of it.

There's no physical feeling, obviously, and we can't hear the engine rev from all the way up here, so there's no way of knowing the course correction worked without waiting for the readouts. We watch the screen with the flight projection on it. I think we're all holding our breath until it beeps and *Titan*'s path shifts back towards Mars.

"Oh, thank God," Dr. Ripley says again, and all of us breathe a little easier for a moment.

The relief is short-lived, however, because a few minutes after our course changes, sending us to safety, the missiles change course too. They're still bearing down on us, and they're very, very close.

"Why are they doing that?" I ask. "How are they doing that? I thought they couldn't be steered after launch."

"That was the Mark 4," Adelaide says, exhaustion in her voice. "These must be Mark 5s. They're still being tested, but I guess Earth didn't want to take chances."

We stare at the screen, defeated. The missiles blink closer. Inevitably in motion, unless acted on by an outside force. Wait.

"Can they speed up?" I ask. "Adelaide, can they speed up?"

She's a little taken aback by the vehemence with which I round on her, and I guess I can't really blame her. I kind of surprise myself too.

"No," she says. "They had to choose between direction shift and speed, and they chose direction shift."

"Okay," I say. "What if *we* speed up?"

It hangs there for a moment.

"We can't," says Dr. Ripley. "We've been in our slowdown for approach for days, and because of our course correction, we still might be coming in too fast for our landing."

She's says "landing" because that's easier than "our carefully calculated deceleration so we end up in a gentle orbit and not spread out in a one-centimetre-thick paste that covers a significant portion of the planet or slingshotted into the void."

"So we don't land," I say. "We crash."

"We *crash*." Adelaide repeats the word like it's in a language she doesn't understand.

"*Titan's* not built for gravity anyway," I say. "If we miss our orbit window, we'll wreck at least part of the ship. No one left on board *cares* about the ship, though. We care about the people. Everyone on Earth has already written off the cost of *Titan* for salvage, but none of them give two tin shits about any of us. We crash the ship ourselves, and we *live*."

I feel a rush of excitement at the solution. We're going to live.

Beside me, Adelaide starts laughing, a high sound, and I think she's finally broken—except, when I look at her, I realize it's genuine hilarity, not hysteria.

"What?" demands Ren.

"They're not insured," Adelaide chokes out. We all look at her like she's insane. "They have coverage for things that happen in transit, like the missiles, and they have coverage for cargo loss, but *Titan* isn't supposed to go into gravity so it's not insured if there's a crash."

It's the last straw. Everything that this stupid ship has put us through—the ladders, the inconvenient lifts, the aliens, the goddamn brass knobs—and none of them are insured if we spread them out on a bed of nice red Martian sand. I laugh until I can't stand up anymore. Ren is wheezing and holding on to the console. Dr. Ripley has managed to keep hold of herself, but even she is smiling in spite of everything. We give ourselves a few blessed moments of hilarity, and then we get back to work.

The new math is basically the old math, but faster. *Titan* will speed up until she's going quickly enough that the missiles can't catch her before she hits what's left of Mars's atmosphere. We're betting that whoever is controlling the missiles will blow them up once they realize we've outpaced them, rather than irradiate Mars with whatever the payload of a Mark 5 is. We just have to make sure that we don't crash too close to a dome, and we'll be set.

My head aches as I run the calculations. Math was never my strong suit, but at least this equation is pretty straightforward, and I have Ren and Adelaide to back me up. Eventually, we get the solution and Ren enters it into the autopilot, setting us on our final course.

"Now we just have to make sure that air-recirculation is reinforced enough to survive," Ren says. "And we'll have to separate it from the rest of *Titan*'s systems to make sure there's no conflicting programming. And it leaves us with the problem of taking those aliens with us to the planet's surface. They can probably survive a crash."

"Can we detach the whole thing?" Dr. Ripley asks. "I mean, they built *Titan* in sections, right? And that one is completely self-contained. If we make it a true escape pod, push it out at the last minute, it'll land separately from the rest of the ship and as far away from the fuel tanks as possible. And maybe the fuel tank explosion will be enough to take out the aliens."

Ren looks at me. We aren't that lucky. But there's merit to the idea, and I'm the one here who knows *Titan*'s systems best.

"It's not a terrible idea," I say. "Air-recirculation crashes. Mars spins enough that the rest of *Titan* crashes behind us, and Earth blows the missiles early rather than take out a zillion-dollar planetary investment. Probably."

At this point, I'll never assume the aliens dead unless I've cut them into pieces myself. But we are going to live, regardless. I have decided.

There's no window, but the viewscreen shows us what we'd see if there was one and if *Titan* flew without spinning, but let's not get too technical. Mars is big and oddly welcoming in front of us. I forgot how close we are because, in space, close isn't usually good enough. It had been out of my reach, so I hadn't thought about it. But now it's here, almost close enough to touch.

"This is not at all like I planned," Adelaide says. "But I'm glad we're almost there."

"Let's make it the rest of the way," Dr. Ripley says.

Ren and I work on the code that will separate air-recirculation from the rest of the ship. I hope that Dominic is doing okay. He could have come through the airlock right after us, but I know why he hasn't. He doesn't want the seal to be in the middle of a cycle when we need it to come back. He's holding the door open. It's his best job. I'll have to be sure to tell him.

Ren finishes her plan and Adelaide and I check it over.

"That's as sure as we're going to get," Ren says.

An alarm goes off, making all of us jump, but it's only the original countdown, which none of us had remembered to turn off. We're able to laugh about it, problem-solvers that we are, but our nerves are pretty jangly. I run the numbers again and notice a tiny mistake that none of us caught. We forgot to add Dr. Ripley to the number of people that will be in our makeshift escape pod.

I start to say something, but a voice in my head points out that there's no time. If we have to run the whole equation again, we'll be past the point of no return. There's only one option, however much I don't like it. I use the first officer's codes, which let me tap a message on my wrist comm, sending an order like an officer would have sent one to me, and Ren presses the sequence of keys that will activate our approach. The final countdown begins.

I feel very quiet when I step into the airlock and the decon starts up. Ren seems very bright. On the other side, her sisters and Dominic (and his mother) are waiting for us. I keep typing on my comm, trying to make sure I say everything I want to without tipping Ren off to what's about to happen. With thirty seconds left, I undo the fastener and slide it off my wrist.

The cycle completes and the door opens. Ren jumps into her sisters' arms, like I hoped she would, and Adelaide and Dr. Ripley are eager to get out too. It leaves me plenty of time to meet Dominic's happy gaze and then watch it turn to horror as I throw my wrist comm at him and slam the door shut with me on the wrong side.

twenty-eight

DOMINIC

I'm running forwards when I catch the comm. I don't know how I knew, but it doesn't do me any good. I'm too late. The seal is shut between us, and it'll be at least five minutes before I can open it again.

I stand there staring until Ren turns around and sees what's happened. I can see the confusion in her eyes, and then she must realize something I don't know yet, because her eyes fill with tears and she howls with what can only be described as grief.

"What's happening?" one of her sisters asks. I can't even look at them. I just look at Celeste.

She's gesturing at the comm, telling me to read whatever message she's sent me, but I still can't move. I don't resist as Ren tears it out of my hand and reads it herself.

"We messed up the math," Adelaide says, horror in her

voice. "We didn't add Dr. Ripley when we were calculating how many people would be in here."

"What does that have to do with anything?" I demand as Ren throws the comm back at me. This time, I *do* read it.

It only takes a few seconds for me to scan the words, but it feels like an eternity unfolds as I comprehend them. Celeste tells me what's going to happen and how they worked it out, how it might take care of the aliens for us, and how she realized the mistake too late to run the calculations again. There isn't enough oxygen for twenty-one people. There's only enough for twenty.

Dr. Ripley looks like she's about to vomit, like it's her fault, when she's done more to save our lives than almost anyone. I immediately come up with fifteen terrible plans, only three of which involve jettisoning my mother, but Celeste has taken the time to explain that we can't run the decon again. It will take too much oxygen, and then all of us will die.

There's a knock on the glass. I look up and realize that Celeste will have to go back to the flight deck before we separate. She'll have to go soon. I go up to her and she's smiling. It's probably how she wants me to remember her. She's got to be scared. I'm fucking terrified. But we both hold on a bit longer to say goodbye. We can't hear each other, of course, and I don't know how to communicate everything I'm feeling in gestures. Even if I knew sign language, I am not sure I'd be able to find words.

Ren comes to stand beside me, tears streaming down her face. She looks like she wants to fight something, but there's nothing left to fight. We've run up against the laws of physics, and there's nothing we can do about it.

"I'm sorry," Celeste mouths to her, and I know she means that she's sorry she dragged Ren out here away from (most of) her family only to leave her. That just makes Ren cry harder, and she turns into my shoulder. I wrap an arm around her without thinking.

Celeste nods. *Take care of her*, I understand, as if Ren won't be the one taking care of me. Then she turns and walks through the airlock, shutting it behind her and sealing herself onto the fragile flight deck.

I turn around and yell, almost shrieking in frustration. It echoes around the deck, filling all of the space that our bodies don't take up. The dead alien has been pushed into the corner, so I can't even kick it. I'm alone with my rage and despair, even though there are other people in the room.

A huge sound—metal tearing in ways it's not supposed to—brings me back to myself.

"We're separating!" yells Ren. "Find something to hold on to."

Titan was built in pieces, and now the piece we're in is breaking away, leaving the ship—and hopefully all of the aliens—behind. We never did find the queen, but it's too late now.

Free of *Titan*, we're not going to have a soft landing. If the math is right, we won't have a ship on top of us, and I have to trust the math. None of that makes me feel better right now. We're secure, the walls around the air supply as strong as they can possibly be. Celeste has nothing but a room full of dead bodies.

It starts to get warm, which isn't reassuring, but Ren yells in my ear that it's normal. The heat means we're slowing down. The slower we go, the better our chances. She's split between reassuring her sisters and comforting me, and I realize that I don't even know where my mother is. I look around and see her clinging to a pipe a few metres away from where most of us are holding on.

A high-pitched whining sound begins, and everything shakes. This is the part where the math works even as the engineering might fail. Mars doesn't have a breathable atmosphere. We have to land intact, and then we have to last long enough for a rescue team to come and get us, or at least throw a dome around us. We're going to make one hell of an impact, so I have no doubt they'll notice our arrival. And Celeste has given us all the time she can for them to come and rescue us.

The shaking intensifies. The heat intensifies. My arms ache, but I don't let go. None of us do. Celeste sacrificed herself for us, and all of us are going to live to honour her. Even my mother. I hold her comm in my hand, determined that her acts and words will make it to the surface in one piece, even as she doesn't.

I don't remember the impact. I am told it was spectacular.

I come to hearing the sound of metal on metal and the heat from the friction as what's left of *Titan* is cut apart. The pipes are a mess. I can tell that even before my eyes refocus. I blink a lot. I probably have a concussion. It seems to be taking a long time for the rescue team to get through the hull, which makes sense, I guess. You don't want those things to be flimsy. I don't feel a rush of gratitude when I see them reaching down for me. I might eventually, but right now everything hurts too much.

A medic checks me over. He's talking to me, but the sound of his voice is in and out and I have trouble focusing on it. I try to follow the light he's holding in front of my face, but it's too much work. I *definitely* have a concussion. All those injury-free years of lacrosse, and I finally hit my head during a spaceship crash. I try to laugh, but I can't. Everything hurts too much.

A second medic comes, and the two of them lift me onto a stretcher, which is pulled up out of the wreckage on some kind of cable. Free of all that metal, I can hear a bit more clearly. I remember that Ren and her sisters were near me and I look for them. I remember Adelaide and Dr. Ripley. I remember my mother. One by one, I pick them out of the crowd.

We're under a dome. It's massive. I almost can't believe that this sort of thing is an emergency structure, but I guess they don't really plan for small emergencies on Mars. If something went wrong, they might have to fit a lot of people in here. I guess covering part of a spaceship isn't too much of a problem, even if it's something new.

Part of a spaceship. But not just the air-recirculation section I came down in.

"The missiles." I can barely understand myself, and I have to fight to sit up because the medics are pushing me down. "Did the missiles hit?"

"You're okay, young man. Dominic Reubens, right? That's what your wrist comm said," one of them says. "*Titan* broke up in high orbit, but inertia is going to have pieces raining down on us for a while. We have a system for that kind of thing. Well, it's for meteors, but it's the same principle. You don't have to worry. The big pieces came down with you."

"Where?" I demand.

The medic gives up trying to keep me down, apparently deciding that my emotional well-being requires that I look around.

"Just over there." He points, and it takes effort, but I manage to follow his direction.

The twisted metal remains are barely recognizable as *Titan*, but I know they must be. It's under the same dome we are, so the salvage teams have already begun picking it apart. I know there will be an argument over the crash and if it was really necessary, because people always argue about stupid things when other people are dead.

I lie back down, hoping that someone else, one of the adults, is conscious enough to tell whoever is in charge here about the aliens. Adelaide must have a lot of pull. She'll take care of it.

I know better than to fall asleep, but I'm about to happily drift off with my painkillers when we all hear a cry go up from the salvage team. Someone screams for a medic, and I find out that I have enough strength left to stumble after them. My own medic follows me, yelling my name as he picks his way through the wreckage, but he doesn't catch up until I sit down on a hunk of something, my adrenaline waning.

It's the captain's ready room, the smallest enclosed space on the flight deck, and somehow it has landed mostly intact—though it can't possibly have been vacuum-sealed, even with all the doors closed.

I expect them to pull out a body.

I look away. I don't want to see Captain Bernard again, gaping hole in his chest and now smashed to pieces by re-entry. But they called for a medic. They think someone is *alive*. And Captain Bernard was very obviously not.

They pull her out, singed and smashed around but whole. Her uniform is torn, and there's a cut on her head that looks awful, but she's conscious. I don't know how it's possible, and I almost don't care. She's alive, and she's alive enough to sit up on the stretcher they brought her and hold her own oxygen mask to her face. I can already hear the word "miracle" being whispered around me, and it is. Somehow, against all odds, Celeste survives.

But space doesn't do odds. It leaves no room for chance. There are possibilities and there are limits, and that's it. It is cruel and more absolute than an earthquake. Her oxygen would have been limited. The impact would have been immense. It would have been much hotter in the captain's ready room than it was in air-recirculation.

And yet, she's alive.

I'm thrilled, but it doesn't make sense.

She looks up over the top of her oxygen mask and finally sees me in the milling crowd. She smiles, I think, but I'm not really paying attention to her mouth.

I'm concussed. I'm exhausted. I'm definitely not entirely sane. But I swear that, for a moment, her eyes flash a bright, unwelcome, impossible purple.

And I know what that means.

ACKNOWLEDGEMENTS

Sometimes the pieces come together. I've been in publishing long enough to follow my gut, and about halfway through my first phone call with David Purse, I knew that *Titan* was a project I wanted in on. Working with someone who didn't just listen to all of the changes I wanted to make to his outline but got genuinely excited about them was awesome. And when I said that last part and he said ". . . That's a sequel!", I could hear his enthusiasm across the Atlantic.

It was an absolute gift to work on an entire project with a Canadian team at Tundra. Peter Phillips was on board immediately and asked the right question ("Can we dial up the horror?"). It was so much fun to add ever more tentacles to this manuscript. Let's do it again with Book 2. But let's not change tense and POV halfway through this time.

I don't think I have ever had a project where Josh Adams sent more emails on my behalf. This one was a challenge, for reasons that had nothing to do with writing, but having the best agent definitely makes it easier.

Thank you to the team at Tundra Books: Sam Devotta, Evan Munday, Sophie Paas-Lang, Catherine Marjoribanks, and Jennifer McClorey, and also to Tom Roberts for the outstanding cover.

Special thanks to Amy Hetherington, Shannon Gibney, Chandra Rooney, Erin Bow, Katherine Winchell, and Eric Smith for various and sundry. And, strangely enough, thank you also to one of the worst bosses I've ever had for dragging me up and down the Ottawa Rift Valley in 40-degree (Celsius) heat, thereby ensuring I would never, ever forget it. Apologies to the Library of Parliament. I think we just got it fixed up.

Titan of the Stars began about a hundred metres off a dock in Lake Muskoka, found its shape in a flower-filled Lisbon flat while pro-Palestinian marches filled the streets, and was finished off in my new office.